AN
IRISH
BOOKSHOP
MURDER

AN IRISH BOOKSHOP MURDER

Lucy Connelly

Bookouture

Published by Bookouture in 2024

An imprint of Storyfire Ltd.
Carmelite House
50 Victoria Embankment
London EC4Y 0DZ

www.bookouture.com

ISBN: 978-1-83525-717-3
eBook ISBN: 978-1-83525-716-6

To Lizzie Bailey and Shannon Houchin, thank you for being my friends.

'Believe nothing you hear and only one half that you see.'

Edgar Allan Poe

ONE

I stood in front of the navy front door and looked up at our new home. The spring breeze ruffled my hair, and the fresh scent of the sea assailed my senses. I rubbed the shamrock key ring in my hand, hoping for a little of its luck to rub off on me. The house had a beautifully kept, small front garden. I glanced at my twin sister and hoped we had made the right choice in moving to Ireland.

When the letter arrived from our grandfather's lawyer, we were shocked. We had no idea he existed. Our mother never spoke of our father, and we didn't ask because it always made her sad.

Our grandfather had left us this house and his business, a bookshop on the main street in the town of Shamrock Cove, Ireland. So far, the place had been nothing short of magical. The situation and the town were so surreal that I had to keep reminding myself this was really happening.

The navy house with white trim wasn't the ramshackle shack I'd expected. The Tudor-style home had a picket fence, with roses and other blossoms trailing over the side. It sat in a court with several other houses, all with their own beautiful gardens and well-kept homes.

There wasn't a chipped bit of paint among them. While all the houses had thatched roofs, each one was painted a different color. Number three Hidden Way Lane with its beautiful garden and homey feel was right out of a postcard. I didn't have a green thumb, and my twin would be busy with the bookshop we'd inherited along with the house. I had no idea how we'd keep up the garden, but we'd figure it out.

I'd been nervous when the solicitor said he didn't have any pictures of the house where our grandfather had lived. The solicitor had been in Galway, and our grandfather had met him there to do his business, so he didn't know the village itself.

I'm a writer, and I'd imagined all kinds of scenarios, from a shanty to a crumbling old building. I loved the house instantly, and I'm not that sort of person. It usually takes me a bit to warm up to places and people. I was the opposite of my sister. Strangely, it felt like home. And from a die-hard New Yorker like me, that was saying something.

There was only one way to find out though, and with one last squeeze of the key ring, I handed it to my sister and stepped back, letting her be the one to open the door. As I took in the view of the inviting foyer with its hickory grandfather clock there was a harrowing scream.

My stomach plummeted as I dropped everything and ran to save my sister.

My sneakers squeaked on the wood floors, and I nearly slid into the banister. Lizzie's body shook as she stood in a doorway on the right side of the foyer. Her blue-gray eyes were wet with tears.

"Lizzie, are you okay?" I called out. She turned to me, her

face so white I feared she might faint any second. She pointed into the room.

I ran to her and then glanced over her shoulder. I swallowed hard. "Dial 999," I said softly. Then I turned her away from the white-haired woman on the floor. "Not 911. Okay? 999." She stared straight ahead.

"Lizzie," I said sternly. Her head snapped toward me. "Call 999. Go sit on the stairs. I'll be there in a minute." I handed her my phone from my pocket.

I checked on the elderly woman on the floor. She had white, perfectly coiffed hair, and was dressed in a lavender sweater set with matching pants. She was still warm, and she had a pulse. I put a finger in front of her nose and felt her breath. Thank goodness.

"Tell them she's alive and to hurry."

I didn't want to move her if she'd fallen, but I grabbed a blanket that was folded over one of the cigar-leather, winged-back chairs in front of a large, gray-stoned fireplace. I placed the teal fabric under her head. I glanced around, found some matching teal pillows on the leather sofa, and put those under her knees.

From the deeply etched lines on her beautiful face, she had to be close to seventy. She was well-kept, and her hair had formed a white halo above her head. While I'd had training for CPR, I wasn't sure what to do with her since she was breathing.

"Ma'am," I said. "Can you hear me?"

She didn't move.

As much as I wanted to check on my sister, I felt a sense of duty to stay with the poor woman until help arrived. I put my hand over her heart. The beat was strong and steady, just like her pulse.

I sat holding her hand. I didn't know who she was or why she was in our living room, but I was worried about her. A dog barked behind me, and the woman's eyes fluttered open. Then she sat straight up and screamed. Extremely startled, I jumped and let go of her hand.

I was on the floor, and the large dog moved forward and growled at me. Well, he was more of a horse. He placed himself between me and the woman. I'd been so focused on her that I hadn't seen him there on the other side of her.

"Good doggie," I said nervously, trying to get my heart rate to return to normal.

"Oh. My. You gave me a fright," the woman said.

"Likewise," I said and reached out to help her up.

The woman on the floor waved me away. "I'm fine. I'm fine. I just had one of my spells. Bernard here woke me up. I wanted to make sure everything was ready for you here at the house."

Well, I'm not sure scaring us to death is the best welcome.

I smiled.

"It wasn't the plan to scare you to death," the woman said, seemingly reading my mind. She smiled. "I'm so sorry for the bother." She patted my hand in a grandmotherly way.

I liked her.

"Let's get you off that rug." I tried to take her arm, but the dog growled fiercely.

"Bernard. She's family," the woman said.

The dog moved back a few inches, and then I swear it smiled.

She waved me away. "I'm fine. I apologize again for scaring you," she said. "I'm Mrs. O'Malley, a dear friend of your grandfather's and your neighbor. I came over to make sure the cleaner did a good job with the house. She's a good girl, but she's young. You must be Mercy," she said. "I recognize you from the jacket of your books. Though, you're much prettier in person."

My mind was still in a fight-or-flight zone, and it took me a minute to process everything she said. "Thank you."

"Where's your sister?"

Lizzie was probably a mess. The last thing she needed was

another stressful event. In the last six months, we'd been through the deaths of our mother, as well as Lizzie's fiancé and his daughter. Ireland was our fresh start, but this wasn't exactly the beginning I'd expected.

"Excuse me," I said, and then took off. She wasn't on the stairs.

"Lizzie?" I called out.

"In here," she said. Her voice didn't sound shaky, so at least there was that.

I found her in the kitchen, sitting with a cup of tea.

I knelt by her chair and took her hand in mine. "Are you okay?"

Her eyes were watery, but she squeezed my hand. "I am now. I have a cup of tea. The kettle was already on."

Mrs. O'Malley entered, and I pulled out a chair for her.

"Well, aren't you two peas in a pod. Except for your hair and eye color, you look exactly alike."

My hair was much darker than my sister's and usually in a ponytail. She was more fond of the messy bun.

"We get that a lot," I said. "We're just different enough that most people can tell us apart, but when we were younger, before my hair became darker, we were nearly identical."

"Are you sure you're alright?" I asked again.

"I'm fine," my sister said. "Go sit and I'll cancel the ambulance."

I did as she asked. More because my legs were a bit wobbly. It had been a long twenty or so hours since we'd left the States, and we'd had a pretty good scare so far in Shamrock Cove. It wasn't even nine in the morning yet.

"As I said to your sister, I'm Mrs. O'Malley," she said as she reached across the table to shake Lizzie's hand. "Everyone calls me Lolly. I've been looking after the place since your granddad passed. I'd just come over to inspect the house. And to bring you some biscuits and tea. I didn't mean to scare you," she said.

"It's okay," Lizzie said. Her smile was genuine, but I worried about her nerves. Was this all too much? The doctors had said she was still fragile, but my sister was good at pretending that wasn't the case.

The slight tremble in her hand as she poured two more cups of tea was telling.

"I have narcolepsy, have since I was a child. Fall asleep anywhere, even standing up sometimes. I've never been able to drive, though around here there's no need. It's one of the reasons I stayed put.

"And it's blasted hard to wake me up if you don't know how. The townsfolk are used to it, but I truly apologize for frightening you."

I'd never known anyone with narcolepsy. I'd have to research that. It might be interesting to give it to a character. The wheels turned in my thriller-writing brain about a murder suspect with narcolepsy who fell asleep at the scene of the crime but didn't remember killing anyone.

It could work.

"Right, Mercy?" Lizzie nudged me with an elbow.

I nodded, not sure what anyone had said. I'd been writing in my head again. It happened a lot.

"The Hidden Way Court residents are having a get-together at your bookshop to celebrate your arrival," Mrs. O'Malley said. "Nothing fancy, mind you. We're a casual bunch. We expect a spot of rain this evening, and when that happens, our parties are usually at the bookshop. I hope you don't mind. It was a tradition with your grandfather, and I thought it would be sweet to continue. Also, to help you get the lay of the land before you reopen the shop. You don't mind, do you? I promise it will be grand."

"No, that's fine," Lizzie said.

I was thinking the exact opposite but didn't voice my opinion because Lizzie gave me the you-better-behave stare.

"Won't it be dusty?" I asked.

"No. Our little group has been tidying up. All the neighbors dusted and straightened in anticipation of your arrival. We left the shelving of new books to you, but you should find the place clean. I cannot wait for you to see it. You don't need to worry about anything. I'll use my key to set it up. But if you need anything before then, I'm in number six on the court," she said.

"Is that the last house?" I asked.

Mrs. O'Malley nodded.

"That's so lovely," Lizzie said. "You didn't have to go to all of that trouble."

"It's no trouble at all," she said.

"The court?" I asked.

Mrs. O'Malley glanced at us as if she were summing us up at that moment. Lizzie was the nice one. I'm suspicious and sometimes rude, but they'd all learn that soon enough.

I don't mean to be, but I have a writer's brain. Sometimes, I stare right at people and don't see them because my mind is working out a story.

"Everyone in town calls this the court." She glanced at me. "Don't worry. The neighbors are of various ages and not all old like me."

"You're not—" Lizzie said.

Mrs. O'Malley held up a hand to interrupt. The giant dog leaned into her, and she patted him on the head. "Don't you start with the compliments. I love my age. I've earned every wrinkle."

I decided a change of subject was in order. "What kind of dog is he?" I asked.

"Bernard is an Irish Wolfhound. Though he's small for the breed."

Small? He'd be as tall as me on his hind legs and had to weigh at least 150 pounds.

"Right then," Lolly said. "You'll learn our ways soon

enough. I'm sure you're exhausted from your trip. Don't forget, six tonight at the bookshop. If you need anything, I've left my number and the other neighbors' numbers on the fridge. We're all happy to help you acclimatize. Don't hesitate to reach out. You've no idea how excited we are that you've come to live in our fair town.

"Oh, and remember, we've stocked your pantry and fridge."

"That's so kind, thank you," Lizzie said.

"Think nothing of it."

After finishing her tea, Mrs. O'Malley left.

I rested my head on the worn but beautiful table. "I can't believe they are throwing a party. I planned to be in bed by five," I said wearily. "Maybe two. Or now. Now is good too."

She shoved my arm. "I think we should explore the house, and then we'll take a brief nap, so we're sharp for tonight. It's our first time meeting the neighbors, and I don't want a foggy brain."

"We could claim exhaustion," I said, slumping down further in my chair.

"Suck it up, buttercup. This is our new home, and the neighbors are doing their best to welcome us. The least we can do is show up. I thought I saw a wine shop in town. We should probably grab some to take. I don't want to show up empty-handed."

She was excited and making plans. The doctors had told me this was a good sign. After the depression she'd suffered, and rightfully so, I wasn't sure I'd ever see her like this again.

She clapped her hands. "I can't believe we're in Ireland. Have you looked at this kitchen? Our grandad had good taste. I mean, that stove alone—it's my dream stove. But be careful because it's always on. I hope there is an AGA instruction book. I've always wanted to try to cook on one."

I glanced over at it. Other than it was the same cerulean as the lower cabinets in the kitchen and had a lot of burners, I didn't really get it. But unlike my sister, who was a wonderful cook, I ate out most of the time. I don't think I used my stove or oven once in my Manhattan apartment. The microwave was the way to go for heating up leftovers.

She stood, and then reached down to pull me up. She hugged me hard. I wrapped my arms around her and squeezed back.

"Thank you for taking a chance for me," she said. "I may not always show it, but I do appreciate everything you've given up to do this."

"I'd do anything for you." It was true, and it wasn't because she was the last person left in the world who loved me—even though I didn't always make that easy. "And this adventure is just as much for me. I promise."

What I'd left behind in Manhattan was a string of bad relationships and a loneliness I could no longer abide. Oh, and a stalker who was becoming increasingly scary.

Before the call about Mom's illness, I hadn't left my apartment in two months. With food and shopping delivered, I could lose myself for days in my writing. And I didn't have to worry about the scary world outside the walls of my place where a stalker had followed me on the subway and sent photos as proof. Even though I had friends in the department, the police told me not to worry. They'd been sure it was just an overly excited fan. I hadn't been so sure.

But then the call from Lizzie came in, and my world shifted on its axis. I was on the next plane to Texas. It wasn't until I'd been there a month that I realized how much I missed human connection and spending time with my family.

And thanks to a stalker, I no longer felt safe in the place I loved most: Manhattan. This move was just as much for me as it was for Lizzie.

If we hadn't moved to Ireland, I probably would have gone back to Texas, even though I swore when I left for college years ago that I'd never return—except for holidays with my family. But I'd been wrong. I needed them as much as they did me.

My sister was one of the strongest women I'd ever met. She powered through Mom's illness, making sure we had beautiful memories in those last few months.

But the night of the accident involving her soon-to-be new family, something broke inside her. Everything I'd done to make this move happen had been in the hopes of getting the old Lizzie back. I'd do anything for my twin sister.

She let go and grabbed my hand. "Come on, like the old days, let's go find our room. Oh, and I call first dibs."

I'd forgotten that. With each promotion our mom received, we'd moved to a bigger house. That was until she'd bought the ranch. At every new home, we'd race to find our favorite rooms, and my twin always won.

If I had my books, I didn't care where my bed might be, but the way her space looked was important to her. And she'd always been the faster runner.

Downstairs, facing the front door, there were two living areas off to the left. One was more formal, where we'd found Lolly. The second one was a den with a widescreen television. The room was painted navy and had a cozy feel with fluffy knitted sofa pillows and warm, fuzzy blankets draped over the back of the leather chairs. The furniture was traditional and timeless, and nothing seemed terribly outdated, which was a surprise.

I'd been expecting dusty old recliners and furniture from the fifties. And lots of tchotchkes. The type of things I wrongly believed an older Irish gentleman might own.

The house was social-media worthy; it was neat, uncluttered, timeless, and beautiful. I was falling more and more in love with every door we opened.

The door under the stairs turned out to be a hallway. There were four rooms on the bottom floor on this side. One was a study with a fireplace and dark wood on the walls, which gave it a very moody feel. A beautifully carved desk had been positioned for a view of the garden.

"It's not super posh like the office in your apartment, but what do you think?" She eyed me warily as if my answer meant everything. "Not exactly the Central Park view from your penthouse."

"I love it," I said truthfully. "It's moody, and tailor-made for a mystery author." As soon as I'd walked inside, I'd felt at peace. Like I could look at this view for many, many years.

She let out a breath. "We can paint if you want or fix it up however you like."

There was a window seat that looked out onto the garden. It was wide enough to sit with a book or my laptop. The furniture, including the deep couch centered in front of the fireplace, fit the place. It was large, comfortable, and totally unexpected, as was all of this cottage.

A designer friend created my home office to go with the rest of the penthouse. But it had never fit my personality. This room did.

"Nah. I mean, maybe working in a place that is so different will help spark my imagination."

She grinned. "It does have a 1930s Agatha Christie feel. It's a bit more antique than the rest of the house."

Lizzie was right and, honestly, I wasn't sure what felt like me anymore. I'd been every bit as numb as she was the last few months. "Maybe that's why I love it. Lots of character. Let's see what these other rooms are like," I said.

Down the hall on the right was a well-appointed bedroom with a much larger closet than I'd expected. The bed was comfortable, and we both tried it out. The door off to the left was a small bathroom. It had a clawfoot tub, a sink, and a toilet.

And there was a small separate shower. The floors were marble, as were the walls.

"It's kind of small," Lizzie said.

I laughed. "Do you remember my first apartment with the toilet and shower out in the open next to the kitchen?"

She snorted. "Mom's face. That I will never forget, I thought she was going to drag you out of there and back home."

Mom hadn't. But I did have to call her three times a day to let her know I was alive. She'd been so proud of me when my first book sold. She and Lizzie had flown to New York to celebrate. That seemed like a lifetime ago.

"I miss her." My voice croaked a bit.

"Me too," she whispered. "Come on, there was one more door in this hallway."

It was shaped like the round hobbit door at the bookstore. We'd peeked in the windows when we'd been searching for the secret entrance to the court. But this one was painted a deep green. The handle was stiff, but when I put some force behind it, it opened.

I gasped, as did my sister behind me.

"I can't believe it," I said as my mouth dropped open.

TWO

Past the deep green, rounded hobbit door at the end of the hall
was one of the most beautiful home libraries I'd ever seen.
Every wall of the huge room was covered in bookshelves, except
for a mantel and fireplace at one end. Cushy chairs were spaced
near a round reading table. I couldn't have designed a more
perfect room.

"Mercy, it's so wonderful," Lizzie whispered behind me.

I knew why she was whispering. The beautiful room
inspired a sort of reverence.

Then she gently shoved me out the way. "He has... I mean,
had incredible taste." She ran her fingers along the spines of
several books. There was a large round window at the north side
of the room that looked out onto the back garden.

"Is that ours too?" I pointed out the window. I hadn't realized there was a back garden as well. She was still caressing the
books. I put my hands on her shoulders and moved her toward
the window.

"Oh. Wow. This place keeps getting better. Are those
gardenias? I didn't think they'd grow in Ireland."

"Well, now you have a garden and a bookstore to tend. You're going to be very busy."

Lizzie smiled, but it didn't quite reach her eyes. "Thank you, Mercy. For all of this." She sniffed.

If she cried, it would break me. She had no idea how many hoops I had to jump through to make this happen, and she never would. I hoped that sad smile would someday be a happy one.

"I promise to help you water, but you know that's about as far as I go with the gardening. I'm like the villain Poison Ivy in the *Batman* comics, only I kill plants instead of people."

That made her giggle. "Yes. Water only, and just when I say, okay?"

I hugged her. "Promise. And thank you, too. I wouldn't be here without you."

"I'm going to head upstairs and rest for an hour or so," she said. "Then I'll head into town and get the wine. You set up for work. Let's be ready by five thirty Irish time, okay? Set an alarm on your phone."

Lizzie had a thing about punctuality. Our mother had been the same way. For some reason, that gene missed me. I was never late on purpose, but my mind tended to wander, and I often lost track of time. I gave her a salute. "Yes, ma'am. But can we run to the pub first? I could use some carbs before bed."

"That's a great idea," Lizzie said.

True to my word, I was ready when she came downstairs several hours later. Of course, I'd set three alarms to make it happen. One to wake me up from my nap. Another to remind me to get out of the bath, and the last one to ensure I was in the front living area by 5:29. Like I said, when I'm working on books in my head, I have to set reminders for the real world.

Lizzie had put her hair up in a messy bun and wore a cute boho dress, a jean jacket, and knee-high brown boots.

I'd opted for my cliché writer garb, which was black everything—jeans, boots, and top. Literary people in New York wear a lot of black. It's practical for a city that can be messy at times. For me, it was more that I didn't have to think about what I had to wear. If everything was black, it pretty much went together. But I'd also found a pair of Mom's diamond studs. I wanted her with me tonight.

My sister scrunched up her nose. "You are beautiful, as always, but we're going to introduce color into your wardrobe here in Ireland."

While she leaned toward pastels and primary colors, I was quite fond of my black wardrobe.

I snorted. "You can try."

She gave me a crooked smile. "Come on. Let's go meet the neighbors."

We locked our front door and stepped onto the path leading to the village. Circling the court was an enormous stone wall. On our way to the house that morning, we'd gone around the block a couple of times before finding the secret entrance from the alley behind the shops on Main Street.

On this side, the entry was easier to see. Someone had painted a flowered mural around the door.

She paused and turned back toward the court.

"The gardens are intimidating," she said. "I'm not sure I can keep up. I didn't even know some of these flowers grew in the wet, chilly climate of Ireland."

It was spring and chilly, so even I understood what she meant.

"I bet it's from all the dead bodies buried under the flowers," I said.

She shivered. "Stop it, mystery writer. Now that's all I'll be able to think about." She laughed to take the bite out of her words.

It was raining lightly, and I held a silk umbrella we'd found in the stand near our front door over us as we went around the corner to Main Street. At the top of the block, there was a glimpse of the rocky sea beyond the cliffs at the end of the street.

Along Main Street were stone and pastel-painted buildings that had most likely been here for hundreds of years. Even though they had to be weather-beaten, they appeared freshly painted and clean. It was a storybook village and belonged on a postcard.

We reached the bookshop, and I looked up. The sign above the hobbit-like, cobalt door was black with gold lettering. *Leabhair agus Seaniarsmaí*. I'd looked it up before we arrived, and the Gaelic translation was "Books and Antiquities." Kind of on the nose for a name, but who was I to judge names in Ireland?

I'd always loved the smell of books, and that's what hit me first as we stepped inside. Leather and a bit of cinnamon mixed with lemon cleaner.

It wasn't the tiny, dusty bookshop I'd expected. Lizzie would probably describe it as magical, and I'd have to agree. There were also antiques and oddities for sale, but most of the space was filled with books from the ceiling to the floors.

The walls were painted azure blue, and the black shelves gave the space a cozy but elegant feel. The lights overhead and lamps on the tables spread around gave the place a soft glow. It was the sort of store one could get lost in for hours.

"There they are," Lolly O'Malley said as she approached us. She wore purple from her headband to her flats. Maybe it was her signature color, as she'd been in a lavender sweater set and pants when she'd been laid out on our floor. "You two look as fresh as daisies."

"Thank you." Lizzie leaned in for a fake kiss on each cheek, and I followed suit.

"Let me introduce you to some of your neighbors."

We were a few minutes early, but there was already quite a crowd. They watched us approach with a variety of expressions. One older gentleman with a long white beard bared his teeth. Perhaps it was his attempt at a smile, but I didn't think so.

It appeared only some were happy about our arrival.

"This is Rob, and his partner Scott," she said. They reached forward to shake our hands. Scott wore a fedora with a Hawaiian shirt. I liked him instantly, which was saying something. I'm often leery of new people.

"What's the craic?" Scott asked.

"The craic?" I cocked my head not certain of what he meant.

"That's our way of asking what's up," he said. "We're so happy you're here. If you need anything, just ask. We're at number two, which is next door on your left. That is if you're looking at your place from the front garden."

"And I've cooked you a week's worth of food," Rob said. He was dressed in a button-down and jeans. His black hair pulled back in a ponytail. "Let me know when I can bring it over." Like his partner, his smile was genuine. They appeared to be in their late thirties or early forties. I was terrible when it came to guessing the ages of people.

"Oh. You didn't have to do that," Lizzie said, "but it's so sweet of you."

"It's my pleasure," Rob said. "You can probably tell I'm half Korean, but I love to cook all types of cuisine."

"My husband is a gourmet chef," Scott said. "He loves making meals for everyone."

"That is kind," I said. That meant Lizzie, who would be busy with the store and the garden, wouldn't have to cook for a bit. I'd offered to try to learn while we were here, but my sister had tried food I'd prepared and preferred to handle that chore herself. Her exact words had been *Mercy, if there is nothing left to eat on the planet, then I'll be grateful for your cooking. Until then, well, you have many other wonderful qualities.*

I didn't blame her. It wasn't an exaggeration to say I couldn't boil water. I blamed my writer brain, which often forgot mundane tasks when I was deep in my craft.

Mrs. O'Malley led us to another man, the one with the beard. His shoulders were slightly bent with age, and he didn't appear to want us anywhere near him. "This is Judge Michael Pierce," she said. "We just call him Judge or the judge. He lives at number five, next door to me."

He nodded.

"It's nice to meet you, Judge," my sister said. She stuck out her hand, and he stared at it for a bit before shaking it.

"Your grandfather never mentioned you until the end," he said roughly. His eyebrows went up as if he found us suspicious. "I thought you were supposed to be identical."

We were except for a slight difference in our eye and hair color.

Lizzie opened her mouth and shut it again.

"We didn't know anything about him," I said. "So, it's possible he wasn't aware of us until the last minute."

"Still, it seems odd you'd inherit something from a man who didn't know you existed. I was his best friend, and he never mentioned you until he was close to death. We have strict rules about how the homes in the court are transferred. I'll be looking into this. Mark my words." He pointed a finger toward the sky.

Okay then.

"This is Linda and Dave O'Brien," Mrs. O'Malley said as she quickly ushered us onward.

The couple stepped forward and guided us away from the cranky man.

"We're so happy you're reopening the store," Linda said.

Her bleached-blonde hair was curled around rosy cheeks, and she had the friendliest smile. "I thought about buying it myself, just so we'd have access to all those wonderful books."

"But my wife is busy enough with her quilting and sewing shop," Dave said affectionately. His gelled hair was slicked back in a style that reminded me of men in the fifties. He wore a tweed jacket with patches on the elbows. But he had shifty eyes. He glanced from us to the others in the party as if trying to stay aware of his surroundings. It was odd. "It's just up the way from yours."

"Quite right, luv." She patted her husband on the shoulder. "I had to drive to Dublin last week for my latest batch of romances, and I don't like the traffic. When do you think you'll open?"

"They've just arrived, darling," Dave said.

"Of course, I'm sorry," said Linda, smiling at Dave.

"I hope by Wednesday or so," Lizzie said. "Before I open, I need to look at the accounting and check the inventory."

"Smart. Smart," Dave said. "I'm an accountant and did your grandfather's taxes, should you need help. We live in number one. The place has been handed down for seven generations in my family."

"Mind you, I've updated it," Linda added. "I brought it out of the forties and into this century."

Dave squeezed her shoulders. "That you have, luv."

They seemed a perfectly charming couple, except there was something odd in Dave's demeanor. Or, maybe it was just my mystery-writer brain searching for suspects in non-existent crimes.

"Wow, that's a lot of ancestors." Lizzie smiled sweetly. "I'm hoping we can find out more about our family, as well."

"We adored your grandfather," Linda said. "He was just a perfectly lovely fellow."

"That's good to know," Lizzie said. "And thank you for the offer with the accounting."

My sister was a wunderkind with numbers. She had taken Mom's hobby ranch and turned it into a successful lavender and herb business. I had a feeling she could run circles around Dave. But my sister was always kind.

We met several more people who weren't court neighbors but lived in Shamrock Cove. I kept to the edges of the crowd, while my sister was immersed in the thick of things.

No matter where I was, I'd glance over and see the judge watching me with his frown. People like him didn't bother me. I hung out with loads of curmudgeonly old writers. I was curious, though, about why he was so suspicious of us.

"You're like me," Scott said. "Do you have anxiety about crowds?" I may have jumped a little when he spoke, and the wine I'd been holding spilled on my fingers. He handed me a cocktail napkin.

"You'd think living in Manhattan would have cured me of that problem, but it hasn't."

He grinned. "I'm always looking for an exit, and I like these people."

"They are a nice bunch—except maybe the judge."

Scott waved a hand. "He doesn't like anyone. He was your grandfather's best friend, and they argued like an old married couple in the pub. Don't mind him. The story is that years ago, his wife left him for another man who she had a daughter with. I don't think he's ever gotten over it. Or at least that's what Lolly says when she's had too much sherry. All of that was before mine and Rob's time."

"When did you move here?"

"Hmm. It must be nearly ten years now. Time does go by quickly. Rob retired from the restaurant biz and decided to write cookbooks. And I'm a coder, so I can work from anywhere. When his uncle left him this place, we decided to try it out.

"I didn't think I'd like living in a small town, but now I can't imagine being anywhere else." Scott's words reassured me. I really hoped we could make this our home.

"I'm curious about something. Many things, actually," I said.

"Ask away. I'll help if I can."

"So, the only way to live in the court is to inherit one of the homes?"

He nodded. "One of the rules for living here is you must either leave the home to a loved one, or to one of the other neighbors. It's their way of keeping control of things."

"Is that legal?"

"When you signed the dotted line, it was in your contract."

I'd had my lawyer and agent look over the contracts. Since no money changed hands, I hadn't paid much attention to what was in them.

"What happens if they don't leave the house to anyone? Like maybe they died suddenly and didn't have a will?"

"It hasn't happened in about fifty years. If it did, there would be a lottery of sorts. Only long-time residents of Shamrock Cove can apply for it. Then, the court residents decide the winner. Some of us thought we might have to have one for your grandad's place. I don't think he told anyone, except for Lolly, that he'd been trying to find you.

"The judge had already set up the lottery when Driscoll, your grandfather, died, and then wasn't at all happy when... sorry. He was just surprised you existed. Lolly said the old man lost it when the will was read."

Scott cleared his throat. "The judge is an exception around here. Don't let him put you off. We'd planned to only be here a couple of years and now we can't imagine leaving. For a small town, there is an amazing amount of culture from theater and art to the gardens—and the best coffee I've ever had, and I've lived all over the world."

I laughed. "The pub, right?" We'd made a quick run at lunchtime for snacks. That's where we'd found Matthew, a barista after my cold, dark, coffee-loving heart. His brew was golden deliciousness, and the Crown and Clover was quaint in an Irish sort of way.

"Yes, that man knows coffee." He laughed. "I've warned Rob if he makes me angry, I'm leaving him for Mattie. I'm way too old for that kid, but I take my coffee seriously."

"We have that in common." I launched into a conversation about my new machine that was on the way, and Scott was dutifully impressed.

"I'll be visiting often and asking for cups of sugar, so you'll invite me in for a cuppa."

"Any time." And I was surprised that I meant it. He was a kindred soul.

"Oi, you're hogging the guests," a tall black woman in a flowery dress and black boots said. She reminded me of Lupita Nyong'o, who I considered one of the most beautiful women in the world.

She held out her hand, and I took it. "I'm Brenna Sullivan," she said. Her Irish brogue was so strong it took me a minute to understand she'd just given me her name.

"Mercy McCarthy," I offered. "My sister Lizzie is over there." I motioned to where my sister was talking with Linda and Lolly.

"We're happy to have some fresh faces," she said. "I loved your grandad. He was a curmudgeonly old coot, but he made me love the classics. I've read your books though, edge of your seat those."

I smiled. It was always nice for a writer to hear kind words. "Do you live on the court?"

"Aye," she said. "I'm in number four. Though I travel a great deal for work. But it's nice to have a home I can relax in now and again. I'm off to Bali at the end of the week."

"Wow," I said. "I was there once. It's gorgeous. What kind of work is it you do?"

"Photographer. I'm doing a travel shoot there for a magazine."

"Glamorous," I said.

She waved a hand. "It's not. Most of what I do is for trade magazines, boring machine parts, manufacturing, and ships—that sort of thing. But I dig around for freelance work when I need a getaway. Please don't think me rude, but I'd love to do new headshots for your book jackets. The one they're using now does you no service. You're gorgeous."

"Uh. Thanks?" I'd been using the same photo for years.

She and Scott laughed.

"Years ago, when I was first published, they needed a photo fast. I couldn't afford a professional one, so I had my mom take a picture with my phone." That was the truth.

"Well, I'll help you update it as a welcome gift. But it will have to wait until I get back."

"Thanks," I said. "I'll take you up on that."

There was some clinking of silverware against crystal.

"The grand dame is about to speak," she said. "I love Lolly, she's the best thing about living here."

"Hey," Scott protested.

She nudged him. "You feel the same way."

"That I do."

Mrs. O'Malley smiled as everyone quieted down. "I'd like to welcome our wonderful new neighbors, Mercy and Lizzie McCarthy." She pulled something out of her pocket. It was a set of keys, which were also on a shamrock key chain, like the ones for the cottage.

"I'm officially passing the torch of the store from your grandfather to you." She handed Lizzie the keys.

"Sláinte." People cheered and raised their glasses.

While I'd given speeches, accepted awards, and other duties

of an author who succeeded in a challenging business, I'd never been comfortable in the limelight.

My sister, whom everyone considered the quiet one, basked in it. She was smiling so hard—I thought her face might break.

This move had been a good one.

My shoulders may have relaxed a few inches. Lizzie would be okay. I'd make sure of it.

Several people offered their goodbyes around eight or so. I should have been tired, but the nap had helped.

"Let us help you clean all of this up, Mrs. O'Malley," Lizzie said.

"Nonsense. I've help enough." She pointed to Rob and Scott. "You all go home and rest. You've had a long day. And please stop calling Mrs. O'Malley. God rest her soul, but Mrs. O'Malley was my dear ma. I'm just Lolly."

"Thank you, for everything, Lolly," Lizzie said.

"Yes, we are very grateful," I added. My sister smiled at me like she was proud. I wasn't completely devoid of social graces. "Oh, what about locking up?"

"I've an extra set of keys," Lolly said, patting her sweater pocket. "I'll drop them by later."

On our way back, it took us a few minutes to locate the secret door leading into the court, but it hadn't taken as long as when we'd first arrived. We were on the way to our house when there was a loud thump and a moan.

My sister and I glanced at one another and ran toward the noise.

"Ohhhh," someone groaned. "You've murdered me." I knew that voice.

We rushed through the gate and up the sidewalk of number five. The front door was open, and the judge was on the porch doubled over. He grasped his chest as if he was in horrific pain.

"Murderers," he yelled. "I know it was you lot."

"Get a pillow for his head and one for his feet," I said quickly. I'd done CPR training for a book long ago, and it stuck with me. While I hadn't known how to help Lolly earlier, I knew a heart attack when I saw it.

"Judge, look at me," I ordered. He grew pale in the darkness. Someone flipped on a light, and I blinked.

"You've killed me." He reached out a gnarled hand and pointed at me, his glassy eyes accusing me. And then they rolled back in his head, as his body convulsed.

"I need something to put in his mouth."

Someone handed me a large serving spoon, and I braced the handle between his teeth.

"Get a doctor or an ambulance," I screamed. For the second time that day, I was worried about someone dying in my arms.

I realized that Rob had knelt at my side. "What do we do?"

"Keep him from hurting himself," I said. "Hold the handle of the spoon between his teeth. I thought it was a heart attack, but I don't know. I've never heard anyone convulse with a heart attack. But let's try to keep him alive."

He was much more fragile than he looked. When the spasms stopped, I turned him on his back to take his pulse. He had none. My fictional detective's sometimes boyfriend was an EMT. The training I'd taken for that character left me no doubts.

"I need to start compressions." My training kicked in, and I didn't let up until an EMT shoved me out of the way.

"Call it," one of the EMTs said.

My heart pounded hard in my chest, and I found it difficult to breathe.

The judge wasn't going to make it. Tears brimmed in my eyes. Had he been murdered, as he'd claimed?

And, if so, why had he accused me?

THREE

I sat on the garden bench just outside the judge's house while a police officer took in the scene. I was numb, at least my brain was. So much had happened in the last few minutes, not the least of which was I'd watched a man I'd barely known die.

And he'd blamed me. Why?

My stomach twisted with nerves.

A few minutes later, the officer motioned for the EMTs to cover the body. While the judge was wheeled away, the officer came toward me.

"Ms. McCarthy?"

"Yes?" I croaked. I cleared my throat.

"I'm Detective O'Malley. If you don't mind, let's go to your cottage so you can warm up."

"Okay." Warmth sounded good to me. The rain had stopped, but the air was nippy, and my hands were frozen. "Wait. Where is my sister?" I asked worriedly. I glanced around for Lizzie.

"Your neighbors took her home."

I raced away from him and toward the house to check on her.

"Lizzie?" The lights were on, but I didn't see her.

"Back here," she called out.

I ran through the hallway to the back of the house.

She was at the stove, tending to a kettle. Rob and Scott sat at the table, and there was a platter of food in the center.

"Hi," I said. Then I went to her at the stove. "Are you okay?"

She forced a smile. "I'm fine," she whispered. "What about you?"

I nodded.

"The guys brought us some food over," she said in her sing-song voice. "Wasn't that sweet of them?"

"It is," I said.

"Lizzie seemed a bit shaky, so we brought her home," Rob said. "I hope that's okay."

My sister was one of the strongest women I'd known, but after she lost her future husband and his daughter who she loved as her own a few months after my mom's death, I never quite knew how she'd take any upset.

Two months ago, she'd had a complete breakdown—the kind where they put you in a hospital until you get better.

I'd vowed then to spend the rest of my life bringing the joy back into her life. She and my mom had always been there for me. It was my time to be the strong one.

Lizzie never had any doubts I'd become successful. She was the one who kept me going in those early years. She'd even sent me money to float my rent so I could stop waitressing and write. I'd paid her back with my first advance, but I'd never forgotten her belief in me.

I'd never be able to repay her kindness, but this move was an attempt at giving back a little to a woman who always had my best interests at heart.

Detective O'Malley followed me into the kitchen and intro-duced himself to Lizzie.

He did a double-take as people often did when they encountered us together. I didn't mind, as it had been happening all of our lives.

"Kieran," Scott said to the officer. "It is always good to see you."

The detective nodded toward him and Rob. "Good to see you both. If you don't mind, I have a few questions for everyone."

While Lizzie poured us tea, we sat at the kitchen table. Her hands shook, and I didn't think she was ready for twenty questions with the detective.

"I don't suppose this is something that could wait until tomorrow?" I asked on my sister's behalf. "It's been a very long day."

"I'm afraid I need some answers now while everything is fresh in your mind."

His logic made sense, but I was slightly annoyed on my sister's behalf.

"Let us start at the beginning," Kieran said. "The victim was overheard saying that you'd killed him."

I sighed. Of course he'd begin with that line of questioning.

"Here is what you need to know," I said. "I only met the man this evening. Yes, he did say that someone had killed him. I just met him, so, no, I don't think he was speaking to me. We were walking past his house, and I tried to save him."

Though, I was worried I'd acted too rashly and had possibly killed him. I thought he was having a heart attack, but I was exhausted. Maybe I'd got it wrong, and I had killed him by pressing too hard on his chest cavity.

I pray that isn't true.

"I have several witnesses who say he pointed at you—"

I held up a hand. I'd been thinking about this. "He pointed upward but wasn't necessarily doing so at me. Most of our new neighbors stood behind me while I tried to save his life. It could have been anyone. You're trying to accuse me of something I didn't do."

He ran a hand through his hair. "No one is accusing you of anything. I'm only trying to ascertain the facts. A man has died, and I'm doing my job."

"Well, I can't tell you any more than I already have," I said. My hands were fists. "If you believe what the judge said that someone killed him, you should be questioning someone who actually knows him. There's this thing called motive. Other than the fact that he was somewhat rude to me at the party, I have no motive.

"I lived in New York, and I'm a writer. If I killed everyone critical of me, well..."

I wasn't usually so cranky, but it'd been a long day, even with a nap.

I shrugged. "There are so many people in my karma line before the judge. I mean, if I was prone to murdering people who annoy me, I'd start with that one critic at *The Post*. The judge wouldn't have even made it on my top thirty list of people to kill."

The men around the table laughed.

"Good to know," the detective said.

The tea was herbal and probably meant to relax everyone. I added several lumps of sugar and a spot of cream to make it a bit tastier.

"Ms. McCarthy, I need to ask you a few questions too," he said to my sister.

She smiled. "Of course. Please, call me Lizzie. But like my sister said, I had no reason to kill the poor man. He wasn't exactly kind to me at the party, but I've dealt with worse."

The detective sighed. "I don't believe either of you killed him. As your sister so deftly pointed out, you didn't have much motive. And the judge was known to be temperamental with everyone.

"What I need to know is exactly what happened when you came home," he said.

My sister took a sip of her tea and then closed her eyes. "We'd just passed his gate when the judge moaned. It was a terrible sound, and Mercy ran toward his house."

"Did you see anyone? Other than the judge."

She shook her head. "It was very dark, even with the lights in his garden. His front door was open, and Mercy was already helping him before... I could comprehend he was on the ground. I found the lights in his front hall. And I think I yelled for help."

"You did," Rob said. "We were coming through the court entrance and heard her scream."

I must have been too busy trying to figure out what happened to the judge because I didn't remember her screaming.

"She's good in a crisis, my sister, that is. I just stood there while she tried to help the judge." She opened her eyes and then took my hand. "You were amazing."

"He died," I said flatly, as if I was to blame. If I was honest, I'd been disappointed. It was my first time using CPR, and I was worried I'd done something wrong.

"It wasn't your fault," she said. "The point is you tried. I couldn't move until you yelled and told me what to do. Rob and Scott came running. One of them grabbed a spoon from some-where to help keep him from swallowing his tongue."

"We'd brought it with us," Rob interjected. "We'd been carrying some of our dishes from the party home."

The detective wrote that in his notebook.

"And then, uh, oh, I've forgotten her name," Lizzie said. "The one who looks like a supermodel. I'm usually so good with names."

"Brenna," Scott provided.

"Yes. She pulled out her phone and called 999. Rob and

Scott tried to help Mercy with the judge. I don't remember seeing anyone else.

"At least..." She frowned.

"What is it?" I asked.

"While you were over him, I... I didn't want to look. He was in so much pain, and it reminded me of... Anyway, I thought I saw someone in the bushes. Just for a second. But then you yelled for an ambulance, and when I looked back, they were gone."

"Do you remember what they looked like?" the detective asked before I could. "Male or female?"

"No, other than their face was white, I couldn't see any distinguishing features." She closed her eyes. "No. Just a flash of white skin, and then nothing. I could have imagined it."

She opened her eyes and stared at me.

I shook my head. Even on her worst days, she hadn't hallucinated things. I believed she'd seen someone.

"And what did you see?" The detective turned his attention to Rob and Scott.

"We had just come through the gate," Rob said.

"When we heard a scream," Scott finished his sentence. "We ran to the judge's house and tried to help. Mercy was a force to be reckoned with. She was barking orders, trying to keep the judge alive. He was clearly in terrible pain."

"Did you see anyone running away from the scene?"

"No." Rob turned to Scott. "Did you? We were carrying dishes, and I was focused on not tripping on the cobblestones in the dark. We really need to get that area in front of number four patched up. And some lights on the path."

Scott nodded. "I'll talk to Lolly."

The detective cleared his throat. "Did you see anyone, Scott?"

"No. But I was focused on the lane. I wasn't looking near the houses. If someone ran away from the scene, they might have gone along the side of one of the houses and then through the back path."

"The back path?" I asked.

"It's the path that leads up to the castle that runs behind the homes," Rob added.

An easy way for a killer to hide their escape.

Then it hit me. "Wait. The only reason we think its murder is because the judge said someone murdered him. But without any forensics, how can we really know?" I asked. "There was nothing outwardly that made it look like he'd been hit or anything. He looked like he had a heart attack until the convulsions started. He could have died of natural causes."

"Right," the detective said. "But given the circumstances, it's best to ask questions of those who saw what was going on before they forget. If it is a situation that had malicious intent, we need the facts as quickly as possible. As you were first on the scene..."

"Got it," I said. It made sense. I was tired and cranky, and the man annoyed me to no end. But he was doing his job.

"Did any of you see him argue with any of the neighbors at the party?"

Everyone just stared at one another.

"Let me put it this way, was there anyone who seemed unusually upset by the judge's normal, caustic self?"

"We weren't upset," Lizzie said. "But he told me and my sister that we weren't welcome. He didn't believe our grandfather gave us this place. He said he'd be doing some research or something. I just figured he was a cranky old dude. I don't do well with people who make a choice to be rude so I didn't speak to him much."

I smiled. My sister was a proper combination of Texan and Southern Belle. No one ever messed with her. If someone mistook her quietness as meekness, they learned quickly.

And yes, she'd been broken, even the toughest steel

magnolia would have, considering everything she'd gone through the last year. But she was coming back.

"Lizzie is right. He said the same to me. I like curmudgeons, to be honest. Some of my best writer friends are old white guys. I'm used to it. I'm just as curious as the judge why our grandfather never reached out to us when he was alive."

"I saw him arguing rather meanly with Linda, but that's nothing new," Rob said. "And then Dave tried to smooth things over like he always does, and you know how that went."

Since I didn't really know any of them, I wasn't sure what he meant.

"Any idea why they were arguing?" the detective asked. The question had been on the tip of my tongue. Maybe the guy wasn't so terrible at his job.

Rob shrugged. "I think she was upset because the committee he heads rejected her request to paint her shop door fuchsia. She petitioned to do a complete refresh of Main Street —again."

Scott made a face. "Thank God she was denied. That wouldn't be in our color scheme."

"You can't paint your buildings or doors without permission?" Lizzie frowned.

"No," Rob said. "This village loves its red tape and doesn't like change. Often, I'm on Linda's side, but the bright pink would have really stood out. Linda didn't like that your grandad's store was painted black on the outside, but it's an institution. The judge wasn't going to allow any changes to the face of the village, and he was head of the council."

"The judge must have been on Brenna's last nerve tonight, as well. She shot him the finger," Scott added. "Even your grandmother pointed her finger at him and told him to behave." He turned to me. "Lolly is the detective's grandmother."

I nodded my thanks, wondering if I could see any family resemblance.

"Do any of you remember any other noises before you heard the judge moan or Lizzie scream?" the detective asked.

We all shook our heads.

Lizzie's hands were shaking on the table.

The detective glanced at them and then at her. There was a gentle expression on his face.

"I'm sure you're exhausted," he said. "I'll make the rounds to the other neighbors. Ms. McCarthy, thank you for your efforts to save the judge. Whatever happened, you did your best. From what the EMTs said, nothing you could have done would have changed the outcome. We'll know more when the medical examiner and coroner take a look."

"Uh. Thanks." That kindness had been unexpected.

"We should go too," Rob said. "Look, I know what happened tonight has made this an awful day. But... I promise Shamrock Cove is usually a grand place to live. We have our drama, all small towns do, but the people here are good. And we're thrilled that you're here."

I grinned. "Thanks, guys. For everything. And we'll take your word for it—at least for now."

"Goodnight to you all. I'm going to sleep for twenty-four hours." Lizzie waved goodbye.

After they left, I locked the doors. Lizzie had sat down on the steps in the entry.

"Did we do the right thing coming here?" she asked softly.

"Yes," I said with more determination than I'd felt. "Would we be the McCarthys if our arrival hadn't been eventful?"

She smiled. "I guess you're right. It all feels..."

"A bit much," I finished. "I couldn't agree more. But just think of the book fodder it will give me. A mean judge. A woman who falls asleep at the oddest times."

She giggled.

"And think of the bookstore," I said.

She sighed happily. "It is quite dreamy. Almost like a place fairies might live. And we will have fun with our treasure hunt to find out more about our grandfather. And maybe our father. I wonder if he had any pictures around here."

I nodded. "I'm sure we'll find some." My sister headed more toward the fanciful, while I was firmly planted on the dark side. But right now, if she needed me to believe in things like fairies to get through the day, I would.

"The judge didn't seem like a very nice man, but I wish he hadn't died," she said. "Do you think he was murdered? And are you certain you don't see it as some kind of omen?"

"No," I said. "He was an elderly man. He could have died from old age for all we know. But if someone hurt him, it had nothing to do with us."

At least, I didn't think so. Strange things had happened to me in New York the last two years. Items had gone missing from my apartment. There were the random photos mailed to me. And it felt like someone had been watching me every time I left my apartment.

I mostly chalked it up to forgetfulness and my paranoid imagination. But, I had to admit, I'd no longer felt safe in my home.

Had that trouble followed me here?

FOUR

The next day, I woke up to someone banging on the door. It took me a minute to figure out where I was. I'm not a morning person. It takes me several hours and copious amounts of coffee before I'm ready to face the day.

In my thirty-plus years on the planet, that had never changed. I'd become a caffeine addict when I was in my early teens.

People in my life know this about me. The person at the door, not so much.

I opened it to find a giant box standing on two legs. The outside of the box read: Jura Giga Ten. I smiled and clapped my hands together like a child given free rein at the candy store.

"Hello?" someone said from behind the box.

"Oh. Come in. Straight ahead. Can I help you?"

"Just make sure I don't run into anything," the voice said. A smooth Irish accent.

Wait a minute. I knew that voice.

"Detective?"

"Yes, am I too close to the table in the hallway?" He sounded short of breath.

I had no idea why he'd been the one to deliver the box, but it was obviously heavy.

"About another three feet and make a jog to the right. I can help."

"I've got it," he said.

We made it to the kitchen, and he set the box down on the table, then stretched out his back.

"I've never seen one in person," he said. "Do you want help setting it up?"

If I wasn't mistaken, he seemed to be almost as excited as I was. His attitude was quite different from the night before. He'd made me think I was a murder suspect. Though, with a bit of hindsight and some sleep, I supposed he was doing his job by asking his questions.

"Is setting up coffee machines part of a detective's duties?"

He laughed. I was glad he took it the way I had intended.

"In this village, it's probably a law somewhere. So that you know, deliveries aren't allowed on the court before ten a.m. If one comes in, it's usually delivered to the station, and someone will call for you to pick it up."

"I don't remember all of these rules in the contracts."

He chuckled. "Some are unwritten laws of the court. So, do you want some help?"

I shrugged. "Sure, thank you for bringing it all this way."

It took almost an hour, most of which I spent saying, "You should go, I'll figure it out." But we finally got the lights on, and he helped me program it.

After running some water through it, I loaded in the beans. Espresso was on one side, my favorite American blend on the other. I'd packed them in my suitcase. Okay, technically, I'd smuggled them in. But I hoped the man standing in my kitchen hadn't realized that.

"Cortado?" I asked.

"That would be grand," he said.

I pushed the button. The machine gurgled to life and soon the kitchen smelled delightful.

"Impressive," he said as I handed him a cup.

"It should be," I said. "But it's going to be worth every penny. We would have picked it up."

"I was coming this way to check on my gran. I was worried she did too much last night for the party and then everything that happened with the judge. She was the only one in town who could manage him somewhat."

I sat down at the table and motioned him to do the same. "Any news on the toxicology or pathology?"

"We don't move quite as quickly as you do in the States," he said. "And I'm not one to talk about ongoing cases with strangers." It was blunt, but there was a twinkle in his eye.

I held up my hands in surrender. "I didn't mean it that way. For the record, they don't move quickly, at least where I live. The medical examiner's office is often overloaded and under-staffed. I was just curious if he'd been poisoned."

He frowned. "Why do you say that?"

"Well, I was doing some research last night. I found a book in my grandfather's library. At first, I thought he'd been having a heart attack, but then there were the convulsions. I couldn't sleep until I had some idea of what might have happened. His pupils were very small, and he seemed confused about what he was seeing.

"And I noticed the gardens around here are varied with so many types of flowers. And it would be easy enough for someone to make some tincture with foxglove, oleander, hemlock, even azaleas, which can be dangerous. He wasn't exactly a kind and loving person. So..." I stopped speaking when I found the detective staring at me oddly.

"You've given this a great deal of thought," he said. It wasn't an accusation, as there was more surprise in his voice.

"I write about murder for a living. I've trained with and

interviewed all types of law enforcement, doctors, and scientists. One picks things up along the way. He didn't have any external injuries that we could see, so..." I stared down at my cup.

"Poison," he said, as if mulling it over.

"Or natural causes. The internet has made it extremely easy to kill anyone without leaving much of a trace. That's why I asked about the toxicology this morning. If the medical examiner or coroner waits too long, it may disappear from the system."

I looked up at him. He was still watching me. "You probably think I'm a nuisance and telling you things you already know."

He smiled. "Not at all. I was thinking it was nice to have a conversation with someone who is knowledgeable about crime and who has an outsider's view on the court."

I raised an eyebrow. "You aren't following the script, Detective." I smiled.

"What do you mean?"

"In a mystery, law enforcement is always at odds with amateur sleuths. They're constantly being told to stay out of the way."

He shrugged. "I've never found much use for ego. I've worked with the Met, Scotland Yard, and the Garda Siochána. Keeping an open mind helps solve cases quicker."

I'd be doing a search later on the detective. Why had he worked with so many agencies? And why settle for a small village like Shamrock Cove with all that experience?

"Well, I best be going. I need to check on Gran, and she's made cranberry scones. I have to get there before she gives my share to Bernard. She spoils him terribly. My guess, if she's feeling well, she'll be by for a visit."

"Well, I'm no cook, but, thanks to you, I can offer a darn good cup of coffee."

Before he could stand, the front door shut.

Who could that be?

"Hello?" I called out.

He turned to face the kitchen door.

"Good, you're up, I brought you some... Oh, hello, Detective." Lizzie smiled at him and then gave me a strange look. Then she saw the coffee maker. "It's not as big as I thought it would be," she said in an utterly deadpan voice.

I laughed.

Lizzie wore jeans and a light-blue sweater with her boots. She held several shopping bags on her wrists, along with two cups in her hand. "I brought you coffee from the pub. The grocery store was opening when I returned, so I picked up a few things for breakfast and lunch. He was incredibly well stocked with the most beautiful fruits and veggies."

"I feel I'm intruding. It was good to see you both," the detective said. And then he waved goodbye.

She waited until he shut the door. "What was that all about?"

I told her about the delivery and that we'd been discussing the judge.

"How are you feeling this morning?" I asked, as I helped her put away the groceries.

She sighed. "Good. I had terrible nightmares, but then I woke up and looked out in the backyard. Come with me." She took my hand and dragged me out the back door.

We'd stepped out onto the deck the day before, but this time she pulled me into the middle of the yard. "There's a two-seater swing under that tree and a bench in the middle of the rose bushes, which need a good pruning. There are two bird baths, and then come through here on this path."

I followed her through some trees. I hadn't realized the yard was so large.

Behind some of the trees was a circle of flowers and flowering bushes. In the center was a small water fountain. And there was a curved bench to the side. Even my untrained eye could see it was extraordinarily beautiful.

"Look at the door in the tree. It's a fairy garden," she whispered as though not to disturb the fey. "Every house has one. I saw it this morning and asked Matt at the pub. He told me fairy gardens are quite popular here."

I smiled. I didn't believe in fairies, but I loved that my sister had found some magic. Any hopefulness from her was a good thing.

"Very cool," I said. "And very Irish."

She batted a hand at me. "I know you think I'm silly, but I love that our grandfather had one. It makes me feel..."

"Connected?"

"Yes, and that maybe I got a bit of my whimsy from him. You and Mom are both so practical, and we didn't know our dad. I've always wondered why I'm so different from you two."

I laughed. "I don't know how practical I am. I write murder mysteries for a living. But it is beautiful here and quite unexpected."

"I agree. Can I leave you on your own for breakfast? I really want to get to the bookstore."

"Sure. I'll even come help. But I need a shower and a couple more cups of coffee."

"Take your time. I'm looking forward to getting acquainted with the place. Oh, and look at the office. Let me know if there's anything you need in there. I'm planning a trip to Dublin at the end of the week for some odds and ends I'm not sure we'll find here.

"Is it weird that the detective makes home deliveries?"

"Yes."

She stopped on the path, and then turned to me. "This place is kind of weird, but I like that about it. And breathe in that air. We have fresh air at home in Texas, but it's different here. It's like breathing in happiness."

I laughed. "So Ireland is magical and happy. That's a good thing."

"Except for what happened last night, it's a wonderful place. Did the detective say anything about the judge?" she whispered as if someone might be listening.

"No word, yet. He said things go slower around here."

She shrugged. "I guess that's to be expected in a small town."

I nodded.

And Lizzie was off. It was good she had so much work ahead of her to keep her mind busy. But I worried about her pushing too hard.

I was also worried we had a murderer in our midst.

Whatever it took, I would protect my sister.

Two hours later, I headed out of the court. I waved to Rob, who was picking herbs from his garden.

"Come by for tea later and bring your sister. I want to try out some new recipes on you."

"Thank you, that's so kind. You never have to ask twice if food is involved," I said. "Though you've made us enough meals for a month already."

We laughed, and I headed to where the secret entry was on the wall. As I pulled it back, I thought I saw something out of the corner of my eye.

I blinked, but it was gone. I could have sworn there had been someone in the judge's garden.

"I need more coffee," I said to myself.

I followed the path behind the Main Street buildings and found the back door to the bookstore. It was locked.

I knocked.

It took a minute, but Lizzie came to the door. She had two pencils behind her ears, and her hair was a mess.

"Is everything okay?" I asked.

"I've only just now found his record books. He hid them in a puzzle cabinet. It took me an hour to figure out which things to pull to get the doors open. I'm learning so much about him from this store. He was eccentric and security conscious. Now, if I can just figure out where everything is, we'll be set."

"Is there anything I can do to help?"

"Yes." She turned and headed inside the bookstore. After locking the door behind me, I followed. There was an office to the right, and she sat down at the desk, an old door with a piece of glass. The chair she sat in was gothic and looked like something out of a wizarding book.

All the walls had stacked boxes and books against them, going up to the ten-foot ceiling.

This was probably messing with her need for order. While I didn't have her penchant for neatness, even this was a bit much for me.

She rifled through a stack of papers. "This place has so many hidden nooks and fun discoveries, and it's gorgeous. I was so busy being social last night that I missed a lot of what makes it so special."

"I can't wait."

"While you're looking around, I've printed out an inventory list divided by genre. Can you handle mysteries, thrillers, and YAs? If it's on the shelf, put a mark under the column that says shelved. If it isn't, leave it blank.

"Also, he's got storage somewhere with loads more books, but I can't find it. Maybe there is a basement. I haven't had time to look. If you see it, let me know." She shoved the papers and a pen toward me and waved me away.

She was right, the bookstore was glorious.

The store was dark, and I slid a hand up and down the wall, looking for a switch. All I found were some knobs. I pulled my cell out and turned on the flashlight app. The knobs were brass. I turned one, and a soft light came on above.

According to Lizzie's sheets of paper, the mysteries and thrillers were up the copper stairs. The beautifully painted dark-blue walls and shelves gave it such a classy, and, yes, almost mystical appearance. The scents of cinnamon, vanilla, and leather permeated the air. I loved everything about it and felt at home there. It was quite possibly the most perfect book-store I'd ever been in, and that was saying a great deal.

I quickly worked on the inventory list, and I may have blushed when I realized he carried several copies of all my books. When I returned to the office, she gave me a list for the children's section.

By the time we'd finished, it was nearly noon, and my stomach growled.

I found her pushing on walls around the bookstore.

"Uh, Lizzie?"

She had pencils stuck in her ponytail, as well as her ears.

"I look crazy. I know. But I swear this man loves secret doors. I'm trying to find the basement. If there is one. I've looked everywhere."

I headed to the back door and then turned to face the store. There were several cabinets lining the back hallway. There was one that was more like a wardrobe. I opened both the doors. It was empty. I took a chance and pushed on the back panel. The door opened.

"Of course it's through a Narnia wardrobe," Lizzie whispered behind me.

"Do you have a flashlight with you? I can't find a switch."

She shook her head. "Let me see if I can find one in the office. Though, his organizational skills were severely lacking. I was surprised since the house was so neat."

"You forget, Lolly had the cleaners at his place. They may have done some extra tidying. And while the neighbors helped in here, I don't think they bothered with the business side of things."

"True." She headed into the office. I nearly slapped my forehead. "Never mind. I can use my phone." I pulled it out of my pocket and turned on the app. The area was so dark, it didn't help much. I stepped through the wardrobe onto something wooden and creaky.

"This has to be a safety hazard." I finally found the light and turned the knob. I blinked when the overhead came on. It wasn't a basement. I'd read that most places in Ireland didn't have them because the ground was too wet.

There was a step down to a wooden floor. The space to my right was narrow, and I realized it was a storage area that ran under the stairs in the bookshop.

Lizzie followed me in as we squeezed past the maze of boxes. It looked as if it narrowed even more, but at the end of the packages was a small room. It was toward the back of the store, so it had to be near the small restroom on the other side of the wall.

There was a petite round desk with an antique crystal lamp. I turned on the light. We gasped as we saw it at the same time.

The names on the envelope made me blink.

"To My Beloved Granddaughters, Mercy and Lizzie McCarthy."

FIVE

We took the letter home and set it on the kitchen table. While Lizzie fixed a salad, I put the lasagna Rob had made us in the oven for lunch.

"Um," I said, as I stared at the multitude of knobs on the AGA.

Lizzie waved me away and set to work. It was way more confusing than regular ovens, and I needed help with those.

While the lasagna heated up, we sat down at the kitchen table.

The letter might as well have been a flashing neon sign the way we stared at it.

"Why wouldn't he just give it to the lawyer?" she asked. "Why hide it away like that? In a secret room where we might not have ever seen it."

I pursed my lips together and shook my head. "No idea. From what we've found so far, we know he was eccentric. And he liked a good mystery. But seeing our names written in his handwriting makes it all real."

She smiled. "I think I've figured out his bookkeeping system, and eccentric is an understatement."

I grinned back. "It's only been a day. Stop and think about how brilliant you are for figuring it out so quickly."

She waved a hand at me as if I was being silly.

"I mean it, Lizzie. If I had been on my own with all that—well, it just wouldn't have happened."

"Just open it," she said. "I want to know why he didn't contact us all this time. Why didn't we know about him? Mom never mentioned our dad was Irish. Not that she spoke about him much. I have so many questions."

"So do I. Maybe she didn't know anything about him. I mean, she called him the sperm donor. I don't think she ever planned for him to be a part of our lives."

Most kids asked questions if there was a missing parent, and Lizzie and I were no different. Our mom said she fell for a guy, and then he disappeared. The sadness when we brought him up was palpable with Mom, so we just dropped it.

But maybe there would be answers to the questions we'd been asking our whole lives in this letter. Time to find out.

I used a butter knife to slice the envelope apart.

I took a deep breath and pulled out the sheets of paper. I'd half expected them to be typed, but they weren't. The handwriting was almost calligraphy.

My sister shifted in her chair so we could read it together.

Granddaughters,

I must apologize, girls, as I had no idea you existed until about a year ago when an heir hunter found you. By then, I felt it was much too late for me to foist myself upon you. I already knew I was dying, and I did not wish to add to your troubles or inter-fere with your life when you were already going through such turmoil.

The short explanation as to why it took so long for me to discover you is I refused to open my son's things from when they sent them home from the war. Over thirty years ago, he was part of a special UN force sent on a mission. He never returned.

I am sorry to say he went missing in action before you were even born. He was a good boy. All these years, I've assumed him dead. Though, I do not know what happened to him and he may, alas, be gone too. We were never very close. It was my fault entirely.

My dear wife, your grandmother, was the nurturer in the family. I spent my life distracted by books and discovered much too late what was most important in life—family. My last conversation with your father was a harsh one, and I told him to never darken my door again. To this day, I've no idea if he's alive. I thought I saw him once a few years ago in Dublin, but the man disappeared before I could catch him. I truly wish I had an answer for you. It is the mystery I couldn't solve before leaving this body.

He would have loved you and your mother well if he'd known about you. I feel certain about that. I am sorry you did not have a chance to know him. My heart aches with the knowledge that she probably wondered why he never returned. But we may never know. It was only when I found out I was dying that I decided to go through his things. I found letters that had been meant to go to your mother. He was deeply in love with her.

I left the letters from him to her in a drawer in the library—should you wish to read them. I've also left some information about my life and his from the early days. You'll find them throughout my private library. You might find it a fun mystery to play out as you learn about us.

When I had my man research your mother, he discovered you two. Your mother was ailing then, and again, I did not want to trouble you. While I do not have DNA proof yet, I feel the timing of my son's letters and the date of your births confirms my suspicions.

Should you wish to know about your family on this side of the pond, there are also several journals and historical records in the library.

I will not hammer on except to say my most profound regret was not looking at my son's things before now. I would have loved to have known you girls. I am so very proud of your accomplishments, but also that you seem to be decent human beings. Your mother was an amazing woman by all accounts, and she made certain you were as well.

I hope you will spend some time in my lovely Shamrock Cove. It is a wonderful place to heal the heart. When you're ready to know about your family history, my journals are in the library behind the secret door.

Know you are loved, my girls.

Driscoll O'Heyne

P.S. If the judge gives you any trouble, show him this letter. Then tell him I said to stuff it up his old arse.

The last bit made me smile.

Lizzie sniffed and I turned to look at her. She'd pulled a tissue from her pocket and dabbed her eyes.

"I wish he would have reached out. I understand why he didn't but..." She sniffed again.

I patted her back. "In a way, it was quite kind of him. We were dealing with so much and we would have had only a little time with him. I bet he never expected us to move here. Do you remember seeing a secret door in the library?"

I hadn't seen one. I loved a secret door. It turned out I had that in common with my grandfather.

She shook her head. "He must have been truly heartbroken when our dad disappeared to wait so long to look through his things. I'm kind of mad at him. It would have been nice to have some other family. We've always been so alone."

"True, but he seemed deeply regretful about finding out too late."

"Funny what he said about the judge. Maybe they weren't as good friends as everyone says."

The timer dinged for the lasagna, and she jumped up.

"I can get it," I said.

"No worries." She took the steaming lasagna and set it in the middle of the table on a trivet. I grabbed the salad from the counter.

We ate in silence. The lasagna was rich and delightfully tasty. Having Rob as a neighbor was a huge bonus.

"I forgot to tell you Rob invited us for tea later," I said. "Though, I'm a bit confused as to when that is. They seem to call every meal tea here."

She nodded. "Probably around four or five. He gave me his number, I'll text. Do you think Mom knew he'd disappeared during the war? Or did she think he abandoned her?"

I shrugged. "She never wanted to talk about him. She called him the donor, as if she'd always meant to have us on her own. Other than he was a nice man and handsome, she would never say anything else." I stuffed lasagna in my mouth.

"Right, but maybe that's because she thought he abandoned her, and it broke her heart. If Grandad had reached out earlier, at least she would have known the truth before..."

"It's too late now," I said. I hadn't meant for it to come out so harsh. "Sorry, you know I didn't mean it that way. It's just that Mom was already in so much pain by then. I'm not sure she could have handled one more thing."

Lizzie blew her nose with a tissue. "True. And you're right

about her not needing anything else to put pressure on her. God, I miss her. She would find all of this so intriguing."

I smiled. "She would. Like you, I wonder why he left the letter in the storage closet under the stairs."

"It's such an odd little place and well hidden. Maybe he was worried someone might take it if he left it here or in his office. I loved the whole Narnia cabinet. How did you even know to push on that back wall?"

"Every shelf, table, and the office was stuffed to the brim with his strange antiques and books. It didn't make sense that huge cabinet would be empty."

"Is it weird that I love he enjoyed secret spaces?"

"Well, we had to get it from somewhere," I said.

She snapped her fingers. "That reminds me, I noticed this time of year is quite busy for the shop. I'm going to stick with the Wednesday opening. I'm also going to institute a children's story time. Will you be my first reader on Saturday mornings? I want to start promoting that in a few weeks."

I grinned. "Of course. Tell me what you need me to do and I'm there for you."

She winked at me. "I'm going to head back to the store. Do you think the letter is the treasure Grandad spoke of in his will?"

I shrugged. "It's certainly a treasure to us. Maybe he thought of us like that as well. I'm curious about our father. Strange that the government never gave our grandad any information about him."

"Maybe he was a spy or something?"

"You've been reading too many Mick Herron novels."

"True. But our grandfather has given us a treasure hunt and a mystery with our dad."

"Also, true."

"You know the books could be the treasure." My sister was incredibly sentimental, and she blinked away tears. "We both love literature, and so did he. I expected his inventory to be a bit more old school, but it wasn't. This place is magical, and he had a great eye."

"He did."

"And maybe the secret door is the hobbit one that leads into his personal library. But you should look for one in there. I need to get back to the store. Can you clean up here?" she asked.

"Of course. Are you sure you don't want me to come with you?"

She squeezed my shoulder. "I feel like that's my baby, and maybe it's time for you to figure out your work schedule and the office here. After you get some writing done, maybe do a bit of research to see if you can find those journals he talked about."

"In other words, stop procrastinating. It's time for you to get back to writing."

"I didn't say that." She smiled. "I just don't want you to hold back any longer because of all my drama."

I held up a hand. "Our lives are intertwined," I said. "There is no bleeding. We've both needed time to heal. But you're right about me getting back to work. I promise to set up my laptop in the office at least. I might even turn it on. The rest of my computer equipment won't be here for a couple of weeks. And I might be on the hunt for another secret door in the library."

"That's a great plan," she said. "And if you get really bored, maybe do some research on the judge."

I stared at her with surprise. "What?"

She shrugged. "I don't like that people may think we had something to do with his death. You write about a really smart detective. What would she do if she was in our predicament?"

She'd find the real killer. While I knew how to do that in fiction, I wasn't so sure about real life.

"We'll see," I said, but I already had plans to do some internet searches at the very least.

I usually plugged my laptop into a larger monitor to save my eyes, but I'd have to make do until they arrived. I prayed we'd brought the right kind of adapters.

She headed out. After I cleaned up our lunch and put the leftovers away, I grabbed my backpack from my room.

I headed to the study. Lizzie had been so worried about the room, but I loved it. The space was exactly what one might imagine a study looking like in an Irish cottage.

I sat my laptop on the desk and plugged the charger into the adapter. Then, I stood back. When it didn't explode, I cheered. I turned it on. It barely had any juice, but it came to life. I didn't open the document my book was in though.

I searched for the sticky note Lizzie gave me with the Wi-Fi code. Once the internet was set, I typed in Judge Michael Pierce. While I was curious about our dad, and I'd be researching him, I felt like that was something I should do with Lizzie.

The first articles that came up on the judge were some of the high-profile cases he'd prosecuted when he'd been the director of public prosecutions. The legal system was quite different here, but he had a history of difficult cases and precedents that were set.

Either directly or indirectly, he'd been responsible for putting hundreds of criminals behind bars for years. From what I'd read, he also had a reputation for being tough but fair with the Gardai and their procedures.

As a judge, he was big on following the letter of the law. Those types of men made lots of enemies, even if they were respected in their community.

While there were hundreds of names of those who had been paroled or released, I cross-checked a few of the criminals who had recently been released from prison.

If it wasn't someone from the court, why wait until yesterday? And when would they have had the opportunity? Real-life mysteries were much more complicated.

With the sun streaming through the window, the room was stuffy.

I went over to the window seat and unlatched the catch. The cool breeze brought in the scent of roses and hydrangeas, along with an argument. It took a few seconds for me to recognize the voices belonged to Rob and Scott.

"You're leaving again?" Rob sounded angry.

"I told you I had this meeting weeks ago. Why are you upset?" Scott sounded annoyed but not nearly as upset as Rob.

"After what happened, you promised to take me with you when you had to be gone for more than a day. And really, don't you think it'll be suspicious if you leave so soon after the judge's death?"

"Why? I didn't have anything to do with it," Scott said.

"But what if they find those papers?" Rob said a bit more softly.

What papers? What were they hiding?

"They haven't even searched his house yet. Besides, there's nothing we did that will raise suspicion," Scott said. "We don't even know how he died. Unless you poisoned him with one of your concoctions."

"I can't believe you'd say something like that. What if one of them hears you?" A door slammed.

Scott mumbled under his breath.

Oh. My. What are these two up to? I really liked them.

I prayed they weren't the ones who killed the judge.

SIX

I could follow up with Rob at tea later that afternoon to see what he and Scott had been fighting about. The first thing I needed to do was get into the judge's home. If there had been foul play, I felt like the answers might be in there somewhere.

That is if he'd been killed. There was no telling when the toxicology report might come in, but my gut told me he'd been murdered. He'd been so surprised by the sudden nature of his attack. If it had just been his heart, surely he wouldn't have shouted about murder...

While his death was none of my business, I didn't like the idea that the others in the neighborhood might think Lizzie and I had anything to do with it. Not that they would say it out loud. I wasn't sure if it was guilt that I couldn't save him or just morbid curiosity, but I had to know what happened to the judge.

And if I was honest, I desperately wanted this fresh start for Lizzie and myself to go well. That wouldn't happen if people in Shamrock Cove thought we might be guilty.

Once I settled on a course of action, it was impossible for me to do anything else. I just wanted to get in there and have a look around. Maybe I'd find something that would help the police.

Ego, much?

I don't know why, but I had to try and find out what happened. Maybe it was that I was naturally nosy. It was what made me a decent mystery writer. Or maybe it was because I wanted to protect my sister if a killer was running around the place. Besides, she'd wanted me to do some research.

I stared at the search on my computer. I had an idea, but my sister wouldn't like my new plan much.

A half-hour later, we were in the front garden.

"Why?" She stared at me pointedly. I'd explained what I'd overheard and what I'd found on the internet. "Aren't you supposed to be writing?"

"I'm just going to poke around a bit," I said.

"It's breaking and entering," she quite rightly said.

I shrugged. "No one, except us, locks their doors around here. Remember? That's the whole point of having a secret door into the court." I'd checked out the path earlier. It ran along the back of the six houses on the court.

"This is ridiculous," she whispered. "What if someone sees you?"

"They won't," I said. "I'll sneak across the path behind the houses."

"If you get caught, I'm not bailing you out." She crossed her arms.

I smiled. "Yes, you will."

"Fine. I will. But I won't be happy about it. Let's get it over with quickly. You get ten minutes max. What do you need me to do exactly?"

"Just pretend like you're working in the garden, and yell loud if any cops come close to the judge's house."

"I really don't like this. I meant for you to look at things on your computer. That doesn't include breaking and entering."

"So you've said; duly noted."

"I do need to prune those roses." She put on some gardening gloves. I had no idea where she'd found them.

"Just pretend to garden and remember to talk loudly if someone tries to go into the judge's house. It's that simple."

She rolled her eyes. "I don't have to pretend I'm gardening. This place needs work."

"Great, so it isn't a waste of time for you."

"I'd rather be at the store," she grumbled. But she bent over some rose bushes. I went through our house and out the back gate.

The small path along the back of the neighborhood wasn't very wide. The gate on our property creaked when I opened it, and I glanced down the way. No one was there. As I passed Brenna's place, which was next to ours, I paused to stare into her backyard. She had turned it into a tropical oasis. I didn't even know palm trees could grow in Ireland.

As I was about to move on, Brenna came to the door and opened it. I ducked down quickly. I hid behind a hedge filled with bright red flowers. I crawled on my hands and knees to the judge's backyard, which was on the other side of Brenna's, and waited behind a huge apple tree in the corner.

My jeans were filthy, as were my sneakers. And I had small cuts in my hands from the rocky path.

This detective business is painful.

When the door shut again, I peeked over to her backyard. It appeared she'd gone inside.

The judge's gate had a key lock on it.

Of course it does.

I sighed.

The back wall was waist-high, and there was nothing I could do. Unless I climbed over it.

Glancing up and down the path again. I hiked my leg onto the stone wall, straining the seams of my jeans and making me aware of muscles in my groin I didn't know I had.

In for a penny...

The next part of my adventure was one of the many reasons I'd never been particularly gifted as an athlete. I'm a klutz. My pants leg caught on something while the rest of me tumbled to the ground. I landed on my butt with one leg still in the air.

I threw a free hand over my mouth to stifle my groan.

"What was that?" I heard someone ask. It sounded like Lolly, who lived next door to the judge.

"I didn't hear anything," the detective said.

Oh. Great.

My stomach twisted into a knot. The last thing I needed was for him to find me in the judge's garden with my leg attached to the judge's garden gate.

They were in the backyard.

My leg was still up in the air. My pants had caught on the latch. I reached up to try and unhook my leg, but to no avail.

"Maybe you should check. We haven't had a suspicious death in years. People will be curious," she said. "Might be some kids taking a look around."

Bernard growled.

Oh. No.

"I'm sure it's fine, Gran. We just sat down for tea. It's probably just squirrels again."

Crud.

"They are a pest this time of year," Lolly said. "Come here, boy, and settle down."

No matter how I tried to reach my leg on the latch, it didn't do any good.

Finally, I lay back on the ground. After undoing the buttons on my jeans, I shimmied out of them. It was chilly, but I had no choice but to strip.

Thankfully, the sides of the yard were surrounded by a large yew hedge that had grown almost as tall as the roofline of the house. Yews were toxic. Their presence reminded me of the judge, who didn't seem universally well-liked and was a bit poisonous himself.

"Fine," Lolly said. "But promise you'll go check when we're done. I don't want troublemakers stealing the judge's things or messing with the house."

"Sure, I'll check when we're done."

I put my pants and shoes back on while they talked. Since the detective was headed to the judge's house after his tea, I didn't want to try to sneak inside. Besides, if the gate was locked, the door probably was as well.

Until they moved away from Lolly's backyard, I couldn't chance crawling back over the wall. I found a perch near the massive yew and stayed there.

"You knew him better than most," Kieran said. "Do you know if he was having trouble with anyone?"

There was at least a minute of silence.

Then Lolly sighed. "He was a troublesome old coot with more secrets than anyone had a right. He was always messing about with people's lives. You know that as well as I."

"True, but someone in trouble enough to kill him? Especially in the court?"

"Are you asking if one of the neighbors killed him?"

"Yes," Kieran said a little too quickly.

"Now don't you be stirring up trouble here in the court. Look to his past. That's where you'll find the evil, if there is any. Are you sure someone's murdered him?"

"No," he said. "But it was more than a heart attack, so I'm not waiting to investigate. His neighbors weren't happy with him. I heard as much when they talked about him after your party at the bookshop."

"Are you certain?" she asked. "And what were you doing eavesdropping?"

"I wasn't eavesdropping. I was interviewing witnesses. Don't play games, Gran. You hear everything. What's the craic?"

"Are you saying I spy on the neighbors?"

"That's exactly what I'm saying. You've always done it, and we all know."

She laughed, which wasn't what I'd expected.

"Someone has to keep an eye on things, boyo."

"So?"

I was equally interested in the answer.

"He had issues with everyone. Though, I'd take my attention off the newcomers. He gave them the eye, but he wasn't serious about it. Driscoll wouldn't have contacted those girls if he hadn't been related. Michael always complained and put people in their place."

Well, at least Lolly was on our side.

"It is strange that he died the day they arrived," the detective said. "And one of them is trained to kill."

What had my sister said to him? I did have Krav Maga training, but I'd only done it for a book—and to feel safer when I lived in New York.

"I'm sure they were having you on," she said. "That Mercy wouldn't hurt a fly, though I've read articles about her travels and how deep into her research she goes. Maybe she could do someone in."

Thanks, Lolly.

"Anyone else?"

"Michael was the deciding vote on Rob's food truck, which did not go down well with the rest of the court. We'd all wanted him to have his dream. We need to bring diversity into Shamrock Cove in food and culture, you know as well as I. That's how we keep our village healthy and prosperous. Scott may have made a few threats to the judge about that."

"What do you mean?" the detective asked.

"Earlier in the week, Scott tried to talk some sense to the judge, and they had quite the row in the front garden. Brenna had to pull Scott away before they brawled.

"I gave the old blaggard an earful. He was out of his wits. His mind was going, and I don't think he knew it. He'd forget appointments and such. Not like him. Always had a sharp mind, that one. But just over the last year, he'd been on the decline."

"Do you think it's possible he killed himself?"

She snorted. "Too much of an ego, and he wouldn't have picked something so painful. I talked to the boys—they said he was in a lot of pain before he died."

"Anyone else?"

"Linda was always on his nerves, as was that husband of hers," she said. "You know why. Their latest scheme about a Main Street revamp had him up in arms. I heard them yelling at each other at the last pub quiz."

"I thought that was over a long time ago," he said.

"Not in Linda's mind. She isn't one to let things go, and she had revised her plan. She wanted to present it to the council, but she needed his permission. He wasn't about to give it.

"But you and I know, God bless her, she's not clever or capable enough for murder."

Wow. That was mean. I didn't know Linda very well, but she seemed like a nice woman.

The detective cleared his throat.

"And that's not including the rest of the town," Lolly said. "If someone did do him in, you'll have a fair number of suspects."

At least she didn't think I killed the judge, which was a bonus. I wasn't so sure about her grandson.

"He loathed what Brenna did with her back garden and considered her jacuzzi an affront. I quite like it. Good for the bones and these tired old muscles."

"You've been in her jacuzzi?" He sounded shocked.

I smiled.

"Yes, Grandson. We had a bottle of wine, and some cheese. 'Twas a lovely evening. Except the judge spied on us the whole time.

"I came home and slept better than I have in years. Thinking about putting one in myself, but that sweet Brenna says I can use hers any time, and I don't like the idea of digging up my garden. I've just gotten it where I love it."

The detective laughed. I had a feeling that was an ongoing joke.

"But he wasn't all bluster and menace, you know that as well as I. The judge had his good side and helped many people. He just liked things his way."

"True. But most think he did more harm than good," Kieran said.

"I don't know about that. When it comes to the measure of the man, I'd err on the side of good."

I listened for a bit longer while they discussed other folks in Shamrock Cove. When he started to say his goodbyes, I decided to scoot back over the gate. I'd have to try and search the house another time. Careful not to catch my jeans, I hit the ground and hid behind the apple tree in the corner as the detective opened the back door and came out into the judge's garden.

"What is that?"

I made myself as small as possible.

Bernard barked again and then growled. I prayed she didn't let him out her back gate and onto the path.

"What do you see?" his grandmother called out.

"Just a piece of black piece of fabric on the latch. I don't remember seeing it earlier this morning when we had a look around. You may have been right about someone trying to break in."

Great detective I am. I stared down at the hem of my black jeans and frowned. I left evidence behind. If he didn't already think I was the killer, he probably would now.

I waited for him to head into the judge's place and sprinted for our house. Okay, it was more of a slow jog. I'm not much of a runner, though I try once yearly, usually in January. I find it cold and hard to breathe, but I force myself to do it for one week. Then I give up.

I do yoga, and I walk a lot. I decided long ago that was good enough.

By the time I made it to the backyard. I was filthy and out of breath. Just as my sister opened our home's front door, I entered my bedroom.

"I'm not sure where she is," Lizzie said. "Maybe she's in her study. Let me check. Would you like some tea?"

"I've just come from Gran's," he said, as if that explained that he'd already had some.

She opened the door to the study just as I squeaked into my bathroom. I turned on the shower and then stripped quickly. I stuffed my clothes under the cabinet. I'd have to get rid of my favorite pair of jeans later.

"Mercy?" Lizzie called out. "Are you here?"

"In the shower," I shouted. "Be out in a minute."

"The detective is looking for you." She didn't sound happy with me. I didn't blame her. Most likely she was furious for putting her in this position.

The door to the bedroom closed. I rinsed my hands and face in the stream of water. Then I found some new clothes. While most of my jeans were black because I'd lived in New York, I had some dark blue ones as well.

I didn't want him to make the connection to the black fabric, so I wore the blue ones.

After putting on the new clothes, I stepped out. I didn't hear my sister talking to the detective until I reached the hallway. Her voice sounded strained, and that was never a good thing.

Lizzie wasn't much of a liar, and she was probably worried I might be headed to jail. Although, technically, I'd only hopped a fence, and then jumped right back over.

"I hope you don't mind," the detective said as I entered the kitchen. "I made myself a cortado."

I shrugged. "Not at all. You're welcome anytime. And that sounds good." I went over to my new machine and pushed the buttons to make the same drink.

"Is something wrong, or did you just want coffee?" I asked.

"I wondered if you might have seen someone last night along the back path or it could have been this morning."

I shrugged. "Before or after the judge died? Any word yet on his toxicology?"

He frowned. "No, as I said, it may take a wee while. And why are you asking before or after?"

I sat down across from him.

"Do you mind if I finish with the garden?" Lizzie asked. "Forgive me, Detective, but I have a thing about leaving things undone. And then, I need to head back to the bookstore. I've decided I want to finish the inventory tonight. Which means, Mercy, I need you to pick us up some dinner at the pub. Say six-ish?"

Oh, my. My sister was angry. I'd be paying for my little escapade.

"Rob invited us for tea, remember," I said.

"Right," she said tightly.

"I can come help when I'm finished with the detective."

"I'm faster on my own, and you need to work on *your* book," she said.

Ouch.

"Detective." She nodded toward him before she left.

"Is something wrong?" he asked.

"With?" I smiled. It probably came off as more of a grimace.

"She seems upset."

"No. She has a lot on her mind. She's a bit OCD, and by a bit I mean a lot. She's being treated for it."

Shut up. Lizzie would be angry if she heard me talking about her that way. Even if it was true. After the tragedy with John and Audrey, her disorder had become out of control. I couldn't stop her cleaning or obsessing about every detail at the ranch.

One day, about a month after everything happened, I found her in the middle of a field sobbing, and she couldn't stop. Her hands had been bleeding from picking the stems of lavender without gloves.

It had been one of the worst days of my life because I couldn't lose her, too.

That was when she agreed to get help.

"Back to your earlier question, no. I don't think I saw anyone back there. I may have heard some folks on the back path earlier in the evening yesterday before the party... but not today. Why?"

"Uh. I found some clothing on the gate at the judge's house."

"Oh, did someone break in? I thought Shamrock Cove was super safe. It's one of the reasons I wanted to move my sister here."

He frowned. "Safest place in the world," he said.

"I have a feeling the judge would say otherwise." Antagonizing police officers wasn't my usual, but there was something about him. Maybe it was because he was too handsome.

To his credit, he just raised his eyebrows.

"Sorry. It was a joke. People don't always get my humor." That part was true. Few people understood my jokes.

"So, you didn't see anyone?"

"No, though I noticed this morning that, with the shrubs back there, it might have been difficult to see anything. Our backyard is fairly secluded. Could it have been kids from town, maybe? I know I would have been curious if someone had died. I was always morbid that way. Probably why I'm a mystery writer."

Shut up. You know who talks too much? Guilty people.

He sipped his coffee and then set down the cup. "The kids in town know better than to hang out around the court. Only residents, family, and their guests are allowed."

"Oh?"

"Yes, it's in the rules. The path that curves behind the homes, however, is public domain. It's considered part of the castle grounds."

"Who owns the castle? And is it ruins or intact?" It was a fair question. Most castles in this part of the world had fallen into disrepair. Also, I was desperate to change the course of the conversation away from what had just happened.

"It's intact, as you say. And our biggest tourist attraction. It brings a great deal of money to the village."

"I'll have to go see it," I said. "Was there anything else, Detective?"

"No, that's all. Have a good day, Ms. McCarthy."

I followed him out. "Feel free to call me Mercy," I said.

"Feel free to call me Kieran," he said. "Most people in town don't call me Detective."

"That seems disrespectful," I said.

"Not when you have grown up here," he said. "Gran and the rest of the town see me as a wee one riding his bike around, but I saw a few things when I left the safety of Shamrock Cove."

Just then his eyes had the haunted look of someone in law enforcement. I'd seen it so many times in the men and women who did the work most people didn't have a clue about. They saw the worst of life day-to-day, and it weighed on them.

While there were bad cops everywhere in the world, most of those in public service did it for the right reasons. Though, the bad ones were sometimes really the worst humanity had to offer. I hoped Kieran wasn't one of those.

"Might I ask you about your work with the Garda, Scotland Yard, and the Met someday? Just for research," I said. "That is, if you're comfortable talking about it."

He shrugged. "I don't like talking about my work. But find me after a few pints, and you never know."

We both laughed.

As soon as he left, Lizzie came in and threw her gloves on the front table by the stairs.

"Do not do that to me again," she said angrily. She was shaking from head to toe.

Crud.

I hugged her. "I'm sorry," I said. "I didn't realize how upset you'd get. Everything is okay, Lizzie. He didn't suspect anything."

"I'm not cut out for this sort of thing," she said. "If you want to play amateur detective, I don't think I can be involved."

I squeezed her tighter like the doctors taught me. My sister had also developed severe anxiety over the past year. Holding her tight or hugging her was a way to bring her blood pressure down and calm her. I berated myself for putting her in that position.

"Well, if it makes you feel any better, I'm not very good at it. I ripped my jeans and left a piece on the gate. I have a feeling that's why he stopped by."

"Great. You're going to end up in an Irish prison, and I really will be all alone in the world. I nearly had a heart attack.

When he came barreling through the front garden, I had to stall him so you could get back. At least, I'd hoped that was what you were doing."

"I was racing back, and you did a great job."

"Well, was it worth it? Did you find out anything?" And there it was, the innate curiosity that ran through me that was in my twin too. She might be upset with me for risking my life, but she was just as inquisitive as I was.

"I never made it inside the judge's house," I said.

Her face fell.

"But I did get an earful of Lolly while she talked to her grandson. Everyone on the court had a beef with the judge. He wasn't very good at making friends. She also mentioned the judge's past, which I'll check into a bit more. From what I could see, he was a law wunderkind in his early days, but everyone—past and present—hated him. Oh, one more thing. You can't go back to the bookstore. You'll need to get cleaned up."

She frowned. "Why?"

"We're having tea with Rob, remember? He wants us to try a few of his new recipes. And we need to find out if they were angry enough at the judge to kill him."

"Why would they do that?"

I told her about the food truck issue.

Her eyes went wide. "Oh," she said. "So, will there be more snooping at their house? I'm not certain I can take it."

"Nope. It's your kind of snooping. Gossip. You're so much better with the small talk and that's what we need tonight."

She gave me an annoyed smile and headed off.

Scott and Rob seemed to have a good reason to want the judge dead.

But did they kill him?

SEVEN

At about five, we headed over to Rob and Scott's house. My sister was nervous, and her hands shook slightly as she opened the gate into their garden.

"Stop thinking so hard," I said. "We're just here for a friendly chat and to try some recipes."

"I'm not cut out to be a detective."

"That's fine," I said reassuringly. "Seriously. But you are a wonderful friend, and so good at drawing people out. We just want to learn everything we can about our new friends. It's no different than if we were back home when you'd take long weekends to catch up with the girls at the lake."

Unlike my sister, I didn't have a lot of friends from high school or college. I mean, I wasn't a total social pariah, but I did tend to be bookish and introverted back then. I still was, but my job sometimes forced me to be the center of attention.

She had loads of friends, and she kept up with all of them. I wasn't sure how. That was one of the toughest things she had to leave behind—her support network.

"There you are," Rob said from the doorway. "I was worried you forgot."

I waved at him. "Sorry, we weren't exactly certain when tea-time was."

"Y'all tend to call every meal tea," Lizzie interjected. She only brought out the y'all when she was trying to charm someone.

"Oh, I love that you used y'all. Neither of you sound very Texan most of the time. Or at least what we expect from the telly. But I love *y'all*, it's so inclusive," he said as he ushered us into the house.

"We're going to start without Scott. He had to run into Dublin for business, but he should be back soon. Well, if the trains are running on time."

"There's a train to Dublin from here?" I asked.

"Yes," he said as he ushered us into his home. The furnishings were beautiful antiques and rugs that had to cost a mint. The walls were painted moody blues and deep greens. It felt a bit more like an upscale hunting lodge than a cottage—minus dead things on the wall.

"Your home is beautiful," Lizzie said.

"It is," I agreed.

He smiled brightly and ushered us into the dining room. The table had been set with flowers and brightly colored china.

"Wow," I whispered. "This is fancy."

He clapped his hands together. "I may have gone a bit overboard," he said. "I love entertaining and feeding people."

"It's gorgeous," Lizzie said. "Can I take a picture with my phone? This table design is something out of a magazine."

"I wish Scott heard you say that," he said. "He doesn't understand why I have to have so many dishes, tablecloths, and vases."

"It's how you express your creativity," I said.

He snapped his fingers. "Yes. Exactly. See, you two get it. Just make sure you repeat those comments when the husband gets home."

"Are you already gossiping about me?" Scott said from the hallway.

"These lovely women were appreciating my table scape," Rob said. Then he kissed his husband. "They love what I've done. What do you think?"

Scott laughed. "It's beautiful, honey, as always. Has he been complaining that I say he has too many dishes? Because he does."

"Is that really a possibility?" Lizzie asked. "I'm a good Southern gal. It's important to have the right presentation for every event." She put on a twang that wasn't normally in her voice.

The men laughed, which was her desired effect. My sister was great at putting people at ease.

I was equally good at putting them on edge.

We all have our things. My mom used to say that. Usually, when I hadn't been invited to a birthday party that my sister had.

Your sister has a talent for drawing people into her world. Yours is telling wonderful stories. It all balances out in the end.

I wasn't certain that last part was true. But when I decided to pursue writing full-time, my mother said she had no one to blame but herself. She'd been telling me for years that she loved my stories.

My sister cleared her throat.

I glanced up and found Rob holding out a chair, as was Scott. I'd been wool-gathering and hadn't noticed.

"Thank you," I said to Scott.

"Honey, come help me bring the food in," Rob said.

"Are you writing things in your head again?" my sister asked.

"I was thinking about Mom," I said without thinking.

She blanched.

Ugh. When would I learn to think before I spoke?

"Sorry. Just about how she used to say you were gifted at making friends and I was good with stories."

She took a deep, shuddering breath. "You know, she said the same thing to me when you used to win all the writing and academic awards at school."

"We all have our things," we said together. Then we laughed.

"Don't worry about tonight," I whispered. "Just be you."

She took another long breath. "That I can do." Though her hands still trembled on the table.

The men came back in carrying several dishes. They set them in a semicircle on the table.

"Wow. No one told me we were dining five-star tonight," I said. The dishes were exquisitely presented and smelled delicious. "I thought this was tea. You know with scones and crumpets and things."

The men laughed again.

"You weren't wrong about us calling every meal tea, but we wanted you to get a feel of Irish cuisine tonight," Rob said. "This is more a tasting of recipes for the cookbook, but others are for..."

Scott put his hand on Rob's.

Rob shrugged.

"For what?" I asked.

"A little enterprise I've been thinking about," Rob said. "Nothing much, just a food truck."

Lizzie coughed. I'd told her what I'd overheard between Lolly and Kieran. She sat her wine glass down a bit hard, and it nearly spilled on the tablecloth.

"Are you okay?" I asked.

"Is it the wine?" Scott asked. "That red is a little bold, but the sommelier said it might match some of the spices. I wasn't so sure."

She dabbed her mouth with her napkin. "Everything is fine. I just need to learn how to swallow."

Scott and Rob turned to one another and burst out laughing.

I did the same. My sister acted innocent, but I knew she got the inadvertent joke.

"What are the sandwiches?" Lizzie asked quickly.

"Colcannon mash and champ," Rob said. "I added pork. Oh. My. I forgot to ask. We have shrimp and pork in some of these dishes, as well as beef and several kinds of veggies. I took some of our traditional Irish dishes and gave them a Korean spin. Are you allergic?"

"No," my sister said at the same time I did.

"Mercy and I love all food," Lizzie said.

We laughed.

"Good. I love people who aren't picky," Rob said. "I haven't been able to make anything with shrimp or prawns in it for years because of the judge.

"In addition to the colcannon, we have a potato farl, which is a potato bread. There is also bacon stuffed cabbage rolls." He motioned for our plates and then put a serving of each of the dishes on them.

"The rolls are stuffed with smoked salmon," he said, "and the last bit is my take on Irish stew.

"I just realized this is a tasting menu, and I don't have any hors d'oeuvres or soups."

"Who wants to waste time on those?" I took my plate from him.

"I knew we would be friends as soon as you two walked into the court," Rob said. "And, of course, I wouldn't serve these things together normally. I plan to have theme days with the truck. I'll have two mainstays, but the others will be different each time we're open."

He kept mentioning the truck. The one the judge had shot

down. Without the judge around, maybe he planned to apply again.

I took a bite of the first dish. "Mmmm." I wasn't faking my delight. "Is that kale in the potatoes?"

"It is."

"If kale always tasted like this, I would eat a lot more," I admitted. The dish was also filled with cheese.

"Me, too," Lizzie said.

I took small bites of everything on the plate.

"When you open your food truck, I'll eat at it every day," I said.

Rob smiled. "To be honest, I've been trying to get one going here in Shamrock Cove. But the judge—"

"Honey," Scott warned.

Rob waved a hand. "They're friends. They'll get it."

"What happened? What did the judge do?" Lizzie asked. It didn't matter how much she might complain about my snooping. Her curiosity was every bit as bad as mine.

"He quashed the application with the town council," Scott answered. "It was brutal and unexpected. I may have taken it a bit personally."

"That's dumb," I said. "I know we've only been here twenty-four hours, but every place needs a restaurant like this." I pointed to the dishes.

"That's what I said," Rob agreed. "He was the only one who voted against it, but since the blaggard was the chair... anyway. I know it's terrible that he died, but I'm going to try again. I miss having a restaurant."

Scott's eyes went wide.

Rob turned to his husband. "Not like that. You know what I mean."

Scott smiled at him, but the grin didn't quite meet his eyes.

"Why not open something brick and mortar?" I asked.

The two men stared at one another again.

Then Rob shrugged. "We might as well tell them before they hear it from the gossips."

"If you want," Scott said.

"I didn't mean to pry," I said. *I totally did.*

"It's okay." Rob cleared his throat and put his fork down. "I had brick and mortar in Glasgow and Dublin. They were doing quite well, but the stress nearly killed me."

"He had a complete breakdown eleven years ago," Scott said. "As in, couldn't get out of bed for three months. And tried to hurt himself. I was so worried..."

As in attempted suicide? That was scary and hit a bit too close to home. Not for me, but for Lizzie. I watched her face carefully.

She hadn't tried to hurt herself, but she had said the words, *I don't want to be here anymore.* Which had scared me more than anything else she had said or done.

It was why I'd insisted on a change of scenery and then made it seem like it was all her idea. When the letter came from the solicitor about this place, that was the universe speaking to both of us.

Rob sighed. "It was a scary time. I just cratered under the pressure. I lost my love for the art of cooking, and my mind went to a dark place."

"So, we sold the restaurants," Scott said. "He promised me, never again."

Rob's cheeks turned pink. "He's right. I did make that promise. But then after we moved here, I was inspired by all the naturally sourced food you could get around Shamrock Cove. Farm-to-table is real here. So, I wrote the first cookbook and when that went well—I always want more.

"I love feeding our neighbors but, apart from Brenna, they don't like anything very exotic. I just need—"

"He's him, so of course he wants more," Scott finished.

Rob snorted. "He's not wrong. I don't want another brick

and mortar restaurant. It's too much pressure. But with a food
truck, I could try new foods out and feed the masses, which
happens to be one of my great pleasures in life."

"I thought I was your great pleasure in life," Scott said, but
he smiled.

"You are, love. You are. But with the food truck, I could
work when I wanted to, and I don't have to worry about nights
and weekends. It's more than a full-time job when you're in the
biz. It's your life. And Scott is right, he's my life now."

"And you're mine," Scott said lovingly.

"But the judge crushed your dreams," I said.

Everyone paused.

"The old bastard," Scott said. "He didn't like to see anyone
happy. He also disliked the tourists who visit the seaside and the
castle. He argued that if they allowed one food truck, they'd
have to allow them all in the village. And that would take away
from the businesses that were already here."

"Wouldn't those outside businesses need permits?" I asked.
"I mean, you live here. Seems you would have more of a right to
own a business in Shamrock Cove."

"See. That's what logical and brilliant people think. The
judge was just an arse. If he had any control over things, he used
his power in the worst way," Rob said.

Lizzie made a noise.

"What is it?" Scott asked her.

"I don't know," she said. "It seems like he was a horrible
man. I don't see why someone didn't kill him long ago."

Her eyes went wide. "Oh," she said.

We all busted out laughing.

"Well, the detective isn't certain he was murdered. So
maybe the universe had enough of his crankiness," Scott said.

"How do you know that?" Rob asked.

"Ran into Kieran on the way home from the train. He was

wondering if we saw anyone in the back garden last night or this morning. I was in a rush, but did you?"

Rob frowned. "I was out in the front working on the garden this morning and then spent the rest of the afternoon in the kitchen."

"For which we are grateful," I said. "I'm not sure when I've ever had a better meal."

"Technically, it isn't a meal. It's a tasting," Rob said. "But thank you. We will have you back for a meal, and then you'll know the difference."

"I'm looking forward to that," Lizzie said. "Can I be nosy?"

The men shrugged.

"Do y'all know if the judge had anyone who would really want him dead? I mean, I wouldn't blame y'all after what he did. But I don't see you as killers. Is there anyone else?"

The two men glanced at one another. "Everyone," they said in unison.

"Seriously," Rob said. "While we've heard he was a decent fellow back in the day when he was a judge and lawyer, we all disliked him. Scott sent him an awful letter telling him what an arse he was. We've been worried that when the police read it in his things, they might think we tried to kill him."

"Rob," Scott said.

"What, honey? It's true. If they find that letter... and we're gay. We'll be *prime suspects*. Is that what they say?" He glanced at me.

I nodded. "What exactly did the letter say?"

"I wrote it when I was so angry," Scott said. "Rob was in tears after we learned the vote from the council meeting. He'd put so much work into his ideas, using locally sourced foods.

"I wrote a tersely worded letter and taped it to his door. The next day, I went to apologize. I asked for the letter back. The judge wouldn't hear of it. He told me to get out. That it was enough that 'our kind' had invaded the court. He wouldn't tolerate any more of our outsider ideas."

Lizzie and I gasped.

"No, he didn't," I said. I couldn't abide any injustice, mainly when targeted at those who struggled to be heard.

"He threatened to use the letter to get us kicked out of the court," Rob interjected.

"So, he was homophobic, as well as a jerk," Lizzie said. "I despise people like that."

"And possibly add racist to the list of his not-so-great attributes," Scott said. "Just ask Brenna. We've been trying to talk her into filing charges against the judge for harassment. He flipped out when she changed her back garden and added a hot tub."

Oh, I would be talking to Brenna. She was on my list.

"Lolly says it has nothing to do with our sexuality or the color of any one's skin; he just didn't get along with anyone. He'd even been fighting with her," Rob said. "They were supposed to be friends—well, somewhat. Something happened in their past, at least that's what we heard. But she looked out for him, even though he was rude to her even on his best days."

"The only person he hated more than us, though, was Linda," Scott said.

"True," Rob added.

"Why was that?"

"Linda gets ideas," Scott said. "She's, uh... a—"

"Passionate," Rob added. Then they both laughed.

"We're being rude," Scott said. "Gossiping about the neighbors."

"How else are we supposed to get to know them?" Lizzie asked. "Or to look out for them?"

The men laughed again.

"Right," Scott said. "You should know that Linda has a lot of schemes. She is on every committee in town and sticks her nose in where it doesn't belong more often than not. Most of the time, when people say that, they also say: She means well."

"But she can be a little tone deaf," Rob added. "She can be quite forceful with her ideas. Just don't get on her bad side like the judge did."

"Could she have murdered the judge?" I asked.

The two men busted out laughing.

"He was forever putting the kibosh on her schemes," Rob said.

"Where did you learn the word kibosh?" Scott asked.

"It was on the vocabulary calendar," Rob said. "Linda might have a mean streak sometimes, but she's no killer. She can barely plan a birthday party. Remember the doves?"

Scott laughed. "Pooed all over the food. Poor Dave. He'd really been looking forward to that cake. They're both very kind. Well meaning, if not always exactly on point with their ideas."

Still, I wouldn't discount her. My suspect list was growing by the minute.

Lizzie glanced at me and smiled. She probably saw my wheels turning.

"So that we are forewarned, tell us about Linda's latest scheme, is that what you called it?"

"Aye," Scott said. "It involves you, so it's best you know. I mentioned it before, but she wants to do a Main Street facelift."

"That doesn't seem so bad, except that Shamrock Cove is beautiful already. In fact, I'm not sure I've seen a more charming town," my sister said.

"Exactly," Rob said. "They just repainted everything a few years ago, but she doesn't like the color scheme. Feels like every building should be pastels—inside and out."

I blinked. "She wanted our grandfather to change his store?" It was one of the few buildings that was not pastel. But it would have been a travesty to paint it. The beautiful interior blue was inviting and calming. Even better, it was mysterious.

"Aye," Rob said. "At the mention of painting the three-hundred-year-old brick, the entire town turned against her. The judge called her a few choice names in the middle of the town hall meeting. He reduced her to tears in front of everyone. I'm not sure she ever recovered from the embarrassment."

"Well, it's true. We're laying all the cards on the table with our new friends, who probably think we are the worst for telling tales."

I held up a hand. "No, as my sister said, we're grateful for the warnings. Moving to a new place can be a bit disconcerting at the best of times. It's good to know what roadblocks might come up ahead."

Had our grandfather died of cancer? As far as I knew, they hadn't done an autopsy. Perhaps he'd been murdered by someone too. I hoped not.

"True," Lizzie concurred.

"I give Linda a week," Rob said.

"Before what?" I asked.

"Before she asks you to consider painting your bookshop—inside and out," Rob answered.

"If you give in to her pushiness, we'll never forgive you," Scott said. "That store is perfect the way it is."

I laughed. "We agree with you," I said.

"She's right. Except for updating his inventory system to a new one from this century, I don't plan on changing a thing. But I'm glad you told us about Linda."

"Me, too," I said.

"Just stay on her good side. She's a decent sort, she just has strange ideas sometimes. Your grandfather would have loved you two," Scott said. "He was the best of us on the court. I'd never seen him raise his voice with anyone. He was a classy Irishman, and I can't say that about many of us."

"He was grand, and very accepting of us when we came to live here," Rob added. "He did window displays for pride month. We don't do as much here as you do in the States, but still, that meant something to us."

A knot in my chest that I didn't even know was there released. "I'm relieved to hear that about him," I said.

"He didn't put up with the judge's antics either," Scott added. "He wasn't afraid of taking him down a peg if the judge spoke out of turn or was hateful. He stood up for me and Rob more than once. And he set the tone for the rest of the neighbors. We loved him."

"Oh, that makes me so happy," Lizzie said. "It's getting late, but I'd love for you to tell us more about him sometime. We haven't found any pictures in the house. Or mementos, really. Except for his books."

She hadn't mentioned the letter, and for that I was grateful. It was too personal.

Rob frowned. "I'm sure I have some pictures on my phone from events around town. Until those last few years, he was involved in everything that concerned the town. He used to joke he was one of the forefathers, but it was true.

"Did you know your family has been a part of the court for longer than any of the others?"

"I didn't," I said. "Did you guys know about us? I mean, that he was looking for us?"

Rob shrugged. "When he first found out he was terminal, he mentioned he hired an heir hunter. While he could have left the home to someone in the court, I think he felt like it might be time for some new blood. He was quite open to the lottery in town and bringing someone new in."

"But then I guess he found you," Scott said. "How lucky are we." He reached across and grabbed our hands. "We adore you two. You're going to have a blast here."

They were both so sweet and I really couldn't see them killing anyone.

Still, if someone had hurt Lizzie the way Rob had been by the judge, I'm not sure what I would have done. The old man sounded like a hateful old jerk. And that sort of thing made me angry.

Something about the judge's death screamed premeditated, which meant we couldn't rule out our new friends. I couldn't quite put my finger on why, though. He was old, but if he didn't die of natural causes, I had this sense that someone had put a lot of thought into how to murder him.

And how to get away with it.

Unfortunately, there was far too many people in Shamrock Cove and on the court with motive. And we'd barely touched the surface.

By all accounts, the judge had been an awful man.

But did he deserve to die?

EIGHT

Opening day of the bookstore was nerve-racking for Lizzie and me. I was more worried about her stressing too much rather than how the town would accept us.

"What if I screw it all up?" she said for the fifth time that morning as we stood inside the shop, getting the last bits ready. "I don't know anything about owning a bookstore. Why did I think I could do this?"

She'd worn her hair high in a messy bun with big, black-framed glasses and was dressed in jeans and a sweater with wide sleeves. I'd called the look boho librarian as a tease, but it suited her.

"You're going to love it," I said. "And they will love you. Besides, you know so much more about books than you'd ever admit." It was the truth. While she'd always been more of the outgoing one, we both spent a lot of time reading when we were younger.

It was a passion we shared, and one Mom had encouraged.

She would have loved this place.

Lizzie's alarm went off on her phone. She turned it off. Then she stared at me like a madwoman.

"One minute until we open," she whispered as she smoothed her hair. "Oh. My. I don't think I can do this."

"I'll open for you," I said. "If that is what you want."

She straightened her shoulders. "No. You're using this as an excuse not to work, but I'm onto you. You write the books. I sell the books. You need to remember that." She pointed a finger at me, and it was all I could do not to laugh.

We were competitive in a way that was shocking to some people. If I told her I could do something when she was in doubt about her own abilities, her hackles rose.

I'd said those words deliberately about doing it for her, and she'd taken the bait.

"You can stay, but only if you promise to behave. Don't scare the customers. No judgey faces about their literary tastes. I mean it."

"Aye, Captain." I gave her a fake salute.

"If you're going to be annoying, just leave. Or maybe call Carrie back. I saw her texts buzzing on your phone this morning."

"Snoop."

"Kettle."

She had a point. I'd spent most of yesterday snooping on all our neighbors. Online, of course. But I'd started a notebook that left me with more questions about them than I'd started with at the beginning.

"How dare you evoke the name, *Carrie*."

She laughed, and the tension left her shoulders.

Carrie was my wonderful editor. We'd been working together for more than twenty years and were friends for even longer than that. Fortunately, or unfortunately, she knew me and my insecurities better than anyone.

I owed her pages. And if I didn't answer her texts soon, she'd start bombarding my sister with messages.

"And I promise I'll text her when I take a lunch break." I'd planned on staying this first day at the store—more as moral support than anything.

I knew my sister could handle the business side. But I worried that people might ask too many personal questions about why we'd come here. And was it true we didn't know our grandfather? And why was it that everyone around us died?

I would ask those questions. Yep. But I hoped to steer her away from that sort of thing.

I stood near the stairs as she unlocked the door. Before she opened it, she took a deep, steadying breath.

"Hello," she said as she held the door. "Please, come in."

I hadn't noticed the line outside the door. Maybe ten people filed in. One of the first was Matt, the bartender from the pub. We'd met him a few days ago when we visited the Crown and Clover pub for lunch. We'd bonded over his love of American mysteries.

"Hi, stranger," I said.

"Mornin'. I didn't know you'd be working here, too."

I shrugged. "Just today or when she needs to take a lunch break. We weren't sure how busy it would be."

"You'll be wantin' to call Caro. I bet she'd be happy to come back."

"Caro?"

"Your grandfather's assistant, or that's what he called her. She's a wonder. I think she's been doing some part-time at Linda's. But she was hoping to come back once the store opened."

"Good to know," I said. I wondered if Lizzie knew about Caro. It was the first I'd heard of her.

Maybe she could tell us a bit more about our grandfather. We'd been searching the house but still hadn't found the secret door he'd talked about in his library. Nor had I found the letters.

"Is there something I can help you find?" I asked.

"I'm headed to the mystery section," he said. "Do you have any recommendations?"

"Since you like American authors, have you read Linda Castillo's Kate Burkholder series? I noticed my grandfather carried a good selection. He even has the first couple. The main character is the chief of police in a small Amish town. I love those books and the author."

"Oh, that sounds grand. I'll look. I heard you had a Jura Giga Ten. Is that why you haven't come to see me at the pub the last few days?"

"Guilty as charged. I didn't expect the detective to be such a gossip."

"It wasn't he who told me. You'll soon learn. Word gets around in this town. Someone probably saw him carrying the box to your house. Well, I know they did, because they told me."

I laughed.

"Are you going to reveal your sources?" I tried to sound serious, but I grinned.

He shook his head. "Technically, I'm a bartender. It's against our code."

We laughed.

"I promise to still come in for your wonderful coffee. Maybe we'll come down for lunch. What do you have today?"

"Today's a good day for it—Mam's made her shepherd's pie. None better in Ireland."

"Wow. That's quite the boast."

He smirked. "She is the best. There's a reason they won't let her compete at the county fairs anymore."

I smiled. I loved that this hip, urban dude loved his mom so much.

"Well, now I can't wait to try her shepherd's pie."

"And her apple cake for dessert," he said. Then he picked up the first two of Castillo's series and found a comfy chair.

I was about to head back downstairs when I saw a young

boy sulking by the children's section. He sat on a pouf and had his chin in his hands.

"Is everything okay?" I asked.

He glanced up at me and frowned. "I'm not supposed to talk to strangers."

I held out my hand. "My name is Mercy McCarthy, and I work here."

He stared at my hand for a few seconds suspiciously. Then he grasped my fingers and gave them a half shake.

"I'm Liam."

"Well, I don't mean to pry, Liam. But you don't look happy."

He sighed dramatically. "My ma says I have to pick out a book and read it. She's making me tell her about it."

"Ugh," I said. "Moms. Always so bossy."

"Yeah. She says my brain is going to mush playing video games. But she's wrong. I'm faster than all my friends when we're playing *Deathlord*. You can't be good like that if you have a mush brain."

I bit back my smile. "I'm sure you're right." He couldn't have been more than seven. What was he doing playing video games like that?

He sighed again, and it was all I could do not to smile. "Video games are way more fun than books."

I was offended by that statement but kept it to myself.

"This is a tough case, but I may have a solution. Let's look over here." He reluctantly followed me into the children's section.

I pursed my lips and tapped a finger on the side of my head. Then I found the first book I'd been looking for on the shelf. By the time I'd finished, I had three books for him.

I handed him the first book. "This one is about kids who are trying to solve a mystery at a haunted lodge. There are even puzzles in it that most adults don't get, but kids are great at them."

He glanced at it and then frowned. "It's a pick your path book. What does that mean?"

"Choose your own adventure. Just give it a quick read. You'll know within the first few pages if any of these books are for you." I set two more books next to him on the pouf.

"If they aren't right, come find me, and I'll look for some more."

He eyed the books with as much suspicion as he did me. "Okay," he said.

I left him there and headed downstairs in case my sister needed help.

There was a line at the register of a few people, but they all seemed happy to be there.

"Can I help?" I asked Lizzie.

"Yes, I just learned from Martha here that our grandfather used to wrap the purchases in brown paper and string. I was wondering why he didn't have any bags."

"That's right," Martha said. "He saw books as presents we should open again and again."

The people behind her nodded.

"I love that," Lizzie said excitedly. "Can you help me catch up?"

I nodded. While I wasn't the best at gift wrap, I did a serviceable job.

"Excuse me?" a woman said.

I glanced up to find her pointing at me. Thinking she might have seen my author picture, I smiled.

"Can I help you?"

"No. I mean, I wanted to thank you." She held up the books I'd given to Liam earlier. "My son wants to read them all. He said you recommended them."

"Oh, yes. I hope that's okay."

"It's more than okay. His teacher says he's running a bit behind in his reading skills, and I've been feeling like a failure. I couldn't get him interested in anything. How did you know what he'd like?"

"She's an author," my sister said. "She knows books and people."

"Oh, then I don't feel so bad," the mother said.

"Mam what's taking so long? I need to know what happens next," Liam said as he came downstairs. He had the second book in the *Case Closed* series.

She laughed.

She handed my sister the books to ring up.

"Do you want me to leave *Case Closed* out?" I asked Liam.

"Yes."

His mother nudged him.

He sighed. "Please."

"And what do you say?" She nudged him again.

"Thank you, Mercy, for the books."

"You shouldn't call her by her first name. We discussed this." His mother wasn't happy.

Liam pulled a face.

"We're friends," I said. "We like the same kind of books. And that's what I told him to call me, Mercy."

Liam lifted his head and gave me the: *Thank God, you're on my side look.*

"Oh, then. Thank you, both. I'm so glad you're here. I was beginning to wonder if this place would ever open again. It's my treasure, once a week."

There was that word again: *treasure*. Had that been what our grandfather meant? Maybe he considered the shop a prize for the town. Maybe there was a bit of ego in that idea, but people seemed to be grateful we were here.

. . .

By the time we'd looked after everyone in line, it was nearing lunchtime.

Lizzie sat down on the stool behind the register for the first time that morning. "I wasn't expecting it to be so busy," she said.

"I can watch the store if you want to take a break," I said. "Or we could do something crazy like close for lunch and head down to the pub. I hear shepherd's pie and apple cake are on the menu."

"Yum. That sounds better than the fruit salad I have in the fridge at home. Do you think it will be okay to close for an hour?"

"I think it's expected in a town like this."

After checking both floors to make sure we didn't have any lingering customers, we headed out.

When we walked through the doorway, a hush fell over the pub. That happened on our first visit as well. I wondered if that would ever stop. How long would we be the newbies?

I mean, we were still very new to the village. But it was weird being a curiosity for the townspeople. Matt was behind the bar and turned when the silence fell.

"Ah, you made it. Good on you. I saved your regular table." He nodded toward the back of the pub where we'd sat when we'd come in a few days ago.

Lizzie smiled at people as we moved around the tables to the back.

"That's weird, right?" she whispered as we sat down.

"Yes," I said. "But not every place is like *Cheers*."

She frowned.

"You know, the show with the bar."

She cocked her head. "That old show Mom used to like?"

I sighed. "Yes. It's the place where everybody knows your name."

She just stared at me, and then she smiled. "Ohhhh. So, you walk in, and they know who you are."

"Yeah. Never mind. What are you going to order?"

"Exactly what you said." She hung her purse on the back of her chair. Then it hit me. I'd left my wallet at home.

"You're going to have to pay," I said. "Or I can run home and get my bag. I left it at the house." I was used to paying for things. My sister's business did well, but I'd been lucky enough with my books to make more money than I'd ever spend.

And I liked taking care of her. I'd made all our arrangements to move here and handled the visas and other legalities. Well, I paid someone a hefty fee to do it for me and to expedite everything. I would do it all over again to give her this fresh start.

She waved a hand. "Don't worry about it."

Matt came by to take our orders.

"Can I ask you something?" I whispered.

He glanced around and then knelt beside the table. "What is it?"

"What did you know about the judge?"

He snorted. "A lot. Nothing good. Why?"

"That's what we keep hearing and I guess my curiosity is—"

"What my sister is saying is she's nosy," Lizzie said.

I tried to kick her under the table but missed and hit the table leg instead.

Ouch.

"I heard you tried to save his life," Matt said. Then he stood with his arms crossed. He didn't seem happy about that fact.

I sighed.

"She did," Lizzie said. "She didn't stop until the EMTs showed up. I'm proud of her."

"Good on you," Matt said. "But you needn't have tried so hard. He wasn't worth the effort." Then he turned away. "I'll get your drinks." He was halfway across the pub before we heard the last word.

"What was that about?" I asked.

"I don't know, but maybe you should lay off the detective stuff. If we want to survive in this town, we'll need some friends."

"I know. It's just—"

"What? Why can't you just let the police handle it? Do you feel guilty because he died? You and I both know it wasn't your fault. You did everything you could while I just... stood there."

"You called for help," I said.

"And you performed CPR like a pro. No one blames you. And whatever he said, well, he was dying, right?"

I nodded.

"No telling what was happening in his brain."

"She's right," the detective said as he stood beside the table.

I felt like I'd jumped out of my skin. That dude was a ninja with his powers of stealth. "Still, I need to speak to you at the station. Ms. McCarthy. Follow me, please." He stared pointedly at me.

Well, this wasn't going to end well.

NINE

I sat in the interview room with flowery wallpaper and waited. And waited. The police station was an old cottage that looked like it had last been decorated in the fifties. It looked more like a grandmother's house than a place where law officers worked.

Finally, the detective came in with a stack of papers. And an evidence bag with the torn piece of clothing from my jeans.

This guy is more intelligent than I thought.

"You could have at least waited until I finished my meal," I said blandly. "If they run out of shepherd's pie, I will file a complaint against you. I may do it anyway."

He smirked, but I had a feeling it was to hide a smile. Did the good detective get my sense of humor?

Most men didn't.

"I'd like you to explain why the hem of your pants was found on the judge's back gate." He leaned back and crossed his arms.

"I don't know what you're talking about," I said. And then cleared my throat as that last bit squeaked.

Way to sound innocent.

"If I search your house, I have a feeling we'll find the item of clothing that matches this torn fabric." He stared at me.

"As I've said before, I don't know much about law enforcement here. But at home, you'd need probable cause to get a search warrant. Is it the same here?"

"Aye," he said.

"Even if it were my jeans, and I'm not saying they were, what crime would I have committed? You said they were on the judge's gate. Well, except for the entryway, where I tried to save his life, I can honestly say I've never been in the judge's house."

He seemed to think about this bit of information for a few minutes.

"Let's get straight into it, Detective. What is it you're accusing me of this time?"

"That you climbed over the gate into the judge's garden."

I frowned. "Is that a crime here? Again, I'm not saying I did. I'm just curious."

"Trespassing on a crime scene is." He cocked his head.

"Oh, the reports must have come back. So, it is murder? Darn. I was really hoping it was natural causes. That is a pickle."

Mirroring his actions, I leaned back and crossed my arms.

"A pickle?" he asked, as his eyebrows drew together.

"Yes, do you know what poison was used?"

"I never said anything about poison."

Darn. I'd been trying to trick him into answers. He was a bit too clever for that.

"True. But the reaction the judge had. It was either poison —or an allergic reaction."

My eyes opened wide.

He didn't even blink.

Good for him, keeping things close to the vest.

"I didn't kill him," I said. "Though, if I'd known him long enough, I might have had cause."

He leaned forward. "What do you mean?"

"I've heard a few things," I said. He wasn't the only one who could have secrets.

"What things?"

I shrugged. "Just talk."

"I could cite you for impeding an investigation," he said seriously. "Tell me what you know."

I shrugged again. "I don't know much, except for what I read online about the judge and his past. Oh, and you know from the rumor mill around here. But who knows how much of that is the truth. I don't think gossip should be a line of inquiry for the police."

He sighed. "If you didn't kill him, and you didn't know him, why are you so interested in his case?"

"Show me a mystery writer who isn't interested in true crime?" In truth, I'm the anomaly who isn't interested in true crime. Normally. But he didn't need to know that. "Many of my friends base their books, loosely that is, on real crimes. They like the authenticity it brings."

"But you don't?"

"I just make stuff up, Detective. I try to make sure my procedures are correct, and I do loads of research. But my favorite part of writing is the pretending side of things. But we all see the world through our own lens, and I'm not blind to the crime that happens around us. I just don't use specific cases. Like I said, I make things up."

"So, you'd say you're an adept liar." His eyebrow rose.

I pretended to be hurt. I put a hand over my heart. "You wound me, Detective. Now, are you accusing me of anything? Do I need to call my solicitor?"

He stared at me for a full minute. I held his gaze.

"You are currently not being charged with anything. At least, not yet."

"Then I'd really like to get back to lunch."

"Aren't you at least curious how I know these are the hem of your pants?"

"No, not really." Oh, I was. I really, really was curious.

I'd just stepped into the doorway.

"Your lotion," he said. "It's all over the evidence I found on the judge's gate."

Darn my addiction to Spongelle verbena and coconut. He was right, I loved the scent because it reminded me of spring.

"My lotion? It's quite popular in the States. I'm sure it is here, as well. Odd that you noticed a similarity, though. Didn't take you for someone with olfactophilia."

My back was still to him, but I heard the scrape of his chair.

"Olfactophilia? You made that up."

I turned, and then I smiled sweetly. "Oh, no. It's nothing to be ashamed of, Detective. Many men are sexually aroused by scents. It's quite common. Bye now."

I turned and left. I was smart enough to wait until I made it outside to laugh.

My stomach growled.

Darn him for making me miss lunch.

I headed back to the store, which was open again.

"Thank goodness," Lizzie said. "I've been worried sick. What did you do now?"

"I'm surprised you weren't there to bail me out," I said.

She rolled her eyes. "For the record, I followed you. But the detective assured me he needed to ask you only a few questions. I went back and ate lunch. I brought you some. It's in the office."

"Excellent. Thank you." I rubbed my hands together.

"Did you find out anything?" she asked.

"No. Except that the judge was murdered. I don't know if it was poison or an allergy, though. The detective is better at his job than I thought."

"Good, then you can leave the detecting to him."

I was about to argue when the door to the shop opened. She waved me away as she said hello to the customer.

The shepherd's pie smelled great, but it was cold. Still, it tasted good.

A few minutes later, my phone buzzed in my pocket.

It was a text from my sister. Why hadn't she just come back here?

Go home and write. I'm good. But remind me to tell you what Matt said.

Matt from the pub?

I started to head back out to the front, but she was busy chatting with some people at the register.

Then it hit me: she was happy. The smile on her face reached her eyes. She was in her element.

I let go of a breath I didn't know I'd been holding.

Not wanting to disturb the peace, I left out the back. I double-checked to make certain it locked behind me.

Then I turned quickly to look to my left. I could have sworn I saw someone out of the corner of my eye.

But no one was there.

I shivered.

I wasn't one to give in to flights of fancy. After all, Shamrock Cove was safe. But I could have sworn I'd seen someone. My stateside stalker had made me more than a little paranoid.

Had he followed me here?

No. I'd kept our move to Ireland quiet from the press and public. No one knew we were here except our new neighbors.

I still wasn't used to looking for the special entrance to the court, but I found it easier than the last time.

By the time I made it back to the house, I was out of breath, and my nerves jangled.

I'd had that feeling of people watching me plenty of times in Manhattan because there were always humans everywhere.

When I first noticed I had a stalker in New York, I'd been hyper-aware of everything around me. I'd even contacted the police, but there wasn't anything they could do. A few letters and things going astray in my apartment weren't alarming to them. But it was to me.

Part of that was because whoever it had been was good at it. There were never any fingerprints in my place, and they never allowed themselves to be seen. But I'd sensed them. Because of that, I'd learned to trust that gut feeling I was being watched. I glanced out the window, but I didn't see anyone.

Stop being so paranoid.

This was Shamrock Cove, and even though I joked with the detective, I'd seen the statistics. Most of the crimes happened in the summer and usually involved tourists. Drunk and disorderly, shoplifting, and that sort of thing.

The judge could have had an allergic reaction. Kieran wouldn't say one way or the other. Though, if it were a reaction, why wouldn't he say that and get it over with instead of making it seem like it was something else?

Because it was something else.

And even if he died from an allergic reaction, someone could have done it on purpose.

My phone buzzed in my pocket.

I glanced at the ID, and then pushed the off button. The buzzing stopped, but then it dinged.

Carrie, my editor, had sent a text.

Call me now.

She was tenacious and the text and calls wouldn't stop.

I dialed her number.

"It's about time." That was how she answered. "I've been worried about you and Lizzie. Did you get settled in and is it what you thought it would be? How are her nerves? Are you writing, yet?"

"Hi, you're up early," I said.

"Stop it. And it's eight in the morning here. The time difference isn't that bad. Are you okay?"

As much as I gave Carrie grief, she'd become a great friend. She was ten years older than me and the best editor I'd ever seen. A good part of my success was due to her ability to push me into being a better writer.

"Yes. We're settling in and you wouldn't believe this house. It has the most amazing library. I've never seen anything like it. We had a bit of a rough start, but Lizzie opened the bookstore today. She seems happier than I've seen her in a long time."

"Well, that is good news. What kind of rough start?"

I told her about what happened with the judge. I even told her about trying to investigate.

"Interesting and surprising," she said. "This would make a great story, though not your usual sort of mystery. And here I thought you'd already be bored."

"No. There hasn't been time to be bored."

"And the writing?"

I sighed. I did that a lot.

"It's only been a few days. I was on the laptop yesterday looking some things up for research."

There was silence on the other end. Okay, that had been about the judge and the other residents in the court. *Why did she always know when I fibbed?*

"But I will, and you know once I get going it will be fast." At the very least, I had that going for me.

Again silence.

"If we don't make the deadline and have to pull the book at the last minute..."

"I know. I know," I said. And I did. "I promise you I will not be one of *those* kind of authors."

"People will understand," she said. "You and Lizzie have been through the worst. But I need to do it now. If we carry on and you can't make that final deadline, we're both toast. Do you understand? Your buy-in numbers are fantastic, and marketing is all over this book. But I must let people know now if we can't make that date."

I blew out a breath. While I wasn't a people-pleaser, I didn't like disappointing my editor or publisher. They'd been good to me all these years. But this was business. I had a job and hadn't shown up for it in months.

Carrie was right. It was time to get back on track.

"Give me two days, and I'll send you the first half. With the caveat that I may need to go back and change a few things once I get to the end."

"You're fast, but not that fast."

"I wrote that first half before everything happened with Mom. I need to go back through it. And I will make the deadline. I promise you that. Unless the detective arrests me for the judge's murder."

She laughed. "Don't even joke like that. Though, it would be great publicity. The mystery writer becomes the murderer. Marketing would love it. But are you sure? This is friend Carrie, not editor Carrie. You've been through so much, and people will understand—"

"I know," I interrupted. "But I can do this. I—uh—I need to do it." That was the truth. I was afraid if I didn't get to work fast, I might not be able to do it at all.

Like, ever again.

That fear had been paralyzing me for months.

"Okay," she said. "Two days. In my email, or I talk to the publisher."

I swallowed the lump in my throat. "Got it."

After we hung up, I grabbed a coffee. I usually didn't drink it after two or so, but I needed it to do what I'd promised. I'd meant what I told her about the book.

I sat down at my new desk in the office and looked around. It was a bit stuffy, so I opened the window out to the garden. Birds chirped, and the scent of gardenias and roses planted near the house filled the room.

I settled in and opened the document that held my latest work. But before I began, I grabbed my notebook that I'd been writing things down in where the judge was concerned.

When I started writing professionally, I'd do an info dump of whatever was in my brain so I could feel free to write.

I made a list of all the suspects, and there were far too many. I noted what I'd learned about each of them and things I might want to follow up on later. Everything I'd been thinking went down in that notebook.

It took me almost an hour, but by the time I was done I felt almost refreshed in a way. When I'd done this in New York, my notes had been more about things I needed to remember to do or tasks I was worried about forgetting—like sending my laundry out or eating.

When I was writing, I tended to forget everything else.

Once that was done, I started at the beginning of the book I'd been working on and barreled through making revisions. I pulled up the notes on my computer and the basic outline I'd done. I added to it as I went along so I wouldn't forget the details about the story and characters.

Four hours later, the scent of food pulled me away from my work.

I glanced up to find the window had been closed, and it was

dark outside. Someone had turned on the floor lamps and the one on my desk.

When did that happen?

I followed my nose to the kitchen.

"I didn't hear you come home," I said to Lizzie. She was fussing with things on the stove while reading an informational brochure.

"I've been home for a couple of hours. I closed the shop at five. I'm heating tamales, rice, and beans that Rob made for us. He's talented, and all this Latin food keeps me from missing home too much."

"Yum. What are you reading?"

"I've never used an AGA before. So, it's a bit of a learning curve. Let's pray I don't burn everything. I've learned how to heat things, but I was curious about some other functions. I thought I'd make something special for tomorrow.

"Can you imagine having something like this in Texas that stays warm all the time? We would die from the heat."

I laughed. "True."

I helped set the kitchen table, and it wasn't long before we sat down to a wonderful dinner.

"I have to admit, this is not the sort of food I thought we'd be eating in Ireland," she said.

"We're lucky to have a chef as a neighbor."

"I kind of love those guys already," she said. "I hope they aren't the ones who killed the judge."

My fork clattered to the plate.

She rolled her eyes. "I saw your notebook on your desk. I may have glanced through it while you were working."

"You did?"

I must have been really in it because I hadn't even noticed her.

"Are you the one who turned on the lights and shut the window?"

She laughed. "I haven't seen you work like that in a while. And I remembered that you used journals to dump your thoughts into. I used to love reading them when we were younger."

"Wait. You read my journals when we were kids? They usually don't make sense to anyone but me."

"And me." She smiled. "Must be a twin thing. You didn't talk much when we were kids, remember? Reading your journals was a way to help me connect with you."

I frowned. "I feel violated and manipulated," I said.

She laughed. "You don't."

"I don't," I admitted. "Was I really that introverted? I seemed to have blocked a lot of that out."

"You were. Oh, so, I need to tell you about Matt. One more thing for you to put in your little black book."

I didn't bother pointing out that she'd asked me to stop investigating earlier. As I suspected, she'd just been worried.

"Matt from the pub? What's that?"

"After I went back to the pub, he came to the table and apologized for being short with us."

"Was he? I don't remember."

She nodded. "A bit short with you when you mentioned the judge. The big news is that the old man was Matt's grandfather."

I frowned. "He is? I mean was. And Matt was working today?" And he'd been at the bookstore.

"No love lost there," she said. "He despised the old man. I mean, he didn't say that exactly. When his mom came home to raise Matt alone, the judge refused to help her. That is until a few years ago. The judge bought out her loan at the bank for the pub. Then he tried to insinuate himself into the place. Made her change the menu and wanted Matt to stop with the fancy coffees.

"But Matt had saved up a great deal from his old job. He

bought out the loan for his mom, but the judge never finalized the paperwork. Matt's been trying to get the deed to the place for almost a year. The judge kept stalling."

I frowned. "He should have sued," I said.

She shrugged. "He was pretty broke after paying off the loan. I have a feeling the old man knew that."

I took a bite of the tamales. I might as well have been at home in Texas with those flavors.

My sister's eyes went wide as she took a bite as well.

"That is..."

"Delicious. Reminds me of the ones that old restaurant, El Fenix, had."

She closed her eyes. "Yes. Or remember that lady at the flea market who we bought from on Saturdays when we were kids?"

I smiled. "I'd forgotten about that. Mom would buy two dozen on a Saturday, and they'd be gone by Monday."

"Do you think Matt could have killed his grandfather?" she asked.

Her comment made me blink. "I—uh. I don't know. He doesn't seem the type to commit murder. But people have killed others for less reason. I will say the judge was a piece of work, and he didn't lack any enemies."

"Are you certain the detective didn't accidentally give you a hint?"

I shrugged. "It was more of what he didn't say. The judge died suspiciously, of that I'm certain." I'd be adding Matt and his mother to my list.

"How did the rest of the day go at the store?" I asked her.

She smiled. "I'll be asleep by eight thirty, but it was a good day. The people here are kind. Many of them are long-time customers who come in weekly for a new load of books." She looked very content. "Speaking of our new neighbors, have you noticed how many people around here have red or auburn hair? It's something fun I noticed about the customers today."

I had noticed. I figured it was one of those Irish traits.

"From what I understand, there's also a great library," she said. "It's a bookish town. They have a ton of book clubs, as well.

"I'm going to do some marketing to target those customers. It's refreshing in a time where most people are reading digitally that they like having books in hand, don't you think?"

"It is." I was grateful for those e-book sales, but equally for those who bought my hardbacks and paperbacks.

"Oh, that reminds me." I put my fork down, as my stomach was already full, which meant I'd overeaten. "You might want to go ahead and order more of the *Case Closed* books. Our grandfather only had the first two books on the shelves. My guess is my new friend Liam will be back for more."

"Right. I wanted to ask you how you knew what would get him to read."

I shrugged. "He's like me. Remember those *Goosebumps* books where you could choose your own adventure?"

"You loved those when you were little. I prefer having a straight-up story to follow. I don't like skipping around," she said.

"I like both," I said. "But I also like the idea of control so I can choose the story I want to read."

"But then you'd go back and make the other choices," she said. "You read them every way possible."

I laughed. "You're right. I had to know all the outcomes, which is one reason I write mysteries. My brain has to go through all the clues and outcomes before I can truly craft the book I want to write.

"Anyway, Liam needs that sort of control over his destiny. Though, I doubt he realizes it."

"Oh, that's interesting. Let me guess, his mom was forcing him to read because she's worried he is a bit behind."

I nodded. "Got it in one."

"So, you picked books where he could choose what story he wanted. And books with fantasy or ghostly elements because?"

"He loves fantasy video games, and he's good at them. That means he likes strategy and fantasy."

"I love this," she said. "Teach me your ways."

I laughed. "I heard you with the customers today. You already do it. You asked them what genre they were interested in, and then you asked about their other interests."

She frowned. "Did I? I don't remember that."

I smiled. "That's because you are a naturally friendly and curious person. You want to know about others.

"You did seem happy today."

She pursed her lips. "I suppose I was. I lost myself in the excitement of it all. I'm sure it won't be like that every day, but it was kind of a nice break from—"

"The sadness," I finished for her.

She nodded and then started to gather the plates.

"You cooked. I'll do the dishes."

There was a knock on the door.

She glanced at her watch. It was one of my mom's old Movado's, and it looked right on her wrist. "It's late for a visitor. I hope it's not the detective back to arrest you. I've got these, you go see who it is."

I headed to the front door.

There was a small window at the top of the door that allowed me to look through to see who was outside. I opened it. Brenna was there and she looked worried.

"Is everything okay?" I asked as I opened the door.

"I brought this as a housewarming gift," she said. She held up a potted plant. "And this." She held up a bottle of wine.

"Oh, thank you," I said. "Please, come in."

It was hard for me to believe she was a photographer and not a model. She was tall and beautiful. Today she wore an emerald dress and high-heeled gold sandals.

It was a bit nippy at night for sandals, and I ushered her in.

"Thanks, I won't stay, though," she said. "I just... you don't know me, but I think I need your help."

"Of course," I said. My curiosity was piqued. "Would you like some tea or coffee? Or wine?" I held up the bottle she'd handed to me.

"I'm fine," she said. "But do you have time for a chat?"

"Yes, come on back." I led her to the kitchen.

"Oh, Brenna, how nice to see you," my sister said as we entered the kitchen. She wiped her hand on the dish towel lying by the sink. In the short time I'd gone to the door, she'd already cleaned everything off the table. "I was about to slice up some apple pie Lolly made for us."

I was full of dinner but also understood my sister's need to feed people. It was part of her love language. She and our neighbor Rob had that in common.

"I brought this for you two. It's from the one I keep in my house that is taking over my kitchen." She handed the pot to my sister.

"She also brought us wine." I held up the bottle.

"You didn't have to do that," Lizzie said. She set small dessert plates on the table and pulled the pie from the oven. Then she grabbed some vanilla ice cream from the freezer.

I didn't know we had any of this food in the house, or I may have already eaten the ice cream. I'm bad about snacking while I'm writing.

"We eat our apple pie à la mode. Would you like some ice cream?" Lizzie asked.

"I've never tried pie that way, but yes," Brenna said. There was forced joviality in her voice.

We settled down to eat.

Lizzie and I glanced at Brenna's shaking hands as she tried to eat. My sister then gave me the look.

As twins, we'd always had our own language and facial expressions. It used to drive my mom crazy.

But my sister was usually the one to delve into conversations that might be a bit tricky.

So, I nodded Brenna's way.

Lizzie shook her head.

I rolled my eyes.

"Is everything okay?" I asked. "It's just that your hands are shaking."

Brenna glanced up to find us watching her carefully. "I was hoping you wouldn't notice."

My sister placed a hand on Brenna's arm. "You haven't known us long, but you can tell us anything," she said. She had that reassuring tone that made people feel like everything would be okay.

"I think I'm in trouble," Brenna said. "I'm coming to you because if something happens to me, I want someone else to know."

I frowned. "What do you mean?"

She put her head in her hands. "I'm going to sound crazy. I know that. But I heard the detective questioned you, and I thought maybe..."

"Maybe, what?" I asked.

"You'd understand. You don't know me. We only met a few days ago, but I would never hurt anyone. I just wouldn't. I don't care how big of an arse the judge might have been."

"We've heard he wasn't the nicest man," Lizzie said.

"Oh, that's putting it mildly. He was an awful old git, and I had plenty of reason to wish him harm." She held up her hands. "But I didn't do it. The thing is, I don't know where else to go. I'm not sure who I can trust anymore."

"We'll help you however we can," I said, and I meant it. I didn't know her well, but I instantly liked Brenna at the party. I wasn't usually that way with people.

Though I felt the same way about Scott and Rob.

"Good," she said. "Because I think someone is trying to fit me up for murder."

TEN

Lizzie and I stared at one another and then back at Brenna. Had she really said someone tried to frame her for murder?

"Maybe start at the beginning," I said. "Tell us why you think that."

"I can show you," she said. She pulled something out of the pocket of her dress. It was a small vial.

Was it poison?

"I think I told you I'd been working in Dublin the last few weeks. I'd only been home a few hours before your party."

"I remember you said that." Lizzie refilled her tea and handed her milk.

"Well, I have another shoot in Dublin tomorrow. And I won't be back in time to pack for my trip to Bali. So today, I packed and readied the house for my departure."

I pointed to the bottle. "So, what does that have to do with your trip, and why do you think someone is framing you?"

"The short version is, I love to cook when I'm home. My mum and nan taught me, and I love sharing that food with people."

"You made the piri-piri chicken. I remember asking Lolly

about it," Lizzie said. "It was so good. We're lucky to have neighbors who love to cook."

Brenna gave her a genuine smile. "There isn't much else to do here once the sun goes down." She held up her hands. "Don't get me wrong. After living in big cities for so long, I love it here. But it's why I kept a small place in Dublin when I moved to Shamrock Cove."

"I'm not following," I said. It had been a long day, and I wasn't able to connect the dots.

"I make oils for when I cook. I learned from my nan that infusing oils with certain ingredients can help intensify the flavor in foods, especially meats."

"Okay, I'm with you so far," Lizzie said. "Do you use olive oils?"

Brenna nodded. "Anyway, I keep dates on my bottles because the special oils don't last more than a month or so. Since I'm leaving tomorrow, I didn't want the older oils to spoil while I was gone. It ruins the bottles I keep them in and makes them unsanitary.

"I was about to dump out the garlic oil I used to make the piri-piri when I realized something wasn't right." She took the top off the small vial. "Smell this."

She handed the bottle to my sister, but I reached over and took it from her. "Is it poisoned?" I asked.

"Are you allergic to seafood?" Brenna asked.

We shook our heads.

"Smell it." She motioned toward me. I took a quick sniff. The garlic was so pungent it burned my eyes, but there was something else. Distinctive, like when someone cooks shrimp in the house.

I handed it to Lizzie. "What do you think?"

She closed her eyes and took a whiff. "Garlic and... shrimp. That's an odd combination, but that chicken was delicious."

"Except, it's supposed to be only garlic," Brenna said.

Then it hit me. "Was the judge allergic to seafood?"

She nodded gravely.

"Oh," Lizzie said. "Oh. My."

Brenna slumped down in her chair. She had the weight of the world on her shoulders.

"My food may have killed the judge," she said. "And you have no reason to believe me. You don't know me. But I didn't do it. I swear to you."

I leaned back in my chair. "I believe you," I said.

"You do?" Lizzie and Brenna said at the same time.

"Sorry," Lizzie added. "But we really don't know you. Why would you come to us? You could have dumped the whole thing down a sink and thrown away the bottle. That's what I would have done."

We stared at my sister.

She smirked. "What? It's actually a brilliant way to kill someone if he did die from the allergy. Why would she keep the evidence?"

"Because she didn't kill him, and she wants to find out who did. Right?" I asked Brenna.

"Yes. That and I'm certain someone on the court murdered him. I don't lock the house up when I'm gone. The people who live here check on my plants and help care for the garden. Anyone could have put shrimp extract in my oil. They all knew what I was making. Lolly emailed the list for your welcome-to-the court party two weeks ago."

I frowned. "So, it was premeditated, not an accident."

Brenna's eyes went wide. "I hadn't thought of it that way. And if anyone had searched my house, I would have been the one to blame. The judge was making my life a living hell, and they all knew it."

I thought about what Lolly had said about Brenna's jacuzzi.

"I understand why you're so upset, but can't you just explain it to the detective?" Lizzie asked. "He seems like a reasonable man. Well, except for he keeps arresting my sister for no reason, but I think that might be because he likes her."

"What?" Brenna and I said together.

Lizzie shrugged. "Why else would he work to spend so much time with you?"

"He's got a funny way of showing it." I turned to our new friend. "I'm with Lizzie, though. I don't understand what it is you want from us."

Brenna blew out a breath. "I shifted some things with work and moved my ticket to Bali up. My flight leaves in six hours. I'm asking you to hold onto the vial, and then give it to the detective after I leave. I do not know what the police will think, I'm worried they'll blame me."

Lizzie gasped. "You're making us complicit."

Brenna shook her head. "No, I wouldn't do that to you. I'm going to leave the vial in an envelope on your porch with instructions to give it to the detective. He doesn't have to know we've spoken. I'll say in the note that you two were the only ones I could trust."

"But if he asks us if we spoke to you, I can't lie," said Lizzie. "I'm the worst at lying, ask my sister."

"She's not wrong. And I think your best bet is to tell him the truth. You could have left without telling any of us. You could have dumped the bottle somewhere in Dublin, and no one would be the wiser. That you are coming forward shows you are innocent. Besides, I'm fairly certain they can extradite you from Indonesia. And it will only make you look guilty if you go without telling him."

She rubbed her forehead. "I didn't think about it like that. I'm a black woman in Ireland, you must understand. It's even worse in the States, and—"

"I hear and believe you, Brenna," I said. "But I think coming forward is the only way to go. Think about it. If you weren't so careful about your containers, you might have left that oil for the police to find. The real killer was probably counting on that. And my guess is they probably planned to implicate you in some way so that your house would be searched. At least, if I was the murderer, that's what I'd do."

"Wait. Wait." Lizzie held up a hand. "We don't even know if the judge was murdered. No one has said a word about that or how he died. That's another reason you need to come forward now. If it was from an allergic reaction, then you wouldn't announce that you had the oil that might have killed him, right?"

Brenna rubbed her forehead harder. She had to be worried sick. "I don't know what to do," she said.

I scrunched up my face. "You could take the vial, and we can pretend we never had this conversation if that's what you want. You trusted us, and you don't know us either, but we believe you. We will do what is best. But we can't lie for you. Lizzie is right about that."

"But if I throw away the oil, then the police may not know it was planted or premediated like you said. And what if the killer comes after me? I mean, maybe they meant to blame me, but if I mess that up..."

"They might try to kill you?"

She nodded.

She had a point. "You are certain it was someone who lives here in the court?" I asked.

"Who else would know about my oils or that I would use the garlic oil to make the dish? It has to be someone here."

Lizzie made a face. "I don't like the idea that one of our neighbors is the killer. I was very much hoping it was someone the judge had put in jail."

Me too. If I was honest.

"I have an idea," I said. "Will you trust me?"

Brenna hesitated but then nodded her head.

· · ·

About a half-hour later, Detective Kieran knocked on the door. He held a boxed cake and a bottle of wine.

"Did anyone see you?" I asked.

He gave me a weird face. "I don't think so. Will you explain why you asked me to bring you cake?"

"In a minute. Follow me."

When he stepped into the kitchen, he stopped. "Brenna? What are you doing here? I mean, hello."

"Hey," she said softly.

"Can someone please explain what's going on? And why I had to buy a cake?"

"We wanted your visit to look casual," I said. "Like you were apologizing for the fact you keep arresting me."

"I've never arrested you," he said. "I just brought you in for questioning."

"Right," I said. "Which is why you need to trust what I'm about to tell you is the truth."

"You're going to want to sit down for this," Lizzie said. "Would you like some pie or tea?"

He frowned and then shook his head. After setting the cake box on the kitchen table, he sat down.

"Just tell me."

I explained everything. Including why I thought it was brave for Brenna to come forward. And that we wanted to be here as witnesses for her.

Then he asked Brenna very direct questions, which she answered.

"Is that it?" He pointed to the vial.

She nodded. "I poured the rest down the sink," she said. "It wasn't until I poured it out that I noticed it smelled wrong."

"Did I kill the judge? I need to know. Though, I'm not certain I can live with the guilt." A tear slipped down her cheek, and it hit me. Technically, it wasn't her fault. But I would feel guilty if it was me.

"I can't say," he said.

I opened my mouth, but he held up a hand.

"I only have a partial tox screen so far. But he did have elevated levels of specific things in his body. Any one of which could have killed him. The pathologist isn't done yet. It could have a mixture of those... elements.

"So, I honestly can't say for certain what killed him. It will probably be a few days."

"But do you believe me?" she asked. Then she sniffed. None of it was faked. She was worried she might go to prison.

"I do. We've known each other a long time, Brenna. I know you didn't kill him. As Ms. McCarthy pointed out, you could have dumped the bottle and we'd have been none the wiser. You've done nothing but help us with our investigation."

She took a deep, shuddering breath.

"If the tests come back to show something about the allergy, then we'll know it was premeditated," I said. "And that someone set Brenna up."

"Indeed." He leaned back in his chair. Then he rubbed his chin.

"Then she may not be safe. What if the killer decides to clean up after themselves? Or tries to make it look like she took her own life because she felt guilty."

"Oh. No." Brenna cried out.

He frowned, and then looked thoughtfully at me. "This isn't one of your novels," he said.

"I wish it was," I said. "Then I'd know who the killer is. And for the record, you keep telling me this place is safe, but now we may have a killer on the court."

Lizzie shivered.

"Here's what we're going to do," he said. "Brenna, you head on to Dublin and then Bali. Please do not come back until you check with me. Understood?"

She nodded.

I thought that was very open-minded of him. I had a feeling, if it was me in these circumstances, he'd lock me up and throw away the key.

"You two need to keep quiet about everything you've learned tonight." He pointed to me and my sister. "Can you do that?"

"I'm not very good at lying," Lizzie shouted. "Sorry. Sorry. This is just... a lot."

"It is," he said. "But, Ms. McCarthy, you and your sister's lives depend on you staying mum about everything you heard tonight. We can't let on that we know about the shrimp. The killer can't know we are on to them. Do you understand?"

She nodded.

"Brenna, I want you to lock up the house and give me your key. I'll get you to Dublin and check on your plants and garden."

She swallowed. "Thanks. I'll feel better about that. But are any of us safe? I mean, I've known these people for years. Why now?"

He glanced from Lizzie, to me, and then Brenna. "That's an excellent question."

After they left to get Brenna's bags, I went back to the kitchen. Lizzie kept wiping the same spot on the table.

"Are you okay?" I asked. I took the dish towel away from her.

"I thought when we came here that things would be... less complicated," she said. Small lines had formed around her eyes. She was exhausted.

"I think complicated follows us around," I said.

"Maybe it follows you," she said. "My life was so simple before... I don't think I appreciated it enough. It's scary thinking someone so close by might be a killer." She put an arm around her stomach.

"At least Kieran doesn't think it's us."

"I know people don't lock their doors around here, but do you mind if we do?" she asked.

"Girl, I've lived in Manhattan the last fifteen years, I always lock the doors. But don't worry, Lizzie. I won't let anything happen to you."

She smiled. "I know. Will you stop your investigation now? Whoever it is means business. I don't want you putting us in the crosshairs."

"I'm sure the detective has it well in hand."

"You didn't answer my question."

"I'm not going to lie to you, Lizzie. The quicker we find out who did this, the safer we will be."

She opened her mouth, but I held up a hand.

"I swear I will be discreet, and I won't put either of us in danger. Besides, I'll be busy for the next few days after Carrie's call. I have to remove my amateur detective hat and put the writing one back on for now.

"That and we're dealing with someone very clever. That oil, what kind of person thinks of that?"

She sighed. "A killer."

"One who thought through every detail of that party and used Brenna."

"If I think about it anymore, I'm going to..."

I hugged her hard. "Nothing will happen to us." I would make sure of it.

She squeezed me hard. "Okay, I'm going to bed. Will you lock up?"

I nodded.

She went upstairs. After locking the doors and turning out the lights, I headed to my office.

I was too wired to sleep, but I couldn't quite focus on my novel.

I picked up the notebook where I'd word vomited everything about the case. I wrote down everything we'd learned tonight from Brenna. My mind whirled with possibilities of who the killer might be.

Then I remembered we'd forgotten to add Matt to our suspect list. Family grievances ran deep. I couldn't imagine the cute but nerdy Matt killing his grandfather, but who knew?

And I needed to see those reports on what had been in the judge's system. I had friends back home who were experts and might help me decipher them.

I must have fallen asleep at my desk because a strange noise woke me up several hours later. After peeling my face off my keyboard, I headed to the window.

It was dark outside, except for the solar lights around the garden, and I didn't see anyone.

Maybe I'd imagined it or dreamed the noise. I'd been having weird dreams about being chased through a forest.

I grabbed my phone off my desk, to check the time. It was three in the morning. I'd only fallen asleep for a few hours. I went to check the doors one last time before heading to bed.

I didn't bother turning on the lights. I didn't want to risk waking Lizzie. I slipped on the piece of paper by the front door. It must have come through the mail slot.

I checked the back door and then carried the paper to my office to read it in the light.

It had been typed out, and the paper was of good weight.

But it was what was typed that gave me pause.

I know what you did. I will make you pay.

Well, that can't be good.

ELEVEN

My sister had had enough to deal with the past few months, so I decided to keep the letter to myself. That was made easier because she was long gone when I finally woke up.

She'd left me some scones and a note that mentioned I should focus on work, and she'd text if she needed help with the shop.

Since my fingerprints were all over the note we'd received the night before, I wasn't certain how much use it would be to the police, but I had to talk to Kieran about it.

After grabbing a coffee and a scone, I went back to my office. I'd put the note in a plastic baggie the night before and stuck it in my desk.

I slid it out of the drawer and stared at it. Then I took a picture and tried to discern the watermark on the fancy paper on which it'd been typed. Last night, I'd thought we might be dealing with a brilliant killer. I mean, the shrimp in the garlic oil was brilliant.

But this note didn't scream genius. The paper would be easy to trace, at least to where it was bought or ordered from, and that might soon tell us who the killer was. The detective had been worried about Brenna's safety since she'd been set up as the scapegoat, but what about the rest of us?

I needed more information.

An hour later, I decided to take the letter to the detective.

After showering and putting on real people clothes—not the ones I usually sit and write in most days—I headed down to the station. It felt good, for once, that I wasn't in trouble.

Sheila was at the front desk. "Oi, look at you walking into the station without cuffs."

We laughed. "I know, it's a first. Is the detective in?"

She shook her head. "He's in Dublin this morning. Texted me last night that he needed to get something to the lab first thing. Usually, that's my job, but maybe he had other business there."

Or, maybe he didn't trust the evidence with anyone else and he went to see Brenna off.

"Is there something I can help you with or do you want to leave him a message?"

I very much needed to look at the reports that had come in on the judge. It occurred to me that the detective had never said exactly what had happened, only that what he had so far only told part of the story.

"Would you mind if I left him a note? It's long, I don't mind writing it out myself. I just had a few questions for him. Also, I think I lost an earring here yesterday. Do you mind if I check the interview room?"

She frowned. The phone rang.

"Go ahead," she said. "Here's some paper." She handed me blank sheets. "Just leave the note on his desk."

"Perfect."

"Station," she answered.

Knowing I didn't have much time, I headed straight for the detective's office.

The judge's file sat on his desk blotter. Unlike the messy

main character in my books, the detective was tidy. I pulled my phone out of my pocket and opened the file. Without really looking, I took pictures of everything in there, including the reports and lab results.

Sheila was finishing her call in the front room, so I put the file back in its place and scribbled a note on the paper she'd given me.

I didn't want to leave what I'd received the night before on his desk. Anyone could have taken it if it was this easy to get into his office.

Back at the house, I didn't have a printer yet, and there was no way I could read the files on my phone. So, I downloaded everything to my computer and then opened the files.

The labs didn't make much sense to me, but the medical report was a different story. A small entry said the judge had too much digoxin in his system.

The exact notation was: *Excessive amounts of digoxin and non-specific elements*. What did that mean? Had he taken too much heart medicine, which could often contain digoxin? Did we even know if he had a heart condition? I mean, that's what it had looked like to me when he'd been dying. He'd been grabbing his chest when he was on the ground.

But I didn't see any signs of anaphylactic shock in the reports. If he had been suffering from a reaction, we should have given him an EpiPen. But if he'd been having a heart attack, the adrenaline would have killed him.

I was no closer to an answer. But I did have a friend, Jack, a former ME in New York, who could help me.

I emailed him and told him it was research for a book. I didn't send the reports because I didn't want him to know I was snooping. But I did send him several questions and asked for possibilities.

Jack was used to that sort of thing coming from me.

While I needed to finish revising the first half of my book, I couldn't quite settle.

I locked up the house and decided to walk down Main Street. My plan was to stop in and see if Lizzie needed anything. If she didn't, I'd walk down the hill to the seashore.

When I stopped at the store, Lizzie was behind the counter reading a book.

She glanced up when the bell rang over the door.

"Hey, I thought you'd be busy writing this morning. Linda said she'd seen you at the station. Did something happen? Did the detective arrest you again?"

I laughed. "Is anyone here?"

She shook her head.

"I just went down to make sure Brenna made her flight okay." Yes, that was a lie. I was a much better fibber than my sister.

"Oh. I'd forgotten about that. What did he say?"

"He wasn't there. I guess he took the, uh, sample to some lab in Dublin. I have a feeling he went there to make sure Brenna got on the plane safely. You said Linda noticed I was there?"

"Yes, she came in and bought a ton more romances. She's sweet. After what Rob and Scott said about her, I wasn't so sure. But she was so kind and thanked me for reopening the store. I looked back in the records. She was one of our grandfather's best customers. Anyway, she mentioned when she was opening her shop, she noticed you going into the station."

"Well, that's lovely to hear. But are you sure she wasn't pumping you for information?"

She shrugged. "I decided to forget about what Brenna told us last night. It's the only way I can stop jumping whenever there's a noise in the bookshop. I love this place, but it definitely plays the old building blues."

"How's business this morning?"

"I was busy when I first opened the doors, but it's a Thursday, I'm guessing things will pick up on Saturday. Where are you headed?"

"I thought I'd walk down to the shore. I was up late on the computer, and I didn't get much sleep. I need to clear the cobwebs."

She smiled. "Did you fall asleep on your keyboard again?"

I laughed. "Yep. Do you want to come with me?"

The bell dinged, and we glanced behind me.

Lolly came in with a group of women.

"Hello, ladies," Lizzie said.

"Will you be okay?" I whispered.

She nodded.

I waved goodbye and headed down to the sea. The beach was pristine, and the water was a deep blue. It was nippier here by the water, even though it was late spring.

I breathed deeply, and the salt air was nothing short of delightful.

I could get used to this.

The beach went on for a bit and was surrounded by tall, jagged cliffs. On the other side, a jetty of rocks went out into the ocean. I shaded my eyes with my hands and could make out some figures in chairs at the end of it. They had fishing poles.

I walked up the stairs leading to the top of the jetty. Once I reached the last step, I found a smooth path heading out to the sea. Along it were a few stands. Some were for fish and chips or ice cream, others for beach accessories like chairs and plastic buckets. All the stands were painted beautifully in pastels with colorful pictures of the items sold.

I wondered when the small shops would open. Up here, the full force of the wind hit me, and I shivered.

The men fishing at the end of the jetty waved at me. I waved back.

The place was idyllic. My shoulders dropped a few inches. This was right outside our door, which only made Ireland more magical.

Except for that one thing where one of our neighbors had been murdered, and someone had left a threatening note at my door. Oh, and tried to frame Brenna.

Ugh.

But Lizzie and I needed this change. It had been good for my brain so far. I just needed to help find the killer so we could truly move on with our lives. That had to happen before my sister decided she'd had enough and wanted to hightail it back to Texas.

Even though we'd found even more trouble, I wasn't ready to leave. There was something about this place that felt like... home.

My phone buzzed, and I pulled it from my pocket.

It was a text from Brenna. I'd given her my number that night at the party.

My flight was delayed, but we just boarded. On my way. Be safe. Thank you.

At least one of us was safe. I texted her back and asked that she let me know when she landed.

On the way back, I stopped in at Linda's shop. I wasn't a crafty person, but I did appreciate the artistry that went into making beautiful things.

After Scott and Rob had called her out, I was curious as to why. She'd seemed fine at the welcoming party, and my sister liked her. But people always wore masks.

The shop had colorful yarn and quilts in the window. Everything was quite particular. Nothing was out of place. And much like the bookstore, a bell jingled when I opened the door.

"Mercy, welcome." Linda motioned me inside. She was

cutting some fabric for a customer. Her shop was adorable. Two walls were covered in cubbies with beautifully dyed yarns. There were several long shelves of fabrics, and the items one needed to work on their crafts were spaced in wooden racks throughout the store.

I looked around the shop, admiring many of the quilts on the other walls and above the counter where she worked. The place was cozy and charming. And extremely pristine, as if dust wouldn't dare land anywhere in her shop.

Once she wrapped up the package for the client, Linda welcomed me inside.

"How are you?" she asked. "Can I get you some tea or coffee?" She bustled around the counter. "I don't mind turning on the kettle."

"No, I'm fine. I just thought I'd visit some of the shops on Main Street. Your store is gorgeous."

She blushed. "Thank you. Do you quilt, sew, knit, or crochet?"

I shook my head. "No. My mom used to knit, and I know the work that goes into creating such beautiful things. I don't have the patience for most crafts. It's probably why I write. It's very immediate, even if it's crap, and easy to fix."

She laughed. "Well, I can't imagine what that must be like, and you are so successful. How are you finding our small town? Are you missing the big city?"

"I love it here," I said, and it was the truth. "I just went down to the beach. It's gorgeous."

"Wait until summer. It will be packed with tourists, but it's worth it. That trade is what keeps our little town going."

"Was this always a quilting store?"

Her smile faltered slightly. "Oh, it's been many things through the years, I believe. Before me, it was a watchmaker's place. You'll find that with many of our shops along Main Street. As times change, needs must."

"It's good for the economy to change with the times, I suppose," I said. "But it's lovely you've been able to keep the place's charm. Everything is so beautiful."

"It takes the effort of everyone who lives here," she said. "Some of us are more progressive than others." She said the last part under her breath, but I heard every word.

"I'm always on a deadline, but maybe Lizzie and I can help somehow. I was told you are the woman in the know when it comes to everything that happens here."

She put a hand on her chest. "You wonder sometimes if people are even aware of the hard work you put into this village. I'd happily invite you to some of the committees I sit on. Everything from our many festivals to preservation causes to deciding which vendors are allowed on the beach."

"I just saw the booths up on the jetty."

"Right, those are our permanent establishments owned by Shamrock Cove residents. I'm talking about the small pop-ups allowed on the beach itself. Our coast is popular, and we must be careful to keep the riff-raff out."

I wasn't sure the last time I'd heard someone use the phrase *riff-raff*.

"We are a town that prides itself on being authentic and crime free."

"Oh, then the judge's death must be a big surprise for everyone." Fine, it wasn't the smoothest transition, but I had to test her.

She blinked. "What do you mean?"

"Oh, uh. I heard he died under suspicious circumstances."

Her eyes narrowed. "You're not spreading that gossip, are you? It could be damaging to all of us and our tourist trade. He died of a heart attack. He was a cantankerous old goat, constantly upsetting himself over things that weren't his business. He did it to himself."

I held up my hands in surrender. "Sorry, I heard some

women talking about him in the bookstore. The police seem to think he was murdered." I didn't mention anything I knew. "But I didn't mean to offend you. I just thought you probably knew more than most, since you seem to have your finger on Shamrock Cove's pulse."

She seemed to check herself. "That I do. But I've not heard the gossip. Though, people talk here. It's a small town, bound to happen. But don't you worry. I'm certain the judge died of natural causes. Anyone who says otherwise is speaking nonsense. Now, tell me what sort of things your mother used to knit."

It took me another half-hour to extricate myself from the shop. And when I finally left, it was with the impression that Linda was a do-gooder who only wanted the best for Shamrock Cove and its residents.

She didn't seem the type to murder someone. A woman who believed she was always right, even when she wasn't, maybe. That I could see, but not murder. She wasn't some mastermind killer who'd have the forethought to place shrimp in garlic oil.

I kept her on the list of suspects, but lower down. I mean, she might have been working with her husband or one of the other neighbors.

And now I'm paranoid and making everyone a suspect.

I sighed.

I bumped into Dave, her husband, just outside her store.

"Hello," he said. "Have you been visiting?"

"I have. Your wife has a beautiful store."

It was only for a second, but I swear he flinched when I said wife.

That was weird.

"Aye, it is. Are you settling in? Is there anything I can help you with? Taxes for writers can be complicated."

"I appreciate the offer. I'm set for now. But I will keep you in mind for the future. Linda was telling me about all the festivals."

"Aye, one for every season, sometimes more than one," he said. "And she's involved in them all." He didn't seem happy about that. His eyes shifted to the right and back. There must have been some tension about her over-committing.

"I'm curious what you do for fun in town," I said.

He laughed. "Well, besides the pub quiz, which is great fun, I love golf. Do you play? We have some of the best courses in the world."

"I don't, but that's good to know. Did you hear about the judge's death being a murder?"

It wasn't the greatest segue, but I was curious about his reaction.

Again, he flinched. Then he frowned. "Is that true? I thought he was just old, or it was an allergic reaction." He stared down at the ground as if he were deep in thought. But he could have been lying.

There was something about him that didn't sit right with me, as if he were up to something.

Had he killed the judge? And, if so, what had been his motive?

"It's only rumors I've heard. It seems he wasn't so popular."

"Well, sad to say, that's the truth. He liked to cause trouble. My guess is there is more than one person in town who is glad he is gone." He made the sign of the cross. "Not me, of course. I don't like the idea of speaking ill of the dead. But he wasn't the kindest of men."

"I've heard that. Did you have any problems with him?"

His face twisted for a minute. "He gave Linda a hard time, but no. I personally didn't have a problem with him." His tone made me suspicious. There was an edge there that hadn't been there before.

"Oh, I wasn't aware they had trouble."

Liar.

"My wife tends to take everything personally and worries about what people think."

"Anything specific the judge picked on?"

He cleared his throat. "It's all in the past, right? No need to worry any more. If you'll excuse me." He nearly ran into his wife's store.

What was that all about?

By the time I returned to the house, it was lunchtime, and I hadn't written a word.

I made a cortado and grabbed a cold blueberry scone. Since my brain needed protein, I also took a few slices of Irish cheddar for my plate. I'd never had that kind of cheddar until the other night at our welcoming party, and I was a fan.

I pushed all other thoughts about murder and blackmail from my mind, and then I sat down and wrote.

A crick in my neck forced me to stop a few hours later. That and I needed some water. When I glanced out the kitchen window, Lolly and the women she'd been with earlier walked down the back path.

I wonder why they went that way?

Maybe they'd been up to the castle, which was something I'd promised Lizzie we would explore together.

I was about to head back to the office when someone knocked on the door.

"I got your note," Kieran said when I opened the door. "What happened?"

It had been such a long day that I'd almost forgotten why I'd gone to see him.

"Would you like a coffee?"

He smiled. "That answer is always, yes."

I laughed. "Go get it started. I need to grab something to show you."

"Okay."

A few minutes later, I met him in the kitchen.

"We've got to stop meeting like this, people will talk."

He laughed. It was funny how handsome he was when he didn't scowl at me.

"Gran is taking her late afternoon nap. Brenna is gone. Linda is at her shop, and Dave is headed to Dublin for a client. Rob and Scott are at the pub organizing quiz night with Matt. No one saw me walk up."

I'd talked to Dave earlier and he hadn't mentioned any travel. "Wow, you do know what's happening on the court and in Shamrock Cove."

He shrugged. "Small towns are like that. What is it you needed to show me?"

I placed the letter on the table and waited.

He frowned and then picked it up. He held it to the overhead light.

"Tell me when and how it was received."

"About three this morning. I think it's what woke me up. I'd fallen asleep in my study. It came through the letterbox in the door."

"It's a very specific kind of paper," he said.

I nodded. "I tried to bring it to you this morning, but you were in Dublin."

"Aye. I wanted to get that vial tested quickly and see Brenna off safely."

"Have you heard any more from the labs?" I didn't mention what I'd seen that morning. Except for an out-of-office notice in my email from him, I hadn't heard back from my friend Jack yet. If he was on one of his trips, it might be months before he checked his email.

He shook his head. "I'm worried about this letter. What is it they think you've done?"

"No idea. I was hoping you could help me out. We know I didn't kill the judge. So, it has to be something else."

He stared at me and did that thing where he crossed his arms and tilted his head.

"Well, at least I know I didn't kill him. Even you have to admit this murder took planning. Can you even prove it was murder yet?" I stopped myself. I wasn't supposed to have seen the medical examiner's reports. "That shrimp stuff had to be placed before my sister and I arrived. You can at least admit that."

His brows drew together, but he didn't say anything.

"Whatever. We've, at the very least, proven I didn't have a motive. So, they can't be on me about his murder. Maybe they think I did something else. That's why I asked for your help."

"Is there anything in your recent history back in the States? News reports or something that someone could use to blackmail you here."

I snorted, but then cocked my head. Had my stalker followed me here? No. I'd been so careful about keeping the move quiet. Besides, I'd been in Texas for months. I'd quickly stopped in New York for my winter clothes, but we'd only been there a few days.

His frown deepened.

"It's funny that you always think I've done something wrong. And the answer is no. I have been at my sister's ranch for the last six months, helping her with everything. It's been rough. And I was there off and on when Mom was sick for the months before."

"I did a search on Lizzie and didn't come up with much. Other than her lavender business was quite successful, as is your career. But I know PTSD when I see it," he said. "Your sister has it. Care to enlighten me?"

"It's really her story to tell," I said.

"If I'm going to help you, I need the facts," he said. Then he was silent. That was a ploy by law enforcement. But I was used to uncomfortable silences.

"Please." It was the way he said it that had my shoulders dropping.

"After losing her fight to cancer, our mom died. I really hate that disease."

"Aye," he said.

"Lizzie and her fiancé were supposed to get married about a month after Mom died, but they postponed the wedding. None of us was ready to celebrate much of anything. We'd been close to our mom. She was our rock." My voice caught at the end.

I took a sip of water.

"About six months ago, there was a freak storm in Texas. Right before Christmas, everything iced over, and the power went out. It was rough for a lot of people. Where my sister lived was particularly hard hit.

"Her generators went out in the greenhouses. She was about to lose everything on a project she'd been working on for a new kind of harvest. That's a whole other story. I'll explain another day.

"Anyway, her fiancé was driving to her ranch to bring her some generators when a fire truck, which had been trying to get to an emergency, slid on the ice and hit his truck head-on. There were no survivors. His young daughter was killed as well."

"Blimey," he whispered the word.

"Yep. Lizzie took it hard and blamed herself. My sister is one of the strongest women you'll ever meet. I mean it. She ran that lavender business like a general and is absolutely brilliant at it. People came to her for business advice. She was that good. But the death of two people she loved most in the world, on the heels of what happened with my mom, broke her.

"One afternoon, I found her lying in a field. She sobbed uncontrollably with her hands raw from picking lavender. I got her back to the house, and she promised we could find help the next day. But that night, she drank too much and took some pills. I don't think she meant to try and kill herself. It was more she tried to dull the pain so she could sleep. I found her a few hours later, and when I couldn't wake her...

"I haven't left her side since then. We convinced each other to come here. I think we both needed to get away from all the memories. The ranch and business she had built had become painful for her."

"I can imagine. Still, to come all the way to Ireland."

I chuckled. "I know. When I received the first letter from the solicitor, I didn't even tell her about it. I thought it was some kind of joke. But then, when he called and told me about our grandfather and what he had left us...

"I'm not much into woo-woo stuff."

"Woo-woo?"

"You know, manifesting in the universe sort of thing. I have a healthy respect for the universe and my place in it, but sometimes things are put in our path for a reason.

"When I told Lizzie about it, I thought we'd just come over and check it out to see if it was for real. But she was the one who said she wanted to move here. That she needed to get as far away as possible... I'm talking a lot."

"I'm sorry for you and your sister," he said. And it was easy to see from his expression that he meant it. "That explains the look in her eyes. And the nerves."

"Yeah, she's a lot more sensitive to everything these days. That's why we have to find out what's going on with all of this. She needs this place. I've watched her in that bookstore. She's happier than she's been since I can't remember when. We have to find the killer."

"*We* aren't handling anything," he said. "I understand you

have doubts about my abilities in solving a murder, but I do have experience.

"I can find out what happened with this." He held up the letter. "And with the judge."

I made a steeple with my fingers. "You don't know me well, Detective, but I'm not very good at butting out of things. Especially when it involves the safety of my family. I trust you to find the culprit, but as things keep happening to us—and people seem to talk to me—I'd like to help."

"It's you asking questions that may have prompted someone to send the letter," he said.

He had a point.

"Unless it has nothing to do with the judge. There are lot of rules and expectations in this town. I'm one of those terrible Americans who says what she means. There's no telling who I might have offended."

He chuckled.

"At the very least, you could check the watermark on the paper, right? That's distinctive and a clue."

"Aye. It is. Do me a favor, though. Stop your snooping."

I threw a hand across my heart. "I'm offended. That said, you might also want to look at Matt. Though, I beg you not to arrest him until I find out who sources his coffee."

This time he guffawed. Then he took his cup to the sink. "I'm well aware of the judge's relationship with Matt and his mother. I may have even tried to talk some sense into the old man a few times. But Matty's a good kid. Wouldn't hurt a fly."

"If you say so. If I promise to knock it off with the twenty questions, will you tell me what happened with the victim? Was he murdered? Did I have any hope of saving him? I think that's what bothers me most. Did I do the right thing? You know, adrenaline or no."

"Aye, you mean if it was an allergic reaction versus heart attack. You did everything you could. I can say he did have a heart attack. I can't say yet what caused it. Now, if, you'll excuse me. I need to relieve Sheila. She's due a break."

He left.

I didn't understand why he wouldn't just tell me what the tests had said. But then I remembered the guy had only known me a few days, and he was law enforcement. He was doing his job.

Still, knowing the facts didn't keep me from being frustrated.

I checked my email to see if Jack had answered me. He hadn't.

My phone buzzed with a text from Lizzie.

You'll never guess what happened.

I waited, but there was nothing else.

Now what?

TWELVE

My sister wasn't normally one for drama, and I was worried. I jumped up. I opened the door to run to the bookstore and slammed into Lizzie. I hit her so hard I had to reach out and stop her from falling.

I took her hand and guided her inside.

"What's wrong?" I looked her over from head to toe.

She shut the door and then waved her hand. "I'm fine. I'm fine. I texted you as I was leaving the shop, and then it felt like someone was watching as I came out of the store. So, I ran home."

I'd experienced the same thing.

"You know when the little hairs go on your neck, but no one is around. Weird. I think I freaked myself out after everything Brenna told us."

I didn't want to scare her by saying I felt the same way earlier.

"That is scary. Are you sure there wasn't someone else around?"

She shook her head. "It wasn't until I was in our garden that it stopped. Do you think maybe there are more secret doors or windows or something? Maybe someone was watching me? I sound crazy."

I chuckled. "You don't. Knowing this place, there probably are several. But you're safe and at home. Tell me what the *what happened* message was about."

She followed me to the kitchen. She washed her hands, and then donned her apron. Then she started preparing a meal. I had no idea how she just did that so unconsciously, gathering ingredients and chopping vegetables. It was second nature to her.

"Scott has been in Dublin, but he stopped by the store earlier. He wants us to come to the pub quiz tonight. He says there is not a more important event in town and that it's a great way to meet the locals."

I wasn't much for those kinds of games, though I wasn't terrible at them. I knew a little about a lot of different things. But I wasn't much of an expert at anything.

"Your text sounded like more than that."

"Well, as he was leaving, he ran into Linda. They were pointing fingers at one another and shouting really loud in the middle of the sidewalk."

"Did you hear what they were saying?"

She shook her head. "I had a few customers I was checking out before I closed. The only thing I heard was *food* and *secrets*. Do you think it has something to do with the judge?"

I shrugged. "No idea. Do you need my help with anything?" She put the vegetables she'd been cutting in a big pot.

She glanced over her shoulder and made a funny face. "No offense, it goes faster without you."

"Harsh."

We laughed.

"I'm making a veggie soup. Mom's recipe."

"I'm all about the comfort food," I said. "But what's really going on in your head?"

After adding broth, spices, and water, she stirred the pot. My sister cooked our mom's recipes when she was upset about things, which was why I'd gained a good ten pounds in the last six months.

"This whole thing that one of our neighbors might be a murderer is getting to me," she said softly. "I mean, not so much that I want to turn tail and go back home. But enough that it makes me feel uncomfortable.

"You're probably used to looking over your shoulder and always being aware of your surroundings in the city. And we should always be that way, to be honest. But I'm uncomfortable. I guess, a little on edge. Everything is different here. Even the language to some extent. I nod a lot at the shop but sometimes I don't understand what the customers are saying... That's something I hadn't even thought about. I'm doing that thing you always talk about when you're writing..."

"Word vomiting?" I smiled.

"That's a gross phrase, but yes. I'm telling you all of this because my therapist said I had to tell you when I feel out of sorts, and I do. Big time. But I'm not—"

"Like before," I finished.

She made a check mark with her finger. "Overwhelmed. That's how I feel. I thought things would be so much easier once we settled in—I guess we're still settling in. I need to remind myself of that."

The move had finally hit her. She'd been so desperate to leave her memories behind in Texas, and I wondered if it might take a while for her to realize the enormity of what it really meant to leave the home she loved for a new adventure.

"We can go home at any time," I said softly. "You say the word, I'll make the arrangements."

She turned, and then leaned back against the sink. "No. Don't make it so easy for me. I need you to stop doing that. I made this choice with you. I don't have regrets. That's what I'm trying to say.

"As scary and as different as everything feels right now, I still don't regret coming. Not even the stuff with the judge has scared me off. I love it here. Is it harder than I'd thought it would be, yes. But the people, for the most part, are so lovely. And the place, I love our wide-open plains at home, but there is no comparison to the beauty of Shamrock Cove.

"I love our cottage and the garden. I took a walk down to the sea this morning. The sea. Can you imagine? I've been land-locked for so long, I had no idea the power it had over me."

"I feel the same way about the water," I said.

"And I really, really love the bookstore. Like, I'm not sure I could express how much. From the fairy garden to the secret doors, this place is just magical. I could not be happier to be here. It just hit me hard today that we…"

She wrapped her arms around her stomach. I wanted to go to her and give her a big hug. But I had a feeling she needed to get whatever this was out.

"We left the place, but the memories are still here." She put her hand on her heart. "There was a young girl who came into the store who looked like Audrey. So much so that it took my breath away."

Now, I was the one sniffling. Audrey was her fiancé John's daughter. She was a bright and beautiful girl, and I absolutely adored her. I still couldn't believe she wasn't in this world any longer.

"I'm sad, and I'm sorry. You've done so much to get us here."

"Stop it," I said. "You have the right to whatever it is you're feeling, Lizzie. To quote your doctor, you have been through the wars. And we are always going to have moments that take us right back to the worst times of our lives. And those wounds may take a long time to heal. I can't imagine not missing Mom. I still pick up the phone to call her about dumb stuff happening. And you've lost the man of your dreams. A guy so perfect, he made me believe that maybe there are good men in the world."

"There are, Mercy. Just not the ones you pick." She smiled to take the edge from her words. But she wasn't wrong.

We laughed. "Preaching to the choir, sis. But I mean what I said. If it will make you happier to go home. That's what we'll do. From now on, that's the focus. Our happiness matters."

She shook her head. "No. The focus should be getting on with life—not running away when it gets tough. Remembering and loving those we lost, but knowing they would want us to move forward."

She was right.

"So, tell me what you want."

"I want you to stop tiptoeing around me, but I also want you to stop looking for the judge's killer. My nerves can't take it. I can't lose you, Mercy. You are all I have left. There. I said it out loud."

I didn't remind her that she'd said the same thing earlier.

"I can honestly say I'm not actively looking into the judge's death right now," I said. "I'm busy writing." I didn't tell her about the letter or that the clues and evidence kept landing at our door.

Or the fact that, by the process of elimination, I'd narrowed down the suspect list to Dave, Linda, Mattie and his mom, Lolly and Rob. Dave was the most likely suspect; there was something off about him.

I mean, I'd only talked to him a few times, but people gave off vibes and his had been one of insincerity and something else I couldn't define. I couldn't explain why exactly, but I was going with my gut. Thankfully, he was out of town at the moment, so I felt we were safe.

"Phew. Good. Now, I'm going to freshen up and change. We'll head to the pub after dinner."

"I don't exactly remember agreeing to the pub quiz. I still have writing to do tonight."

She pouted. "Come on, just for a couple of hours. It's a chance to meet some folks outside of the court. I don't want to go on my own. Please don't make me."

I sighed. "Fine. But only because I've finished revising the first half of the book, and I'm on to writing new pages."

"Yay." She clapped her hands. "I'll go get ready. Soup will be ready in a half-hour."

After dinner, we headed to the Crown and Clover. The place was packed, but Rob and Scott waved us over to their table, where Lolly was also sitting. A few tables over, Linda and her husband, Dave, were arguing about something. They sat with a different group of people.

My stomach dropped when I spotted Dave. *I guess he's back from Dublin.*

"Let me get your drink orders," Scott said.

My sister and I ordered black and tans.

"What's that about?" I asked Rob. "I heard she was fighting with Scott earlier."

He rolled his eyes. "It wasn't a fight," he said. "With your grandfather and the judge gone, she's been asking to join our pub quiz team. Brenna had taken your granddad's place. When Linda overheard that I invited you guys to join us tonight because Brenna's away, she wasn't happy that we'd excluded her."

"Why don't you let them join your team?"

He glanced over to Lolly, who smiled.

"Because Dave thinks he knows everything and yet manages to get every answer wrong," Rob whispered the last part. "He's very convincing, though, and Linda is protective of him. Just watch, you'll see."

This felt very high schoolish to me, but the dynamics were fascinating. A new book and cast of characters had formed in my mind. They all seemed perfectly friendly with one another at the party, but as I peeled back the layers, new information came to light.

Stop it. You have to finish the book you're working on.

Still, I didn't want to forget. I typed a few notes into my phone. When I looked up, my sister gave me the eye. Then she smiled as she shook her head.

She'd been around enough to know what I'd been doing.

Scott returned with our pints.

"Good evening, everyone, our first category tonight is geography," Matt said on a microphone.

"I'm out," said Lizzie.

I laughed. "I'm not much better," I admitted.

"Lolly's pretty good with this one," Scott said. "Your grandad was the best. Actually, he was our best overall player. He had an inhuman knowledge of trivia."

"Did he?" I loved hearing more about him and liked that he had a general knowledge of things. He obviously had great taste in books and design. His house was adorable and did not look like an elderly man had owned it for so long.

"First question of the night: What is the capital of New Zealand?" Matt asked.

Lolly's eyes went wide.

"Is it Auckland?" Lizzie asked.

Lolly shrugged her shoulders. "It could be."

"Uh. It's..." I glanced around to find others listening to our convo, including Linda and Dave's table. I took a pen out of my sweater pocket, along with the small notebook I carried around. I wrote down: Wellington.

"I only know because I did a book signing there five years ago, and the woman who drove me around gave me a great history about the place." She thought it would be a good place to set a mystery. People did that to me a great deal, but I never minded.

Scott, who held the electronic tablet where we recorded our answers, looked at Lolly and then Rob. They nodded.

He wrote in the answer.

Matt stared at the tablet on the bar, where I assumed the answers were recorded. "Ten seconds left," he said.

"Okay, all answers have been locked in. The answer for question one is Wellington. Only one team got it right."

Our table cheered.

Dave and Linda stared daggers at us.

Oops.

"Next question: What is the currency of Denmark?"

"Oh, that's an easy one," Lolly said. "Give me the tablet." She wrote in krone.

An hour later, our table had won the first round. Everyone in our little group had contributed something, which made it even more fun.

"We'll take a fifteen-minute break before the second round," Matt announced. "The kitchen has a new batch of chips, come get them while their hot."

"Will you get us some?" Lizzie asked me. "I need the ladies."

I nodded.

Linda came up to me in the line. "Well done, you," she said. Her tone and big smile suggested she meant it.

"I hope it's okay," I said. As soon as I said it, I realized I shouldn't have said anything.

She frowned. "What do you mean?"

"That we, uh, helped out on the team tonight."

"I don't understand. Why would that matter?" She seemed genuinely confused.

"If we hadn't been here, maybe you and Dave could have been on the court's team."

She laughed out loud.

"Uh. No, dear. Is that what Rob and Scott said?"

Now, I felt in the middle of something that I didn't have a clue about.

"I just thought since many of the members were from the court..." I had no idea where I was going with that.

"We have no desire to be on the team," she said. "When your grandfather died, I did ask, but the judge was so rude about it, I didn't make that mistake again. And for the record, I adore Rob and Scott. I know they aren't my biggest fans. Mainly, because I wouldn't do a yarn rainbow in the window last June with my display. But I plan my window displays and yarn orders a year in advance. You saw the butterfly I made for spring out of the colors," she said.

While I had seen the display in the window, I hadn't realized it was a butterfly.

"I am a bit OCD about what I do in my shop. I have control issues when it comes to work, which is why it's best I am my own boss. But I have nothing against gay people. In fact, this June, I am creating a yarn rainbow. I've ordered in special colors just for the display. Rob is one of those people who holds a grudge, and he also likes to get his way. I promise you there is no ill will between me and him or me and you. I like to be friends with everyone. The world is tough enough."

"I couldn't agree more. It's just... someone saw you arguing in front of the bookshop and... I'm sorry, Linda."

"Oh, dear, don't be sorry. You're new. You'll learn the truth about our group soon enough. Just do yourself a favor and never get on Rob's bad side. The man can hold a grudge."

I had to admit, I had seen that behavior from Rob. But Linda had been nothing but pleasant to me.

"I'm hoping when he sees what I've designed for my June window, he'll forgive me for last year. Here, let me buy you some chips," she said. And she did.

"I bet you're glad to have Dave home," I said while we waited for the food.

"Always," she said. "Travel is a necessary part of his business though. He must go where the accounts are. Sometimes I get lonely when he's gone more than a few days, but I have my romance books to see me through."

"Does he get along with everyone?" It was a bold question but one I had to ask.

She laughed, though. "Better than I do," she said. "He helped the judge with his taxes and everyone on the court at one time or another with their financial needs. My Dave is easy to get along with and quite the charmer." She smiled lovingly at her husband.

But Dave gave her an odd look.

That was weird. And it most certainly wasn't loving. Maybe he was angry with his wife about something, but they definitely were not on the same page. If I was right about Dave, I hoped Linda wasn't in danger too.

We came in second in the next round but had the highest number of points overall. Our prize was a complimentary basket of chips and pints for the table.

It was about nine thirty when we finally headed home. I don't drink much anymore, so I had a light buzz. I felt like my shoulders had dropped several inches. That wasn't necessarily a bad thing. The last year had been a tense one, and I didn't have a lot of downtime.

When we made it to the gate of number three, we found the detective on the porch.

"Has something happened?" I asked.

"Ms. McCarthy, I need you to come with me to the station," he said.

"Whatever it is you can ask me here," I said.

"Mercy, I'm not talking to you," he said. "Lizzie, will you come with me?"

There were gasps around me, and I glanced around to find our neighbors watching.

"I'm not sure what you think happened, but Lizzie had nothing to do with it," I said. I was angry with this guy. One minute, he was friendly. The next, he was accusatory.

Lizzie put her hand on my arm. "I'm fine, Mercy. He wants to chat. Right, Detective?"

"Yes, miss."

"Are you certain you don't want to come in for a cup of coffee?" she asked.

"No, we'll need to make this interview a bit more formal."

She frowned. "Lead the way," she said.

"I'm calling our lawyer, barrister, solicitor, whatever you call them here. Do not say a word until I talk to him."

Lizzie shrugged but followed the detective.

"Can't you talk to him? Why does he keep harassing me and my sister?" I asked Lolly, who stood out in the road. She gave her grandson the evil eye, for which I was grateful.

"I'm sure he has his reasons, but I promise to have a word." Lolly frowned at her grandson. "Whatever he wants from her certainly could have waited until tomorrow morning. It's very late."

I left the group gaping behind me and followed my sister to the station. The solicitor hadn't picked up yet, so I left him a message. After the last few days, he was probably tired of my panicked calls.

I left a message that was loud and may have mentioned that we'd been consistently harassed by local authorities.

"Mercy, stop," Lizzie said. I sat down with her in the interview room. The detective came in holding some papers that were inside plastic sleeves.

"We'll be quick about this," he said. "But there is something I will need you to clear up."

"Whatever I can do to help," Lizzie said.

"Though she will be answering no comment until I hear from our solicitor," I added.

"That is her right, and maybe it's good you're both here. I'm not a big fan of games and feel you've been trying to play one with me since you arrived. You're lucky I haven't arrested you both for interfering with a police investigation." His voice was rough, bordering on angry.

I huffed. "Neither of us is playing games," I said. "Maybe you should begin by telling us what you're talking about."

He put two pieces of paper in plastic sleeves on the table.

"Perhaps, Lizzie, you could explain why this threatening letter, the one your sister says came through the letterbox in the wee hours of the morning, was typed on paper used in your shop?"

My sister gasped and then went very white.

THIRTEEN

Lizzie and I sat in the interview room. My sister opened her mouth and shut it again and then turned to me.

"Someone left this for us. And you didn't tell me?" She was furious with me.

"I. Uh."

"If this is you trying to protect me, stop it. Do you hear me?" Her voice became shrill. "I told you it felt like someone was watching me when I came home. You should have said something about the letter."

"Wait. Someone was watching you?" Kieran interjected.

"Yes," she said. "And I've never seen that paper before."

"It's used in your shop," he said. Then he pushed the paper in the other sleeve forward. It was a letter from my grandfather to one of his suppliers. I held it up to the light and found the same watermark.

Lizzie wrapped a curl around her finger. She did that when she was thinking about something. Then she shook her head.

"I mean, maybe it's the same kind of paper, but why would I write myself a threatening note?" she asked.

He leaned back in his chair, watching us carefully. "Perhaps because you've had second thoughts about Shamrock Cove, and you miss your home." He left that hanging. Then glanced from her to me and back again.

"You've got to be kidding," I said angrily. "What are we, twelve? If my sister wanted to go home—and I'm seriously thinking about it right now because of your constant harassment —she would say, 'Let's go home.' Where do you get off accusing us of playing games?

"And why would I even give you the letter if I thought it might implicate my sister? I'm beginning to wonder about your skills as an officer of the law." Okay, that was a bit uncalled for, but I was seething.

He sat forward. "Perhaps, you'd like to try and see it from my point of view," he said. "Since you arrived, the judge was murdered. Someone tried to break into his house. And you claimed that someone sent this, yet it's from the paper used in your shop. If you're trying to play out one of your little mysteries..."

Man, I hated when men minimalized women's work by saying "little this or that." *Ugh.* Also, he just told us the judge had been murdered. I'd known that was the case, but it was good to get confirmation.

"Hold it right there," I said. "How dare you! I mean, really? You're right. You don't know us. My sister and I have done nothing but try to help you with your investigation.

"We can't explain the paper because we had no idea it was even in the shop. We didn't kill the judge. Again, I ask, where is the motive? We'd barely met the man, and I was the one who tried to save his life.

"We didn't know about his seafood allergy or that he had a heart condition. You're barking up the wrong tree, Detective. If you harass me or my sister again, I will report you to every authority possible.

"Wait. How did you get that invoice to the supplier? Did

you go into the shop without a search warrant? I really will have your job."

I couldn't believe I said that. It was the sort of thing people of privilege said when they'd done something wrong and didn't like being called on it. But that wasn't the case here. Maybe I was tired, but it bugged me that he thought we would try to do something like this for attention. I thought we'd made some inroads.

If I was honest, I liked him. I thought we were becoming friends.

To his credit, the detective stayed calm. "Are you finished?"

"For now," I grumbled.

"The piece of paper was from another incident involving your grandfather."

"What kind of incident?"

"A theft at his store," he said.

"I'd like to see the file. Is this something we need to look out for? Or someone?"

"It's an ongoing case..."

"You've got to be..." I growled. I couldn't help it.

Lizzie put a hand on my arm again.

"Kieran – is it okay if I call you that?" Lizzie asked.

"Aye," he said.

"My sister doesn't write *little* anything. She's sold millions of books all over the world. That number might be inching toward billions. In the small moments she has free, she's researching, taking classes, or working with law enforcement so her characters are as authentic as possible. She's very good at what she does and is a much better detective than most professionals. We came here to get away from drama. To get away from painful memories. And you, sir, are making that difficult with your constant judgments and accusations toward my family."

"Lizzie—" he tried to interrupt.

My sister held up her hand. "Do your job. You said the judge was murdered. Find his killer but leave us out of it. We've been here less than a week. I can't explain the paper, though I will search for it at home and in the bookstore tomorrow."

"And what about Brenna?" I jumped in. "We brought that evidence to you. She was going to dump it and head for the hills. Think. Man. Think."

"And in the future, if you need to speak with us, you can go through our lawyer," my sister picked up once more. "You are no longer welcome in our home. The very idea that you could accuse me of such a thing... You need to be better at your job. Officers like you should have instincts about people. And it's obvious you lack any talent in that regard. And I mean it. Even look at me or my sister wrong, and I will set not just one but several lawyers on you. I'm tired of this." She stood and motioned for me to go.

I'd never seen her like this. I sat open-mouthed for a moment until I got up too.

I followed her out, and we didn't say a word until we were inside number three. Then she sat down on the steps just inside the door and kind of folded in on herself.

"Are you okay?"

Her shoulders bounced up and down. And I thought she was crying. When she lifted her head, I saw she was smiling.

"Did you see his face? I don't think he'll be messing with us again." She laughed so hard she could barely get the words out. "That felt so good. It's like all the anger that's been boiling in me for months came out at once.

"Oh, when he said, *little* stories. I nearly punched him in the face. The gall of the man."

I sat down and then wrapped my arms around her. "I'm glad you're laughing. And I know you don't want me to coddle you, but I swear I'll book us the next flight out if you want to go home."

She snorted. "No. I won't let that man push us out of this place. He will not win. Do you understand me? That we would be so duplicitous. We welcomed him into our home. Well, he's about to find out he can't mess with the McCarthys."

"This is not the reaction I expected," I said.

"He flipped a switch in me when he said that about your books, and implied we were trying to play out some real-life mystery. I take back what I said."

I frowned. "What do you mean?"

"About investigating the judge's death. That man is not going to be able to figure it out on his own."

"Hey, I'm not his biggest fan but he does have a lot of experience. He's worked with several law enforcement agencies. I looked him up."

She cocked an eyebrow. "Did you ever wonder why there had been so many? Maybe he isn't very good at what he does, and he keeps getting fired."

She had a point.

"I'm not a detective," I said. "And neither are you."

"That's true, but you write about a smart one. So, we follow the clues like she does. We will have to if we want to clear our names."

"I don't think it's as bad as that," I said.

She scoffed. "Right. Did you see our neighbors' faces? It's embarrassing. Let's talk to Lolly tomorrow and get her on our side. She seems to have her head on her shoulders."

"True. Are you sure about this?" I still had my suspicions about Lolly but decided not to voice them for now.

"The investigating? Yes. But we have to be careful, Mercy. We can't let people know what we're doing. You heard what he said. Someone murdered the judge. And they were very clever about it. We need to be careful."

"Agreed," I said. "Where do you want to start?"

"Let's start in the shop tomorrow morning. We need to find where that paper came from. I've been through every nook and cranny, and I don't remember seeing it there. But we can check again. I mean, we supposedly have another secret door here in the house we haven't found. Maybe it's stored in there."

"Wait. I just remembered something." I left her on the stairs and went to find the letter our grandfather had written us. I'd left it in my desk drawer. It was just as I suspected.

I brought the letter to the stairs.

"It's the same paper," she said.

I nodded.

"I don't get it. Why would someone go to the trouble of using his paper?"

"Because they are doing their best to point the finger at us. Think about it. They had to know we'd take that letter to the police. Maybe they knew about the theft case and that the police would make the connection."

She shook her head. "That's a huge reach. Would you write that in one of your books?"

"Nope. You're right. But I can't help but feel we're all being manipulated by someone's agenda. Whatever is going on has been planned for a long time. And we are pawns."

"I agree. I was kind of mean to the detective," she said.

"If you apologize to him, I will never forgive you. He's being ridiculous. Yes, some of this points to us. The only thing he got right was me trying to break into the judge's house. And I didn't actually do that, and those jeans went in the garbage bin days ago."

She laughed.

"Are you sure you don't want to go back to Texas?" I asked. "We can pack and be out of here by morning."

She scrunched up her face. "No. I noticed something at the pub tonight."

"What do you mean?"

"We had fun, Mercy. We laughed so hard at Scott that we couldn't catch our breath. When was the last time that happened? This is our home now. These are our people. No one is going to take that away from us.

"We'll figure this out," she said. "There's nothing we can't do together."

I smiled.

She was right.

The next morning, I went to the bookshop with her. We turned the place over, especially the office and the storeroom. We went through every box, but we didn't find the paper. She checked the printer, but it was just regular cheap printer stock.

"Maybe we should check the house," she said, and then glanced at her watch. "I have a half-hour before the store opens."

"I'll check the house. You stay here and get ready. Just keep your ears open and let me know if you hear any gossip about our suspects."

"Who are?"

"Everyone on the court."

"Even Scott and Rob?" she asked.

"I don't want to think they could do something like this, but they are both very clever. And how far would you go to protect me from someone?"

She frowned. "I'd like to think I wouldn't go so far as murder, but if they hurt you, who knows?"

"Exactly," I said. "Until we have definitive proof, we can't mark them off the list. We should also add Matt and his mom to the list. And then, I'll do a deep dive into the judge's past cases again."

"If he died from the allergy, it would have to be someone

who knows him," Lizzie said. "But that doesn't mean someone from his past wasn't aware of it."

"True," I said. "Whatever you do, don't push anyone too hard for information. The killer is clever and vindictive. We can't let on that we are suspicious."

"Got it."

Someone banged on the door, and we jumped. Then we peeked through the glass to find the detective.

"What is he doing here?" she asked.

When I went to the door, he held a piece of paper against the glass. *Warrant* was in big letters at the top.

I unlocked the door. "What is wrong with you?"

"Ms. McCarthy, you and your sister need to vacate the premises. I have a search warrant for your store, and I'm working on one for your home."

"You'll be hearing from our solicitor," I said. "But search away. We couldn't find the paper stock. Maybe you can."

His head jerked back with surprise.

"That's right, Detective," Lizzie said. "We've spent the last hour and half trying to find the paper. But you go right ahead. I did warn you, though, if you tried anything else, I'd be coming after you."

Lizzie handed him the key.

"You better not damage a single book or leave anything out of place," I said. "Lock up when you're done. We'll start searching the house. And my sister is correct, our lawyers will be contacting your superiors."

The color drained from the detective's face as we turned and walked away.

Good. He deserved to be taken down a peg or four.

On the way back to the house, I made a few phone calls. The solicitor who had handled my grandfather's estate was appalled by what had happened. He put his best team on it.

Meanwhile, Lizzie and I searched the house. The attic was

creepy, but we didn't find anything except a bunch of boxes and older furniture. Some of the boxes had photos, which we would go through later.

We went through all the drawers in my study and the library. We even checked through several of the books in his personal library. While we did find some of the letters our grandfather told us about from our father to our mother, we didn't see the paper stock. Nor did we find a treasure or a hidden door. Maybe we'd read his letter wrong. Or the treasure was something more esoteric. Strange, though, we didn't find the paper stock.

"I think the killer took the stock to frame us somehow," I said to Lizzie.

We sat down in the chairs in my grandfather's library.

"It's just such a weird and specific thing," she said. "Is it just me, or does none of this make sense? And why is the killer trying to use us? If they'd been planning this for so long, we weren't even in the picture until a few months ago."

"That's a great point. Maybe it isn't specific to us. They could have planned to use whoever might win the home lottery and moved in here."

Her eyes went wide. "If that's the case, it actually makes me feel better."

I frowned. "I don't understand."

"Think about it. We could be anyone. So, the attacks against us aren't personal. We're just a tool."

My phone rang, and I answered.

"He'll not be bothering you again, lass," the solicitor said before I could answer. "His superiors have been informed of the harassment. And the search has been called off. They won't be touching your house."

I smiled. "Thank you." I let out a big breath.

"I'm sorry for all the bother," he said. "Your grandfather loved Shamrock Cove. I assure you this isn't how they normally run the place. He loved it because it was so peaceful there. And they are usually much kinder to strangers."

"I appreciate you taking care of this," I said. "And I guess we'll have to take your word for it when it comes to being accepting."

After I hung up, I told Lizzie what he said.

"Thank goodness. I know you need to work on your book, but can you return to the store with me? Just in case I need to do a quick clean-up?"

"Sure."

When we headed outside, we found Sheila, Kieran's second-in-command, standing by the gate.

"I have your key," she said quietly.

Lizzie took it from her. "Thank you."

Sheila turned to walk away, but then stopped. "The detective is a good man," she said. "There was no reason to call his bosses. He was just doing his job."

"Sheila, I appreciate that you might want to stick up for him," I said. "But he has been harassing us. If he were doing his job, he'd look at suspects who knew the judge. Read the file. I think you'll find the suspicious nature of the man's death could have little to do with us, because we just met him."

"Except, we never had any trouble until you came to town," she said. She wasn't accusatory, more pointing out a fact.

"That may be," Lizzie said. "But we think the killer is trying to fit us up, as you Irish folks like to say. They are casting aspersions at us. Meanwhile, they are getting away with murder.

"This has nothing to do with us. Thank you, for the key. We'll be going."

When we entered the bookstore, Lizzie was happy to find that it was exactly how we left it.

"Do you want me to stay?"

She shook her head. "No, go work. I'll be fine."

"I'm too restless," I said. "Do you have any shelves that need stocking?"

She laughed. "Always."

She gave me a list. I headed upstairs with a box.

I wasn't up there long when the women who'd come in with Lolly the other day arrived.

"Is Mrs. O'Malley not with you?" Lizzie asked.

"No, she's planning the judge's wake," one of the women said. "The police finally released the body. Nasty business. We heard he was murdered."

"Oh, that's terrible," Lizzie said as if she'd just heard it for the first time. "Wait, you said Mrs. O'Malley was planning the wake. Does the judge not have any family?"

"Not any that would care enough to give him a proper send-off," another woman said. "He was married years ago. In fact, that other woman is what broke him and Lolly up. Married Lolly's best friend out of the blue. She's dead now." She made the sign of the cross. "God rest that slag's heart."

"Beth," the other woman said.

"Well, it's true. It was fifty years ago, but I'm not sure Lolly ever really forgave him. Sure, they pretended to be friendly, and she is planning his wake. She's a decent soul. But he didn't deserve her friendship."

"What do they say when things come back to you?" one of the women asked.

"Karma?" Lizzie offered.

"Aye," the woman said. "Though, that would be Lolly's story to tell."

Well, a lover scorned was always a good motive.

Even if the murder happened decades after the fact.

It was hard to get my mind around it, but could Lolly have murdered the judge? And was her grandson covering it up?

FOURTEEN

After Lizzie closed the store for lunch, we headed over to Lolly's house. We knocked a few times and there wasn't an answer. Then we heard a loud bark.

"Is someone here, boy?" Lolly asked her dog loudly.

She gave us a big smile as she opened the door. "Hello," she said. "Come in. Come in." She ushered us into the house.

"We won't bother you if you're busy," Lizzie said. "We heard you were planning the judge's wake, and we hoped we could help in some way."

After she insisted on making us tea, and put out a small plate of sandwiches, we sat down with her in the backyard. Flowers bloomed everywhere, and the place was one of the prettiest gardens I'd ever seen.

Lizzie commented on several of the flowers and bushes, but there was one that held an interest for me. Foxglove. It was known as digitalis and was lethal if consumed. Something the judge had too much of in his system when he died. It was often found in heart medicine, but could also be a poison.

I knew about the beautiful blooms because I'd used them in a tea to kill someone years ago in one of my books.

"You didn't have to do all of this," Lizzie said. "We really did come by just to see if we could help."

"Oh, you are kind," she said. "But I think I have everything well in hand for the wake. I hope you'll come. It's tomorrow night at the Crown. You didn't know him well, but you are a part of the court."

"We will be there," I said a little too eagerly.

Lizzie gave me the eye.

"But please, let us help you," I said. "And we'd like to send flowers. The judge had a lovely garden. Do you know if he had a favorite?"

"Flowers aren't necessary," she said. "But he was always partial to heritage roses. You haven't seen his back garden, but soon it will be a blossoming wonderland. The scents from some of his roses are legendary. I hope whoever moves in will appreciate them."

I didn't mention I'd been back there, but I'd been too busy trying to save my neck to notice the flowers.

"I tell you what I could use help with is his garden. At least until the new tenants arrive," Lolly said.

"Oh, do you know who is moving in?" I asked.

She shook her head. "No idea. In fact, I've been wondering if I should open the lottery. Some of the other court members have already asked if I knew if the judge willed the home to anyone, but I don't. The will is to be read tomorrow morning."

I would have paid money to be there but wasn't entirely certain how to get that invite without looking very suspicious.

"One of the things we've learned is that he was a stickler for the rules," I said. "I'm sure he's done his due diligence."

"I suppose you're right," she said.

"Will you be at the reading of the will?" Lizzie asked.

"I will, though I don't know why I've been asked."

"But you and the judge were friends," Lizzie said.

Lolly laughed. "I suppose you could call us that."

"We were curious about him," I said. "We've heard a lot of rumors, but we were hoping you could tell us who he really was."

"Well, I've probably known him the longest. He wasn't always so..."

"Cranky," I offered.

She smiled. "No, he was always a grump, even when we were younger. It was the way he looked at the world. There was always something wrong with it in his eyes. Too much crime. Too much of everything. Too many people in the world."

"I heard a rumor earlier that you used to date," I said, slightly embarrassed to bring it up. Lolly was one of the kindest souls I'd ever met, but we had to get to the truth. And she had a long history with the judge.

She laughed hard at that. "Yes, a hundred years ago, or so it seems. Broke my heart back then, yet at the same time it was the best thing that ever happened to me."

"I'm sorry," Lizzie said. "My sister is good at nudging bad memories to the surface."

I gave her a look, but she just shrugged. She probably wasn't wrong. I did tend to push people's buttons.

"How was it the best thing?" I said, hoping to prove Lizzie wrong.

"Back then, he thought I was tainted because of my naps. He didn't want children who might have an affliction."

She must have been talking about the narcolepsy.

"Saw it as some kind of defect. He ran off with my best friend. And was he in for a surprise when she announced she didn't want kids! Even though he thought there were too many people in the world, he wanted a family. Never did have one of his own. And then my friend ran out on him because he made her feel the same way he had me. That she was broken somehow. Turned out he was the problem."

"That's awful that he was so mean to you," Lizzie said.

Lolly laughed. "Oh, love. If he hadn't gone off to Dublin and married, I might have ended up with him. That would have been terrible. After blaming the women in his life, it turned out he'd been cursed and couldn't have children of his own."

Now, I was confused. How was Matt the judge's grandson?

"No, because he left, I met and fell in love with Dougan, who was the best husband and partner a woman could have. We had our babies, and now we have grand and great-grandbabies.

"My Dougan loved me, and we had a wonderful family. I still miss him so."

"He sounds like a wonderful man," Lizzie said. "So did you finally forgive the judge?"

Lolly smiled. "We Irish can hold a grudge, but by the time he returned to retire in his mother's cottage, we were too old to remember those past hurts. And I feel like the good Lord punished him enough by not giving him the one thing he wanted most in the world; a family.

"It took a few years, but when he moved back in the eighties, we became friends again. My Dougan was very ill then. The judge helped. He kept us fed and took care of the gardens so I could look after my husband. And he was there to help me through the end, which is honestly one of the hardest things I've gone through. We celebrate death around here, but loosing Dougan... I might have lost myself if it hadn't been for the judge. He wasn't all thorns that one. As much as he could be a pain in the arse, he did good in the world as well."

Like most people, the judge sounded like there were many sides to him. But this was the first time I'd heard anything kind about him.

"Do you mind if I ask something really rude?" I knew I was pushing it, but I desperately wanted her opinion.

Her eyebrows went up.

I held up a hand. "Do you know who might have wanted to murder the judge? Your grandson keeps trying to implicate us."

She frowned. "My grandson is just doing his job. I should be angry with you for calling his bosses, but I can understand why you did."

"Technically, we just called our lawyer," Lizzie said. "He was the one who called the bosses. For some reason, Kieran has it out for us. I don't know if it's because we're new or what. Sorry, I know you two are close."

"Aye. There isn't a better boy in the world. But he is one to follow things by the book. It's what makes him good at what he does. And contrary to what you might think, he is an excellent police officer."

I did not share her views, but I wasn't his grandmother.

"Why are you so curious about what happened? As you said, the judge had nothing to do with you."

"I blame Kieran," Lizzie said. "Since he keeps bothering us about the judge, we feel it necessary to arm ourselves with information."

That was true.

"Well, I didn't kill him, if that is what you are thinking," she said. But then she smiled.

"Oh, no, we don't believe you did," I said. "That's why we're here. You know everything that happens here." I still had my suspicions, but we needed Lolly on our side.

"Aye, I do keep my ear to the ground. The judge was a busybody and was in everyone's business," she said. "And he did not like change. He was determined to keep this town precisely as it was. I tended to agree with him in that respect. But some of the neighbors took issue."

"Like Rob and his food truck and Linda's revamp of the Main Street buildings?" I asked.

She smiled. "You have been busy. Yes, but all of that has

been going on for a long time. The food truck is a good idea. But forcing pastels on four-hundred-year-old buildings is not."

"Yes, I can understand your opinion," I said.

"It's odd that his death happened the day you arrived. I imagine that's why my grandson has been following your movements so closely."

"But we didn't have anything to do with it," Lizzie said. "We didn't meet him until that night. And Mercy tried to save his life."

"I don't think I ever thanked you for that, Mercy. From all accounts, you did your best."

I nodded. Though I still felt a pang of guilt. I wished I could have done more, even if he wasn't the nicest fellow. He'd died painfully.

"I've said it before, and I'll say it again. I think my grandson should look to the judge's past. He was ruthless regarding the law, and some people hated him for it. He gave the maximum penalty for most crimes. My guess is it's all a coincidence that it happened after the welcome party."

"I might agree with you," I said. "Except, it feels like someone around here is trying to put the blame on us. We think the killer is someone he knew very well."

She frowned. "Are you saying someone on the court, did it?" She laughed hard. "You're right that it is most likely someone he knows, but I can't imagine it being one of us."

"I haven't seen all the evidence, but I think the killer might have wanted it to seem like an accident... That's why they tampered with the oil. That and they wanted to create a reaction in his body. One that he wouldn't be able to fight if he had too much of his medicine in his body. The suspect definitely did their research."

Lizzie stared at me strangely. I'd revealed too much and hadn't meant to in front of Lolly. I'd been thinking out loud.

I did that a lot when I was writing.

"What's that?" Lolly asked. "Why would you think that?" She frowned.

"Oh, uh." I shrugged. "No idea. I haven't seen the lab reports. But when I was trying to save the judge, something was going on with his heart in those last minutes. The anaphylactic shock might have brought it on."

"He may have eaten something right before he left," Lizzie offered.

"I'm just confused about everything that happened that night," I said. I tried to cover my butt because I wasn't supposed to have seen those reports. I didn't want Lolly to share what I knew with Kieran.

Lizzie rolled her eyes at me. I did the classic talking-too-much-to-strangers-about-a-case thing that drove me nuts when other writers did it.

"I don't feel safe," Lizzie interrupted. "I thought this was the last place we'd have to worry about crime but..."

"Ach no, I promise you are perfectly safe," she said. And then she fell asleep. Right there in the middle of the conversation.

"Lolly?" I reached out to touch her, but Bernard, who had been by her chair, sat up and growled.

"What do we do?" Lizzie stood.

"Let's leave her for now," I said.

We tried to pass near her chair to go back through the house, but Bernard growled again.

"Let's go out through the side gate."

"What are you doing?" an angry voice asked as we stepped through the gate that went from the backyard to the front.

"Leaving your grandmother in peace," I said. "She fell asleep while we were chatting."

"Why are you here?" the detective asked. His hands were on his hips.

"For the record, we were here to see if we could help with

the judge's wake," Lizzie said. "We were having tea, and she fell asleep."

"Then why not come out the front door?"

"Bernard wouldn't allow it," Lizzie said sharply. "Now, let us go. You shouldn't be anywhere near us without our lawyers."

He took a step back. And my sister stomped past. I'd never seen her like this, and I liked it. She was usually the calmer of the two of us.

As I walked past, he opened his mouth and then closed it.

"I'm very disappointed in you. I thought you were one of the good ones," I said. I had no idea where those words came from, but I meant them. "Perhaps you should try living up to your grandmother's expectations."

The next day was hectic. I'd sent the first half of my book in the night before, and by the time I woke up, Carrie had notes. She always had notes, even if she loved the novel.

Then, I went to work on the second half. The words fell out of my head. So much so, that I was surprised when my sister came home that evening and knocked on the study door.

"Is that what you're wearing to the wake?"

I frowned and then glanced down at my clothes. I was still in my oversized T-shirt and yoga pants that I put on when I woke up.

"What time is it?"

"Five," she said. "The wake begins in an hour."

I saved my document and then shoved myself away from my desk.

"Did you eat today?" She followed me to my room.

"I had an apple this morning and, I think, some cheese. And coffee. I had a lot of coffee."

"I'll make you a sandwich," she said. "Hurry up, though. I've never been to a wake. I don't want to miss it."

I showered quickly. Even though my hair was wet, I pinned it on top of my head in a bun. I wasn't sure what one wore to a wake, and my clothing options were limited until the few boxes we shipped arrived.

I settled for matching black slacks and a blouse and then threw on a blazer.

I found Lizzie in the kitchen.

"Better," she said. "Here. Eat this."

"Won't they have food at the pub?"

She nodded. "It's a wake, Mercy. I don't think anyone is expected to feed the people who go. I mean, I looked it up in one of the Catholic books in the store. It's like the viewings we have at home. Where people come to pay respects to the family, but the coffin will be there. No one wants to eat or drink with a coffin in the room. I think it's weird they didn't do it at the church or a funeral home."

"I've been to one at home," I said. "For a writer friend. The coffin was at the pub, and there was a lot of food and booze." It truly had been a celebration of the man's life.

"Just eat the sandwich."

I did as she asked.

Fifteen minutes later, we walked to the pub. The wind off the sea brought the salty air to us. It was refreshing, if a bit chilly.

"I'm still surprised they didn't do it at the church," she said as we passed the bookstore. A beautiful cathedral was at the top of Main Street, just a few blocks up from the shop.

"I'm excited to get an answer to a question that's been driving me crazy," I said the words without thinking.

She stopped. "You can't question people tonight. It isn't proper and is too big of a risk with an audience around. What if the killer overhears you?"

"I thought about that. But we never found out how Matt is

the judge's grandson. We can ask casual questions and still get the answers we need."

She cocked her head. "What do you mean?"

"Lolly told us the judge was cursed and couldn't have children. So, how is Matt's mom his daughter?"

"Oh. Ohhh. Yes, okay. You can ask that question. We need an answer. But don't go poking the bears."

I snorted. "As if."

"Oh, you if. You if all the time," she said.

We laughed.

When we arrived, Matt motioned us toward the back of the pub. There were a few people in the front of the bar, but I had a feeling they were tourists. None of them looked like the crowd who stopped talking and stared at us whenever we came here.

"He was so mean," I whispered. "Do you think anyone will show up?"

When we turned the corner, I had my answer. Most Shamrock Cove residents had to be in the room at the back of the pub. It was packed.

Thankfully, the space was huge, with cathedral ceilings. At the far end of the room was a casket, but it was barely visible through the crowd. No matter how the residents felt about the judge, they came out to pay their respects. There was a coffee and tea service near where we had entered. We veered off to grab a cup.

Even though I've spent a fair amount of time living in the city, I'd never grown used to crowds. Lizzie and I stayed on the periphery of the room for that reason.

"Can't believe the old coot is gone," one man said. I didn't recognize him. "Best poker player I ever met, though."

The people around him raised their glasses and said, "Aye."

There was a clinking of glasses. People started taking seats that had been lined up in neat rows in the center of the room. Since there were several elderly residents in attendance, Lizzie and I remained standing with some others.

A man in priest's robes stood by the casket. "Friends, thank you for seeing off the judge. He did not want a formal affair, so we will keep things simple. If you want to come forward and say a few words, you are welcome."

A young woman moved to the front of the room. "Hello," she said. "My name is Susie Tennison. The judge helped me get my son back from my awful ex, even though it wasn't his case. I know he could be cantankerous, but he believed in the law. In my eyes, he was a good man, and I will be forever thankful." She put a hand on the casket and then bowed her head.

An elderly gentleman with a cane, with the help of a younger man, made it to the front. "When he was a young solicitor," the older man said, "the judge handled my case against someone trying to steal my business from under me. He had no reason to help me, but he did. He believed in what was right and fair. Say what you want about him, but he was a good man."

More than ten people spoke out for the judge, and there wasn't a cross word among them. Most of them expressed how grateful they were for his sense of justice and how he had helped them. We saw a different side of the man through their eyes.

Though, every word they spoke was another side of the man than what we'd heard from others in town. I thought they were done with the speakers when the detective made his way to the front of the room.

"Many of you know I was doomed to be a criminal," he said. Everyone laughed.

What had he meant by that? He seemed so straight and narrow. *Narrow-minded, maybe.*

"If it weren't for the judge, I might have taken a very different path. He wasn't the easiest man to get along with, but he set me straight. I owe my career to him and my very good life to his wise words." Then he sniffed and nodded.

He raised his glass. "Death is nothing at all. I have only slipped away to the next room. I am I, and you are you. Whatever we were to each other, *that* we still are. Sláinte."

Everyone said sláinte, and then drank from their glasses.

It was odd to see the detective emotional. And I wondered what he'd meant about being a criminal. Everyone had acted like it was a joke.

Lolly read a verse from the Bible. Then, the priest said a few words and a prayer.

When it was over, no one was in a hurry to leave.

"Not a bad send-off," Rob said from beside me. I hadn't seen any others from the court, except for Lolly.

"I've never been to a wake," Lizzie said.

He smiled. "Some are a bit livelier than this with more gargle and a lot of dancing."

I assumed gargle meant more booze.

"That's how we want to go out," Scott said as he joined us. "A big party. But this fits the judge. He wasn't much of a partier."

The two men laughed like it was some inside joke.

"I was surprised there were so many people here," I said.

"We liked to give him a hard time, but he helped many people," Scott said. "Did you figure out who killed him yet?"

Lizzie gasped. I nearly spilled my coffee.

"What?" I asked.

"The rumor is he was murdered," Rob said, "though we don't believe it. And you two were asking us a lot of questions when we invited you for tea the other night. We decided you're pretending to be Nancy Drew. What we can't figure out is why the detective keeps hauling you off to jail. Did you kill him? We heard women from Texas were dangerous." Rob laughed like that was the funniest thing in the world. Scott joined him.

I sighed. "No, we didn't have a reason to kill him. Kieran doesn't seem to like us very much," I said. "And we aren't investigating anything. I have no idea what you're talking about."

I guess we hadn't been as discreet as we hoped. Probably because we'd never had to solve a murder before. "And in my defense, I'm a naturally curious person. I always ask a lot of questions."

"She's right. If it feels like she's asking a lot of questions, it's because she has some book in her head, and she's cast us all as characters," Lizzie said. She always had been quick on her feet. "She does it all the time."

"Oh, that is good news," Scott said. "I've always wanted to be a character in a book or telly series. You mentioned you had trouble getting back in the groove of writing. Has Shamrock Cove inspired you?"

I nodded. "It's going well now. I guess I'm curious because one of the times we were called into the station, we learned the judge was indeed murdered." I said it on purpose to gauge their reactions.

The shock was evident.

"Murder?" Scott whispered. The two men looked at one another and shook their heads. "So, it's true?"

"That isn't possible," Rob said. "We would have heard about it."

"The detective hasn't said anything in public," Lizzie said, "but my sister is telling the truth. I don't think he meant to let it slip. But we both heard it."

"Hard to believe something like that could happen on the court," Scott said. "I don't think we've had any crime..."

"Until we moved in," I said.

"For the record, we know it wasn't you. But it could have been someone in this room," Scott said.

"That's scary," Rob said as he glanced around.

The shock and fear on their faces made me believe they had

nothing to do with the judge's demise. Even though the cooking oil may have helped lead to the judge's death. Neither Scott nor Rob could have been that good of an actor. They were truly surprised and alarmed.

Well, that's two people who have moved to the bottom of the list. I didn't have definitive proof yet that they didn't do it, but the shock on their faces spoke loads.

"We were surprised everyone said such nice things about him," Lizzie said.

"People always say nice things about the dead," Linda said as she came up. Her husband Dave was by her side.

Rob frowned and Scott's eyebrow went up.

"What? It's true. We all pretend he was a pillar of the community, but we also know the truth. He may have been a good man to many, but he had a cruel streak."

"Linda," Dave said. "I don't think now is the time."

"I'm not one to speak ill of the dead. I just feel we should be honest about who he was. But, I suppose, he was like most of us. None of us is perfect. Least of all me, or any of us really."

She sniffed and walked away.

"Sorry," Dave said. "She doesn't do well with any sort of death. Always tends to say the wrong thing. I think she might be the most upset of any of us."

From the look of sadness on her face, it looked like she was truly upset.

Could Linda be the killer?

She seemed sweet, and I couldn't see her as a killer. Her husband, on the other hand...

"Were you friends with the judge?" I asked Dave.

"I would not have called us friendly," he said. "But I got along with him better than my wife did. I should go after her."

We watched him follow Linda.

"I know what you're thinking, but..." Rob said.

"What?" I asked.

"She may have hated the old goat, but she doesn't have the moxie to kill someone."

"No more than we did," Scott added. Then he turned to face me. "Are we suspects?"

Lizzie choked on her tea, and I patted her back.

"You'll have to ask the detective," I said. "Nothing to do with us. We should pay our respects, Lizzie."

"See y'all, later." She waved at the two men.

"So much for keeping our investigation a secret," she whispered as we made our way to the casket.

"Right? And we're going to have to work on your poker face."

"I've never had much of one, it's why you can't ask me to lie," she whispered.

I smiled at her.

"Who do you think gets the judge's house, now?" she asked as we stood by the casket whispering. "The rules on the court are so confusing. Since, he didn't have any family, what happens to it?"

"He left it to Gran," said the detective behind us.

We didn't scream, which probably wouldn't have gone over well at the wake, but we may have jumped a little.

"We weren't asking you," Lizzie said. "But I thought it had to go to family."

I turned to face him. "What she said."

He smirked. "There is a loophole where the house can be left to someone who lives on the court. If it were left to no one, there would be a lottery. The residents of Shamrock Cove would be allowed to put their names in, and then a few would be drawn. Members of the court would then vote on them."

"Interesting," I said. "But what is Lolly going to do with another house? Her home is so lovely."

"She's gifting it to me," he said.

"You'd take a home that should have gone to Matt or his mom?" I may have made a face.

"I haven't taken anything. I only said he bequeathed it to my grandmother, who, as a court member, can bequeath it to a member of her family. I just found out an hour or so ago. I'm not sure what we'll do about it."

Oh. God. Now the detective might be our new neighbor.

"There is something I need to say to you both." His voice held quiet strength.

"What now?" Lizzie's chin lifted in defiance. It was everything I could do not to smile.

"I'd like to apologize, even though I was doing my job. I understand that I could have been more considerate."

"Did Lolly or your bosses insist you apologize?" I asked.

"Neither. I tend to be focused on evidence, and I don't always consider how following it might affect those involved."

"So, you don't think we killed anyone?"

He sighed. "I never did. I was only following up on what I'd found. And you must admit it was strange that someone would use the very paper your grandfather bought for his shop."

I nodded. "We can all have tunnel vision," I said. And feeling a bit sorry for him, I held out my hand. "Friends?"

He stared at my hand for a few seconds and then shook it. "Aye. Better to have you on my side than against."

My sister and I laughed.

"You're learning," I said.

"I should make the rounds." He nodded and then headed through the crowd.

"Well, that was unexpected," I said.

"Agreed. But are you thinking what I am?" Lizzie asked.

I nodded.

Why hadn't the home gone to Matt or his mother?

FIFTEEN

After we spoke with the detective, I went in search of Matt. I was curious what he thought about the judge's house going to Lolly and her grandson. He was behind the bar, stacking glasses. He'd disappeared shortly after people spoke up for the judge.

"Hey," I said. "Are you doing okay? I noticed you snuck out soon after the detective spoke."

He put the cloth he'd been using to shine the glasses down on the bar. "Hard for me to hear nice things about the old man." Then he shrugged. "He gave my ma and me hell. For no reason, really. Well, except that she was my gran's."

"I'm confused."

"The judge wasn't really my grandfather by blood. He took in my ma when her mother, his ex-wife, died. She was about fourteen, and her real father had taken off. Social services called the judge, and he took her in."

So they aren't genetically related. That part of the puzzle finally fell into place.

"Ma always says it was the worst thing that ever happened to her. That's when he moved from Dublin to here. From what she says, there was always a mutual dislike between them. He resented her from the beginning."

I'd been wondering how Matt and his mom came to be since Lolly had said the judge couldn't have children. Now, I had the answer.

"So, you aren't upset about the house going to Lolly?"

He laughed. "Uh. No. No offense, but it takes a certain type to live on the court. Ma and I are more free spirits. We don't like rules and people telling us what to do."

"I think my feelings might be hurt." It was a joke, but he'd made a good point.

"Present company excluded," he said. "You're creative, so I know you get it. Besides, Ma loves living above the pub. She likes being able to roll out of bed and go to work.

"And I'm quite fond of my little cottage by the sea. Waking up to that view every morning is nothing I'll give up any time soon."

"Oh, where is that? The other day, I was at the beach and didn't see any seaside homes."

"About a fifteen-minute walk up the coast. A cluster of small cottages on the high cliff. I bought it when I moved back home. So, no. We didn't care about the cottage."

"What about the pub?" I asked, wondering if there was something else.

"Yes, his death did help us get complete control of the pub. I'd paid back Ma's loan he gave her. He only needed to file the papers, but he was being an arse about taking his time. I think it's because he felt like it helped him have some control over my ma and me. Anyways, Lolly told us that she's already told the solicitor to file the papers for us. So, the pub is ours free and clear again."

"So, he didn't leave you all anything?"

"Contents of his house if we want it. I haven't been there in years. I don't know that I remember wanting anything out of there. But Lolly says we have a month to take what we want.

"Mum was surprised that he left us anything. And I think Lolly plans to give the house to the detective. He's the right sort for the court. He likes his rules."

"That's the truth," I said.

We laughed.

I excused myself to go to the ladies, but something blocked the door leading into the hallway where the restrooms were. I pushed as hard as possible, but the door wouldn't budge.

"What's wrong?" Kieran asked.

I jumped a bit. The man was far too sneaky.

"I can't get the door open. Something is blocking it on the other side."

"Let me try."

He pushed hard, his muscles straining through his shirt. The door budged just a crack, but it was enough for me to slide through.

"Here, let me go through." I stepped through the crack and stopped. I swallowed hard.

"What is it?"

I sighed. "It's Dave. And I think he's dead." Bile rose in my throat and my stomach churned.

"There's another entrance off the kitchen, I'm coming around. Do not touch anything," he ordered.

He needn't have worried. I was paralyzed by the fact that there was a dead guy in the hallway. Dave was face down, but his body was at an odd angle like he'd just fallen. There was no blood, for which I was thankful. His right arm reached out as if he'd tried to stop himself from slamming into the ground.

I took my phone out of my pocket and took some photos. I have no idea why. Just that if I were blamed for his death, I'd have something to look at to prove my innocence.

As I put my phone into my pocket, Kieran came around the corner from the kitchen.

He checked for vitals and then shook his head. Then he was on his phone telling Sheila to bring evidence kits and the coroner.

"Can you tell how he died?" I asked.

"No."

He glanced up at me. "Why don't you head home," he said. "I'll talk to Mattie and his mom about closing the pub. There is nothing we can do for Dave now. If I need something from you, I'll stop by later."

"I didn't kill him," I said. My voice was a whisper.

He stared at me for a full thirty seconds. I know because I counted them.

"I know you didn't."

"Any chance it is natural causes?" I asked.

He shrugged. "Too early to say."

I nodded, but I had a horrible feeling that *someone* had killed our neighbor.

Later that evening, Lizzie made us hot cocoa, and we sat across from each other, eating the chocolate chip cookies she baked when we returned home. My sister bakes when stressed, another reason I'd gained some weight while living with her.

We'd discussed Dave's death ad nauseam and had moved on to the detective moving into the court.

"Technically, I guess it's a way to keep the court tied to the families who originated here," I said.

"Having a policeman so close by isn't such a bad thing," she added. "But how are we supposed to solve the murders with him watching our every move?"

I grinned.

"What?" She stuffed half a cookie in her mouth.

"It's just funny you've done such an about-face concerning the investigation. We don't know that Dave was murdered. But if he was, it isn't safe for us. We need to be careful."

She made a face. "A woman can change her mind, and that was before I realized he was determined to pin it on us. I thought that night with Brenna that he'd finally come around. You found Dave's body. He might try to fit you up for that one as well."

"I don't think so. When he told me to go home, he was genuinely concerned by whatever he saw on my face."

"Shock, most likely."

I nodded.

"Do you think it was just a coincidence, and maybe it was natural causes?"

I shrugged. "My head wants to say yes. But my gut says no. The two deaths are related."

"Maybe because it would make a better mystery for a book?"

"Could be. But for him to die at the wake, that's just too much."

"Since you didn't see any outward trauma, do you think he was poisoned like the judge?" Lizzie asked.

"Possibly. Maybe he discovered something about the killer."

She pursed her lips. "He seemed like a nice guy, not that we spent much time with him. And he appeared to love his wife."

"Poor Linda. She was so in love with her husband."

Lizzie nodded. "I'm not the only one a little scared that people are dropping like flies around here, am I?"

"No." I took a deep breath.

"So, what's next? Because I know you won't stop investigating."

"Well... it will probably be a while before we find out what really happened to Dave. Lolly most likely will find out before anyone else. So, we'll chat with her next.

"But I think I should continue to investigate who might have killed the judge and why."

"It's even more dangerous now. And you said the detective doesn't think you did it."

"Right, but now he has two deaths on his hands. At least they aren't moving the judge's stuff out until the end of the month. That gives us a couple of weeks. I still need to get into his house. I'm sure the detective searched it, but..."

"What?" she asked.

"It's a stretch, but what if all of this was a ploy to get control of that house."

Her eyes went wide. "You can't suggest the detective killed the old judge to get his house. I mean, I'm not the guy's biggest fan, but he seems straightforward. And then why kill Dave unless he discovered something?"

"We have to think about all possibilities. Who stood to gain the most from the judge's death? From what we learned from Matt and Kieran, most of the money went to charities. The contents of the house to Matt and his mom. But the house went to Lolly, and then the detective."

Lizzie chewed on her lip.

"I'm just saying it's a possibility. We have to consider everyone and think about it. If he weren't a law officer, we'd put him at the top of the list."

"True," she said. "I just don't see it. Even though he's annoying to us, look at how people treat him. He's well respected and seems to be fair."

"Seems to be... that's the phrase we need to be wary of, and why does he keep pointing the finger at us?" I didn't believe he did it, but I had to play devil's advocate. The detective was too much of a rule-book follower. Maybe he hadn't been in his past, but it was easy to see now.

Even if I didn't want to admit it, he was a good guy.

Lizzie shrugged. "Technically, he's not pointing. Just... no you're right."

I picked up my third cookie. I needed to stop, but these were mom's recipes and so intrinsically linked to my childhood that it made it feel like she was here with us.

"But let's focus on the party the night we arrived. Did you overhear any conversations with the judge?"

She closed her eyes. "He spoke with Lolly. They were talking about some literary festival coming up. But it was benign. Oh, I do remember him calling Scott a cheater. Something like, 'If it isn't the rose stealer...'" Her eyes opened. "What do you think that was about?"

The rose stealer. I shrugged. "No idea, but I'll add the question to our list. We know about Rob's food truck. Then, Linda's revamp of Main Street."

"And do we believe Lolly didn't know she was getting the house? I'm certain the judge must have said something to her."

"You're right about Lolly, I'll keep her on the list. He wasn't the greatest guy, and she had a reason to knock him off. More than one. Maybe she wanted her grandson closer. Or maybe she never did forgive the judge for leaving her."

Scorned lover was a great motive, but it had been years ago. That and even my suspicious mind couldn't imagine Lolly as a killer. "From the way she talked about that situation," I said, "it seemed like he did her a favor. Do we really think it was Lolly?" My gut said no, but I still had no proof.

"I guess not," Lizzie said.

"Rob and Scott were so shocked by the news the judge had been murdered. They'd have to be world-class actors to fake that reaction."

She scrunched up her face. "Yep. So, at least that's a few off the list. But who would want to kill Dave? He seemed to be pretty easygoing."

"You're right. How does he fit in with the judge?"

"This is terrible to say, but maybe it was natural causes? He wasn't in the best of shape." She rolled her eyes. "I can't believe I said that."

"But you're right." He had a rounded belly, which seemed harsh to say, but perhaps it was a heart attack.

"Poor Dave. I can't believe he's dead."

"He was one of my top suspects," I said. "But, unless he died of natural causes, then the killer has to be someone else."

She sighed.

"What is it?" I asked.

"Tonight brought back Mom's celebration of life and how much she meant to everyone. Gosh, I miss her. If someone wasn't threatening us, she'd think all this would be so fun."

"She would," I said. Mom loved a good mystery. It's probably one of the reasons I went into the genre. "We need a game plan—a real one. We have to start crossing people off the list.

"It has to be someone who knew about Brenna's recipe. She said there was a list of dishes in the email. It had to be someone who knew her ingredients and had access to her house."

"Linda, Matt, his mom and Lolly all cook," she said. "But how would Matt and his mom know how to get into Brenna's, or what oil she'd use in a recipe? Unless they were close, and we didn't know it."

"True."

"And would Linda hurt Dave? She seemed to love him so much."

My sister had a point. "Maybe it's just a coincidence," I said. "His death was sudden."

"But your eyes say it is too much of a coincidence."

I sighed. "What could the judge and Dave have in common that someone would want them dead?"

She shrugged.

"If we can figure out that answer, we might discover our killer."

She shivered.

"This is all so confusing."

"Even though we've marked Rob and Scott off the list, we need to find out what the thing was about the roses," I said. "I'm going to leave that to you, since you're the gardener."

She frowned. "I'm not great at the detecting part of this. What if I say something wrong?"

"Just start talking about gardening. Have you met you? You're a lavender farm owner. You could talk about flowers and plants all day."

"True."

"So, just do that. Tell him you heard about his prize-winning roses. And then see where the conversation lands. Don't ask him about the judge. See if he mentions whatever the gripe between them might have been."

"That is a good idea," she said. "I also think we should throw a housewarming party. People still do that right? In lieu of gifts, we'll ask for recipes and cuttings."

"That's brilliant," I said.

"I can't take credit. I was thinking about all those Agatha Christie books you made me read."

"Made?"

She laughed. "Okay, that first book you made me read was a gateway drug. Anyway, her Inspector Poirot had a habit of putting all the suspects in one room and then drawing out the killer. We'll have to wait a bit, so that Linda doesn't think we're being disrespectful to the memory of Dave."

"That's a good idea. Maybe we could throw it in honor of him. Include the court, the detective, and Matt and his mother."

"That whole thing about the pub and the loan is confusing to me," she said. "Why would the judge hold on to that paper-work? If they didn't get along, he should have wanted rid of them. I think he secretly cared about Matt and his mom. Why would he have helped the mom in the first place?"

"So, you're saying the judge might have been a jerk, but maybe he had a soft middle?" I asked. "Yeah, that makes sense. I guess we did hear about a different side of him tonight from those who spoke at the wake."

"I wouldn't say, soft, exactly. But maybe he felt responsible in a way. I mean, did Matt's grandmother not have any other family she could have sent her daughter to? I don't know. It just seems odd. That he'd take her daughter in, given she left him."

"He's a conundrum for certain," I said. "I'm still trying to right my mind with what everyone said about him tonight. He did seem to help many families either stay together or for parents to get their children back."

"Yeah, there did seem to be a theme. So, he wasn't all bad. When should we have the party? I'm ready to get this over with one way or another."

I frowned. "We need to invite everyone on our suspect list, which includes those on the court who are still alive, and Mattie and his mom. Let's check with Lolly first. We want to make sure we aren't in conflict with anything else happening in the court or in town. You need to talk to Scott about the roses. You can tell him about the clippings and recipes. And ask if you might be able to get one of his famous rose plants."

She nodded. "How about you?"

"We'll need to give our condolences to Linda and find out what she has planned for Dave. And I have to get into the judge's house tomorrow night. Less chance of being seen under the cover of darkness."

"Oh, God. That means I'll have to be lookout again. That makes me nervous. Why would I be working in the garden at night? What if we offered to clean the judge's place before the detective moves in?"

"Too obvious, and why would they let us? I can't see Lolly letting that happen. No, I need to sneak in, and you don't have to be working in the garden. You could just be sitting on the bench out front. Or you could be looking at the solar lights. I noticed one of ours was wonky."

"Oh, that's a good idea. But what do I do if anyone heads toward the judge's house?"

"Follow them and talk very loudly. Give me time to get out the back."

"I wish you hadn't told me. Now, I won't be able to sleep." She picked up another cookie and then put it down. "I know what I said about snooping, but we are in this together. I hope we survive the process."

She made a good point. This was dangerous, but I didn't really see any options.

SIXTEEN

The following day Lizzie and I knocked on Linda's door. We were loaded down with baked goods my sister had put together and some flowers. But it was Lolly who greeted us at the door.

"Bless you," she said. "Come in."

"We don't want to intrude if Linda isn't feeling up to company," Lizzie said.

"No, come on back, we're in the kitchen."

We followed her through the house, which was decorated very much in a formal but homey style. There were quilts hung on the walls, and ornate Queen Anne styled furniture. The layout of the house seemed close to what we had, with the kitchen in the back. But the décor was more grandma chic.

Linda sat at an old wooden table with her hands around a mug of tea. She wore a housecoat that looked straight out of the 1950s. Her usually coiffed hair was mussed, and she was devoid of makeup.

When she glanced up, her eyes were red and her skin blotchy. She gave us a watery smile.

"We're so very sorry." Lizzie hugged her. My sister always knew what to say in situations like this.

I squeezed Linda's hand. "We can't imagine what you must be going through," I said.

"Thank you," Linda said. Her voice was shaky. "I can't believe he's gone."

"Have a seat," Lolly said.

"I heard you found him," Linda said. "Did he say anything to you before he passed. Did he have any last words for me?"

I shook my head. "I'm afraid he was... already gone by the time we found him. Do the police know anything yet about what happened?"

Lizzie kicked my shin under the table, and it was all I could do not to yell ouch.

"Kieran was around last night to ask questions, but no." Tears streamed down her face. I felt terrible for making her cry. "I haven't heard a word. Dave had a problem with his heart. A-fib. I just assumed his bad eating caught up with him."

"That's so sad," Lizzie said. "He was so young."

"Aye," Lolly added. "Prime of his life. But these things happen. The Lord has him a good one with Dave."

"Thank you for that, Lolly," Linda said. "I just can't believe he's gone. It doesn't feel real. I know I keep saying that," she whispered as tears waterfalled down her cheeks.

Lolly pushed the box of tissues closer to her.

"Is there anything we can do for you? Or help in any way?" Lizzie asked.

"Dave never wanted any fuss. Not even a wake," she said. "He didn't believe in such things. He couldn't wait to leave the judge's. I... I thought he'd gone home. He'd hinted he didn't feel well." She sniffed. "But I thought it was him making excuses to get out of helping with the clean-up after the wake. When Kieran told me what happened, I couldn't believe it. I still can't."

Lolly gave her shoulder a squeeze.

"Once we get the body back, he'll be cremated," Linda

continued. "He wanted his ashes thrown into the sea he loved so much. He always wanted a sailboat. He talked about that a lot. Just one of the many dreams he had..." She sniffed again.

Lolly patted her hand. "At least you had his love," she said softly. "He was a good man and he looked after you."

Linda nodded.

"I know you don't want to do anything, but Lizzie and I feel we should honor him somehow. He was kind to us," I said. "He offered to help with the books and such. We were thinking of just having a small get-together. He seemed to really love the court and appreciated that his family had lived here for so long. If we could hear stories about him from the others, we'll be able to get to know him better, which is something we'd like, if it's okay with you."

I was surprised by how plausible that sounded.

Linda blinked several times. "You want to throw him a party?"

Lizzie cleared her throat. "A party seems inappropriate. No, it's more of a get-together to talk about the good old days sort of thing. But, of course, only if that's okay with you."

She sat there for a full minute without saying anything and I couldn't read her face. Even Lolly didn't seem to understand what Linda might be thinking.

"That's sweet," Linda said. "Dave always loved our garden parties."

Lolly's eyebrows went up, but she didn't say anything.

"Then it's settled. Maybe next weekend? Unless that's too soon," Lizzie said.

"No. That's fine. Thank you."

"We'll take care of everything," I said. "All you have to do is show up."

"You are both so kind, thank you."

There was a knock on the front door.

"We should go. You've got more company," Lizzie said. "But please let us know if you need anything."

We passed Rob and Scott in the hallway. They were loaded with even more food than we'd brought.

The people on the court were wonderful about caring for one another. Except for the fact that one of them might be a killer.

They paused.

"How is she?" Rob whispered.

"In shock, I think," Lizzie said. "Just a heads-up, since there will be no wake, we thought we'd hold a get-together to honor Dave."

"There's no wake?" Scott frowned.

"Linda said he didn't believe in that sort of thing. He didn't want to do one. But she agreed to let us throw a little thing for him next weekend."

"Well, let us know what we can help with," Rob said. "Anything you need."

"Thanks," Lizzie said. "Let's catch up later."

They headed down the hall. We'd stopped in front of what looked like Dave's office. I peeked my head into the room.

"No," Lizzie whispered forcefully. "We are not snooping right now."

I sighed. "Fine. But tonight, we hit up the judge's place. No argument. We've got to find out what's going on. What if Dave was murdered like the judge?" I whispered back. "You have to admit two heart attacks so close together is highly suspicious."

She pulled me outside before I could say anything else.

"That woman just lost her husband, Mercy. This isn't the time."

"Unless she's the one who killed him?"

Lizzie rolled her eyes. "You saw how close they were. They loved one another."

"Most murders are committed by the people the victim is closest to," I said.

"But Linda? Really? Mercy, that's a reach even for you. I'm not discussing this with you right now. Go home and write." She stormed off.

I did go home, but my mind whirled with possibilities. I couldn't settle. I went into our grandfather's private library and searched for the secret door. Finding none, I started to go through his books to find more letters. I was desperate for news about our dad.

Hours later, when the alarm on my phone buzzed, I was thumbing gently through a first edition of a Thomas Hardy novel. The annoying ring told me it was time for me to explore the judge's house. I had to find answers.

Or maybe, if I got caught, I'd end up in jail.

SEVENTEEN

Under the cover of darkness, I snuck through a back window into the judge's house. My poor sister had been a shaking mess when I'd left her in the garden. She'd begged me to be careful, but I had to do this.

The back door had been locked, but I'd brought my lock-picking kit. Years ago, I'd taken lessons from a locksmith, but I was rusty. Before I tried that, I decided to check the kitchen window. It had taken a bit of maneuvering, but it slid over enough for me to crawl inside.

There was a musty scent of a place that had been closed for too long, mixed with lemony cleaner. After unlocking the back door so I'd have a quick exit, I turned on my flashlight. I'd already decided to look for a study or office. The judge's files, I felt certain, would give me some answers.

As I went along the hallway, it helped that the house plan was like ours, with large rooms off to the left and the stairs on the right. I went through the door under the stairs. His study was in the same place as mine. However, this room was much messier than the rest of the house, which had been quite tidy.

My hands shook with nerves, and bile rose in my throat. I

liked to think I was brave, but breaking and entering was new to me. If the police caught me here, they would look no further for a suspect.

There was a desk and a table against the wall where the windows were. The heavy curtains had been drawn so I felt safe using my flashlight to dig through files that were piled everywhere.

I was about to sit down when there was a thump from upstairs.

I straightened and then turned back to the hallway.

"Is someone here?" I whispered cautiously. There was no answer. I waited almost a minute before moving again but didn't hear anything else.

These were old homes, and they made noises. I chalked it up to that.

I sat on his chair and started with the files on his desk. After flipping through several, I came to the one concerning the Crown and Clover. What Matt had said was true.

According to the files, the loan was paid off, but the judge hadn't done the paperwork to transfer ownership. Still, I took a few pictures with my phone, so I didn't have to steal anything.

I was surprised the detective hadn't boxed and taken all these files to the station. The killer could have snuck in here and stolen the evidence at any time.

I shivered.

I didn't find anything else in the piles on the desk, so I went through some of the drawers.

But when I turned the chair, I accidentally knocked off the scales of justice on a cabinet behind the desk. It clattered to the wood floor, making a horrible sound.

I sat there stunned for a few seconds, and then shut off my flashlight and prayed no one heard the noise.

Nothing happened.

I continued my search.

I was surprised to find only one large accordion folder in the right drawer labeled, *The Court*. Within the folder were individual files on several of the court's residents. I picked up the one on Rob first. There were several bits of research on food trucks. Then a sternly worded letter to Rob, as to why his truck would be undesirable. It was in legalese, but the gist of it was the truck would be an eyesore in their beautiful town.

No wonder Rob had been upset.

I took a few photos, and then put the file back. I was surprised to see there was one on Scott. In that one, there were several copies of letters the judge had written to various gardening competitions saying that Scott had no claim to the rose he presented in competitions.

There had also been several letters back to the judge from those competitions. All of them stated that though they had investigated the claims, they were found to be without merit.

Since the judge had gifted the plant to Scott, and then Scott had been the one to graft the new rose with another one, the judge's rights to it were null and void. I knew nothing about gardening, but it appeared Scott had been in the right and that the judge was bitter that Scott had received the credit.

As a lawyer, I'm sure the judge would have found some kind of loophole, but it looked like he hadn't responded again. I put the file back. Scott had to know what the judge had been up to, but I wondered if he knew the full extent.

While the judge had been petty and mean, I didn't think the guys had killed him over a food truck or roses. The looks on their faces when we'd mentioned murder had said it all.

When I opened the file on Linda, I was surprised to find it had nothing to do with Main Street. It was a divorce decree.

I blinked. Linda and Dave had been so lovey-dovey and supportive of one another. But they were getting a divorce? That didn't make sense.

I was about to take pictures when I saw a file on our grandad and another on me and Lizzie. What were those about?

A gate creaked outside.

"Detective? Is something wrong?" Lizzie said loudly out in the garden.

Crud. I'd been so engrossed in the files—I hadn't heard them.

"My gran heard a noise. I need to make certain no one has broken into the house," he said.

And then the front door clicked.

I didn't have time to run into the kitchen. He'd see me pass. I grabbed the files involving my family, and then climbed underneath the desk. Trying to make myself as small as possible, I pulled the chair in as far as it would go.

I'd just have to wait him out, and then I'd run home.

Footsteps creaked down the hallway on the wood floors. Then the study door opened a bit more.

It was all I could do not to scream, my nerves were so jangled.

Hold it together, Mercy.

Please, don't come in. Please, don't come in.

"Mercy, I know you're in here."

Oh. Darn. I held my breath.

"Just come out."

How did he know it was me?

"I can smell your vanilla perfume. I know you're under the desk."

I sighed. I was in big trouble.

EIGHTEEN

Before I crawled out, I stuck my family's files in the back of my jeans, under my T-shirt and bulky sweater. I had to stop wearing perfume and lotion if I was going to go around playing detective.

I stood in front of the desk.

"Tell me why I shouldn't arrest you on the spot?" he asked. He flipped the light on, and I blinked.

"Because it will make you look even more guilty when I tell my solicitor you're the prime suspect." It was the first thing that came out of my mouth and quite possibly not the smartest thing I'd ever said.

If he were the killer, I was in considerable danger.

His jaw dropped. And then he started laughing. He laughed so hard, he bent over and supported himself by putting his hands on his thighs. "What?"

I took a deep breath. "My sister will know it was you if you kill me."

His eyebrow went up. "While that particular thought has crossed my mind more than once since you arrived in town, why would I want to kill you?"

"I'd feel better if we had this conversation with solicitors and witnesses," I said. "Feel free to arrest me again."

"First, why don't you tell me what you're doing in the judge's house."

"I'd rather be arrested."

He straightened and then leaned against the door to the study and crossed his arms. "Tell me."

"I thought I saw someone come in here, and I decided to check it out. When I first came in, there was a noise upstairs."

"And you didn't think calling the police might have been a better choice."

I mirrored his actions and crossed my arms. "Not if the head of the police is a suspect."

He snorted. "I don't believe you really think I killed the judge. Tell me the truth and I won't arrest you—yet."

"You inherited the judge's house, which makes you a prime suspect, so I don't really trust that you will do your best to find the killer. Meanwhile, my sister and I are being targeted by someone who wants to frame us for the murder. And you seem to want to blame us for that. I decided to take matters into my own hands."

He crossed his arms. "You seem very interested in motives. What would be mine?"

"You stood to gain the most. Well, Lolly did. You may have helped her knock him off."

He laughed then, so hard that he bent over from the waist again.

Jerk.

"That might be my favorite thing you've said so far."

"You got his highly sought-after house," I said. "Why are you laughing?"

"I didn't kill the judge," he said through snorts of hilarity.

"Says you."

"First of all, my gran and I had no idea she was in the will until the solicitor called her in for the reading. Your grandfather was the judge's witness, by the way. No one was more surprised that she was a beneficiary. Then she called me just before the wake and asked if I might be interested in moving into the judge's place. So, we had no motive to kill him."

"I only have that as hearsay from you," I said. "It doesn't prove she didn't know about it. And even if she didn't, there are other reasons for wanting to kill him."

He smiled even bigger. "My gran is going to love that she was a suspect. Please, tell me the other reason."

"I'm doing your job for you, Detective. Since you seem blind to finding the real killer."

That shut down his smile. "Excuse me?"

Whoops. What if he was the killer, and I'd just really made him angry?

"Tell me why you suspect my gran." He waved a hand. "Beyond inheriting the house, which I assure you she knew nothing about until the will was read."

"Unrequited love, revenge, there is more than one reason Lolly might want the judge dead. If the judge was poisoned, that is something women most often use to kill."

I pointed to the drawer where I'd found the court files. "And then there's an entire drawer of suspects in here. Each of them had a reason to want the judge dead. Yet, you left all the evidence here. What if the killer was the person I saw come in here, and they came to steal the files that might prove what they'd done—or at least *why* they'd done it."

"My staff already made copies of everything the day of the murder. That's why the files are in such disarray. We haven't had time to put everything back in the file drawers. We don't have enough storage space at the station to keep everything, so we uploaded pictures of all the evidence online."

That had to be a time-consuming process, but it made

perfect sense, given the size of the small cottage the station was in.

"Have you been through all the evidence? Because I've seen some things in these files that give me pause."

"We've just begun," he said. "As you can see, there is a fair amount to go through."

"Is everything all right?" Lizzie asked nervously from the hallway. "Some of the neighbors are out front. I... uh, don't know what to do. If you're going to arrest her, just get it over with," she said.

"Thanks," I said.

She shrugged. "Well, what else would happen? You were caught bre—"

"Checking on a neighbor's house, as I was telling the detective," I interjected. "He says Lolly also saw someone coming in here."

My sister blinked and then nodded. "Oh. Us too. I was scared, but Mercy insisted on checking around back. I didn't know she'd come inside."

It was all I could do not to laugh. For the first time in her life, my sister had lied. She hadn't done such a bad job of it either.

Kieran ran a hand through his hair. "You, go out the way you came. I'll lock up behind you. If I arrest you again, I'll probably lose my job. And not because you'd be blackmailing me."

"Blackmail?" Lizzie said. "Who said anything about blackmail?"

"Just go." He waved his flashlight at me. "Lizzie, I want you to invite me back for coffee in front of everyone. I have a feeling I'm going to need some."

It didn't sound like he planned to arrest me or kill us. I didn't need to be asked twice. I scooted out the back door and then over the gate.

Someone jumped out as I passed Brenna's house and

knocked me into the apple tree. I whacked my head hard and stumbled to the ground, twisting my ankle as I fell.

I tried to see who it was, but they were dressed all in black, and too far down the back lane before I could turn to look. I helped myself up using the tree trunk.

Someone *had* been in the house. Then they'd been waiting for me. What was that about?

I shivered and the creepiness that came with my stalker in New York slithered through my body. Then the sky opened and dumped buckets of cold rainwater on me. I could barely see a few inches in front of me.

"Really?" I shouted to the heavens as I limped to our back gate.

By the time I returned to the house, Kieran and Lizzie were at the table.

"Hey, what happened to you?" Lizzie rushed to me.

The detective jumped up to help her, but I waved them away.

"Someone jumped me by Brenna's house."

"What?" he shouted, and then he was out the back door.

I still had the files in the back of my pants, and I was drenched.

"Someone attacked you?" she asked worriedly.

"I don't know if it was an attack or more they shoved me out of the way. Maybe they thought the detective was just behind me. I need to change. I'll be back."

"Are you okay? Why are you limping? Wait, are you bleeding?" She touched my head.

I shrugged. "I need to hide these files before he gets back."

Her eyes went wide. "I thought you weren't going to take anything. Pictures only, remember."

"They are files about us and our grandfather."

The back door opened, and the detective came in drenched. Though he'd been wearing a mackintosh, so, it was only his coat. I'd noticed many people in town wore them almost all the time, probably because Shamrock Cove was known for its lush scenery and heavy rainfall.

"Did you see anyone?" Lizzie asked.

"No. Are you all, right? You're bleeding."

"I'm fine," I said.

He took his jacket off and hung it on one of the hooks by the back door.

"Get cleaned up, and let me know if you need any help," Lizzie said. "Detective, why don't you have a seat? I have some cookies, and would you like coffee or tea? Or perhaps something stronger. Our grandfather kept a fair amount of whiskey around the place..."

Her voice drifted off as I made my way to my room.

By the time I reached the bathroom, my ankle ached, and I was shivering uncontrollably. I peeled off my sweater, which was thick enough that the files were only slightly damp.

I hid them in a cabinet under the sink. Then I stripped down. I turned the shower on and rinsed myself off with the hottest water I could stand.

By the time I'd finished, my ankle had swollen to twice its usual size. I threw on leggings that came just past my knees and a huge Vassar sweatshirt. It was one of my favorite writing outfits.

I limped back to the kitchen.

Lizzie shook her head as she handed me a bag of ice and two towels. "Prop your foot on the chair."

I did as she asked and then hissed when she put the bag of ice on my ankle.

"How's your head?" she asked.

"Fine," I said as I touched it lightly. There hadn't been much blood, but there was a small bump.

"You should probably be checked for a concussion," Lizzie said as she fussed around me.

"I'm fine. My pupils aren't dilated and think the blood was from scraping the bark."

"Why would someone be waiting to attack you?" Lizzie asked.

"That is a good question," the detective said.

I shrugged. "Your guess is as good as mine. I thought I heard someone upstairs in the judge's house." I remembered my lame cover story. "I mean, that was why I was there."

"Any sane person would have run away then," my sister said.

"It was just a thump and then nothing. I thought maybe I'd imagined it."

"Since you seem determined to investigate..." he said, pulling out his policeman's notebook. "Why don't we start at the beginning, and you tell me what you've found."

"I don't think you should tell him anything," Lizzie said.

"Is that because you believe I'm a suspect?" he asked.

Her eyes went wide.

Then he explained what he had told me. Until I could confirm with the solicitor who read the will that no one had known its contents, I had to trust he told us the truth.

"If I'm giving your sister the benefit of the doubt, can you not give me the same courtesy?"

Lizzie stared at him with a wary look. "I guess."

"As I said, we've been reviewing the judge's files. Not that I have to explain, mind you—but we started with his past cases. Several of the criminals he'd put away have been released in the past year and a half. We are working our way to the present.

"So, no, we haven't been through all of the evidence."

"Right. But as we discussed before, someone had to know about the shrimp allergy," I said.

"You're hung up on that," he said. "And you're right, what happened with Brenna's oil makes it feel like it is someone here on the court. But the judge's allergy is something everyone in town knew about."

"But to sneak into Brenna's house…"

He held up a hand. "Most people in Shamrock Cove don't lock their doors. It isn't something we share with tourists, but it's a well-known fact here in the village. The judge's killer was clever and probably has a history of criminal activity. That's why we've begun our investigation with his past cases."

"That goes against everything we discussed a few days ago," I said. "How would they know Brenna's movements or what she was fixing for the meal?"

"The allergy only exacerbated the problem," he said.

I leaned forward on the table. "What do you mean?"

"That isn't what killed him."

"What did?" Lizzie asked the question before I could.

"He'd taken too much of his heart medicine," he said. "If we hadn't found the shrimp in his system…"

"Too much? That doesn't make sense," I said. "I'd only met him that night, but he was sharp. I mean, he didn't seem the type to overdose accidentally. Could someone have made certain he took too much? Like, maybe dosed him earlier? Or…"

"Or what?" Lizzie asked.

"There is foxglove in your grandmother's garden," I said. Then I stared at him.

He blinked. "I don't understand. It's poisonous… oh." He smiled. "I can assure you my gran didn't kill the judge."

"Says you," I said. "Maybe she doesn't share everything with you."

"Anything is possible," he said. "But you're wrong about her. There isn't a kinder soul in the world."

I didn't disagree. Lolly was the most welcoming person in Shamrock Cove.

"It could be two killers," Lizzie proposed. "One made

certain he had too much of his heart medicine. The other that his allergies kicked in."

"Why don't you start by telling me what you found in the files," he said. "The things you thought we missed."

I told him about the letters concerning Scott's roses, and some of the other things. "But the big kicker was the divorce papers between Linda and Dave." I saved that last bit to watch his reaction.

I wasn't disappointed.

"What?" He coughed.

"Our Linda, the one who owns the quilt store?" Lizzie asked. "But they seem so close." She was as bewildered as the detective.

I pulled out my phone. "Oh, darn. I forgot to take a picture of that one."

The detective frowned.

"If Linda didn't like the judge so much because of his views about the village, why would he have her divorce papers? And why hasn't she told anyone? She seemed truly upset this morning?" I had so many questions.

"The woman just lost her husband," he said.

"Right. And she seemed to be in shock, but..." I couldn't explain it.

"What?" Lizzie asked.

I shrugged. "No wake? Maybe they really were getting a divorce."

"Or, maybe she changed her mind," he said. "She and Dave did have a bad row a few months ago. She could have gone to the judge when she was angry and then changed her mind."

"Was the judge the type to blackmail someone?"

Kieran shook his head. "No. There was a reason he was so good at what he did. He believed in the law and had a squeaky-clean record himself."

"I'm having trouble seeing her as a killer," Lizzie said.

"When she was in the bookstore, she was so happy and positive. And she loves this place and the people in it. Besides, she's in love with romance. She bought a lot of them."

"So, we should be looking for a thriller or mystery reader?" I asked.

She shrugged. "I'm just saying, she seemed to be in love with life. Everything is wonderful in her world. I sort of admire people with that outlook. People who love happy endings. I used to be one of them."

She stared down at her hands. That last comment had hit a nerve. I reached across and took her hands.

"Can you tell me how big the person was who knocked you on the ground?" he asked.

"No. They came at me from the side and then were well down the back path before I turned around. And then the heavens opened. What I don't understand was—why wait at all? They might have risked being seen by you," I said.

"That scares me the most," Lizzie said. "Now, they know you were in that house."

"She isn't wrong," Kieran said. "Someone thinks you know something or that you saw something. Now, is there anything else you've been hiding?"

"No," I said. "The judge was old school with his paper files, but I noticed a printer in his office. Did he have a laptop or desktop?" I asked.

"He did have a laptop. We haven't been able to crack his password protection yet. We're waiting for one of the techies to come from Dublin to help. It could be a few more days. I could take it there, but it'll do no good. They have a backlog right now."

"Mercy can help you. She can hack anything."

I rolled my eyes.

"Is that so?" the detective asked.

"I've never done anything illegal," I said. "But I have spent a fair amount of time with hackers for research. I did learn a few things along the way. In my first couple of books, before the series I'm working on now, my heroine was a hacker."

"Do you always research your books so well?"

"She does," Lizzie said. "It's why the characters are so believable. That's how she knew CPR. That's how she knows about poisons and hacking."

My sister was not helping. I knew she was proud of me, but sometimes she pushed things too far.

"I know a little about a lot of things," I said. "But I do fully immerse myself in my lead characters' professions. It makes it easier to write from their point of view."

"Interesting," he said. "I hope you understand that you've fully put yourself in the killer's crosshairs now. Whoever that was behind Brenna's house knew you'd be coming that way. They've been watching you."

My stomach twisted.

My sister shivered.

Crud.

"From now on, I'd appreciate it if you'd come to me with the information you discover. But please stop your snooping. You're putting your and your sister's lives at risk. I don't know who is doing this, but I'm certain they mean business."

He wasn't wrong.

"I'd like to check your story about the will first," I said. "Before we decide to trust you."

Lizzie threw a hand over her mouth to hide her laugh.

"Gran has the solicitor's number. I'm sure she can put you in touch." He didn't seem upset about the fact I didn't trust what he said.

"What about the laptop?" Lizzie asked. "I promise you she can crack it."

I shook my head. "At the very least, I know people who can help me."

"Criminals?" His eyebrow went up.

"No idea what you're talking about."

Lizzie snorted.

"Right." He shook his head. "Stop by the station tomorrow morning. We'll see what we can do."

"And Dave? Do you know what killed him?"

He shook his head. "The preliminary report says heart attack, but we do not have the other tests back yet."

"Isn't that too much of a coincidence?" I asked. "Two heart attacks so close together?"

"Aye. I must be going. Please try to stay out of trouble."

I ducked my head to hide my grin. "Noted," I said.

He left.

"Are you sure your head is okay?" Lizzie asked.

I nodded.

"Good, because I feel like punching you in the face." She pointed a finger at me. "I nearly had a heart attack when he walked into that house. Why didn't you run away?"

I shrugged. "There wasn't time. I hid under the desk, but he smelled me."

"What?"

"My perfume. He recognized it."

She smiled. "In a weird way, I think he likes you," she said. "Otherwise, you really should be in jail this time. I can't believe I let you do that. My heart is still pounding. And now, if whoever knocked you down is the killer, they are going to be suspicious of you."

"They already were. Remember the threatening letter?"

She frowned. "We never did find that paper. Odd that our grandfather wouldn't have kept it somewhere here or at the store."

"I agree. Which means the killer stole it on purpose. Maybe to throw off the police. No one around here locks their doors. So, anyone could have come in here at any time."

"I'm not sure my heart is ever going to slow down. We need to be careful."

"Be aware of your surroundings at all times, Lizzie. Oh, that reminds me. Have you talked to a woman named Caro? I kept meaning to ask and I forgot."

"Is she a suspect?" Lizzie looked confused.

"No. Matt mentioned she used to help Grandad with the store. I think she wanted to come back. She's been helping Linda out. Maybe ask her to work with you at the store. I don't like the idea of you being there alone all the time."

"Well, I could use the help. The place, thankfully, is much busier than I expected.

"Oh. I was surprised that Linda was filing divorce papers. That was weird. They seem like they were meant for one another."

"I agree. Maybe a situation where when they cooled off, they changed their minds."

"I can't see her as a killer," Lizzie said.

"You're right. These murders took planning and a great deal of knowledge. Not that she's dumb in any way. She's so good-hearted. I can't see her hurting anyone.

"Do you need help at the store tomorrow?" I was curious to go through everything I'd taken pictures of and the files I'd taken.

"Nah, the store is my thing. Writing is yours. I'll check with Caro tomorrow. Besides, you also need to help hack the judge's computer."

I rolled my eyes. "Thanks for throwing me under that bus."

"Yeah, I wasn't thinking. He's so nice when he isn't arresting you that I sometimes forget he's a policeman. He was very worried about you while you showered. He kept wanting me to check on you. He was sincere about that. I will say, I don't think he's the killer. He seems to genuinely care about the people here. You also have to consider that the killer is someone from outside the court, but who may be familiar with the residents. From what he said, the judge had a lot of enemies. It doesn't get more personal than someone tossing you in prison for most of your life."

"Good point," I said. "I don't disagree. But I have this sense that it's someone closer than the detective thinks. I can't shake that gut feeling."

She shivered. "I hope you're wrong."

"Me, too."

But what if the killer was so much closer than any of us believed?

NINETEEN

The following day, I woke up to the shrill ring of my cell. It had taken me forever to fall asleep. And then Lizzie had woken me up every two hours because she was worried I might have had a concussion.

I didn't.

I think she finally gave up around four. Maybe because I'd said something incredibly rude.

I glanced at my phone. I was surprised by the time. It was nearly ten.

It was Carrie calling.

"How much further are you in the book?" Carrie asked, before I could say hello.

My stomach sank. I'd been fairly unfocused while trying to write it. Maybe it sucked.

"Is it that bad?" I asked. *Crud.* I should have made them wait before I turned in the first half. Her notes hadn't been bad, but I always caught more after revising a few times.

"No. It's one of the best things you've written. I want you to hurry and get it to me. We need to send it to some influencers. And I sent it to marketing, they've booked you a tour here, and over there, talk shows, big events. The most comprehensive tour you've ever done."

I blinked. "You sent marketing a half-written book?"

"Yes," she said. "I'll be honest, part of it was to get them off my back. But more so that it's a great book. They are all great, but this one has more stakes emotionally. It's absolutely the best."

Was it? I couldn't judge the books I wrote or compare them with other novels I'd done. I was too close to the stories.

"Can we agree right now that you'll never do that again?"

She sighed. "I never make promises. I needed to prove to them that this book was worth the wait. You know how cutthroat this business is. And while the bosses understand what you're going through and that you're one of our best sellers..."

"We still need them to back us with marketing."

"Exactly. Now, how are you?"

I was in the bathroom staring at the mirror. I had a huge bruise on the side of my forehead where I'd hit the tree.

"I'm fine."

"You don't sound like it. What's going on?"

"Nothing. I'll get to work on the second half. I will make the deadline." It would take a lot of coffee, but I would do it.

"Hey, you know I'm only doing this because I love you."

I snorted.

"Not fair."

True. She'd been there for me from the beginning. And while she wasn't the type of person who would say it, she was the one who made me who I'd become as a writer. I'd learned a great deal about the craft from her.

She'd also been there for Lizzie and me, after everything happened. She'd helped plan everything and stayed with us for several weeks after the funerals. Carrie was a wonderful editor, but an even better human being.

"Like I said, I'll make the deadline no matter what."

She chuckled. "I believe you. Now, go finish the book."

I planned to do that, but I'd told the detective I'd be by the station first thing. So, after a cup of coffee, and a shower, I headed that way.

Even though we were edging from spring to summer, it was nippy. I went back inside and grabbed my jacket. Lizzie and I would need to invest in macintoshes at some point.

At the station there was a man I hadn't seen before manning the front desk. I waited while he was on the phone.

"Miss, can I help you?" he asked when he was done.

"I'm here to see the detective," I said. "He asked for my help with something."

"Ms. McCarthy?" He wasn't that much younger than me, but the way he said my name made me feel like I was old.

"Yes," I said.

"Right. The detective expected you earlier. But he left the information for you in the interview room. He's out on a call."

"Okay. Do you mind if I head back?"

He smiled. "I heard you know where it is."

I chuckled. "That, I do."

"Would you like a cuppa?"

I held up the travel mug full of coffee I'd brought with me. "I'm good," I said.

In the interview room, I ignored the flowery wallpaper and focused on the file folder and laptop in front of me.

There was a note attached to the front of the file.

This is the judge's personal information. In case you need it to identify the password.

I assumed that had come from the detective, though there was no signature.

It had been about ten years since I'd done anything like this, and I almost called one of my friends to help. I'd worked with, and learned, from a couple of great hackers, two of whom had gone legit and worked for government agencies.

But first I wanted to test my skills.

I skimmed the file about the judge. He was a smart man, who believed in the law. But he'd also been older. Older generations tended to use simple passwords.

The username was already in there but without the judge's thumb, access to the password was a no-go.

After trying a few combinations that didn't work, I tried to go through a back door and was promptly shut down. Encryption software for even the simplest laptops had come a long way the last decade.

I tried another way in, and that didn't work.

Before calling my friends in the States, I went back through his file.

"Any luck?" the detective asked.

I jumped a little. More because I'd been so focused, I hadn't heard him come in.

Then an idea came to me. "What's your grandmother's birthday?"

He frowned. "June twentieth," he said. "Why?"

I typed in LollyO'Malley206 and boom, I was in.

Maybe the judge had still held a torch for her.

"I'm in," I said.

He pulled a chair around. "How did you do that?"

"Sheer dumb luck," I said. "It had nothing to do with skills. So far, most of the files are the same as the paper ones in his office."

"Check his texts and photos. We were never able to find his phone. And I'm still waiting for permission from the phone company for his records."

There weren't many texts. It looked like the judge had deleted them all or wasn't into texting.

There were hundreds of photos though, that had been uploaded.

We went through them together. Occasionally, he'd ask me to tag one to print out.

When we finished with those, he asked if I could get into the emails.

"I can try. But most sites are pretty well protected from the average hacker, and I'm not even average. There are probably five-year-olds who are better at this than me.

"Do you know what service he used?"

"Hold up." He pulled out his phone. "The judge emailed me a great deal when he wasn't happy with someone."

He gave me the email address.

I tried the same password, but it didn't work.

"He printed a lot of the emails," I said. "I saw them in the files. He was old school that way," I said. "I don't think he trusted anything digital."

"Aye, you're probably right about that."

"Wait."

I tried a couple of things, and then when that didn't work. I hit the find my phone app.

"I tracked his phone," I said. "After all this time, I'm surprised it still has battery."

"Where is it?"

I clicked to make the search area bigger.

"I could be wrong, but it looks like it's in his house."

He frowned. "We've searched the house a couple of times," he said.

I shrugged. "That's where it's pinging."

"I'll do another search."

"I can help."

"Nay, I've got it. You've helped us a great deal by getting this open."

I wrote down the password using the note on the file.

"May I ask why you tagged these specific photos?" Some were of flowers and gardens. Others were people at events. Some of them included the court neighbors.

"I don't really have an answer for you. I just wanted to examine them closer," he said.

"So, you've come around to my way of thinking?"

He turned to me. "What do you mean?"

"That it is someone close by. The photos you picked out are of gardens and people in the court."

He shrugged. "I'm looking at all possibilities. I have Sheila and James running down leads from the past. I've turned my focus to those in Shamrock Cove who may have had trouble with the judge. As you said, those who have motive."

"And opportunity. If it was someone from the outside, they'd need to stay somewhere, right? They'd be noticed as a stranger."

He nodded.

He'd never admit I'd been on the right track, but at least he'd listened.

"Okay, well, I should get to work on my book. If you need anything else, let me know."

"Ms. McCarthy," he said. He stood in front of me, blocking the way.

"Yes?"

"Thank you," he said. "I know we've had a bit of a bumpy start."

"A bit," I said.

He smiled. "I'm grateful for your help this morning. Good luck with your book."

"Good luck with your search."

As I was leaving, my phone rang.

"I need your help," Lizzie said before I could say hello.

"Is something wrong?"

"What? Oh. No. I need you to handle the shop while I talk to Caro, who used to help our grandfather in the bookstore. Do you mind? It won't take more than a half-hour, hour at the most."

"Okay. I'll be there in a bit." I crossed the street, and as I was passing Linda's shop, she stepped out.

"How are you? Did you get arrested again? That might be a record for a resident of the court." She smiled.

"For once, I was being helpful. How are you? I can't believe you're working."

"I'm not. The shop isn't open, I couldn't sit at home any longer. I'm happier among my fabric and quilts."

"Linda, I'm really sorry about Dave. I can't imagine what you're going through. You two seemed so close."

She bit her lip. "Our marriage wasn't always perfect, but we loved one another. I'm not sure what I will do without him."

"Will you still live on the court?"

Her eyes went wide. "Of course, this is home. I can't imagine living anywhere else."

I nodded. "I've only been here a couple of weeks and I must agree. I need to get to the shop to help Lizzie for a bit. But you let us know if you need anything."

Linda smiled, but it didn't reach her eyes. "Thanks. Were you successful in helping the detective?"

She seemed curious, but I would be as well. I shrugged. "I hope I helped. Kieran doesn't seem to like me much. I think it was more him keeping an eye on me and Lizzie."

She smiled. "I sent Caro down to speak with your sister. Even with business about to pick up with the season, I can't use her in the shop much these days."

"Well, that was kind of you." I wanted to bring up the divorce papers, but there was just no way to do it without being obvious.

"Not a problem. What happened to your face?" She pointed to the bruises.

"I had a fight with a tree, and the tree won."

She laughed.

"Oh, did you get the invite for the dinner on Saturday?" Lizzie had texted that she spoke with Lolly earlier in the morning and had sorted it out.

"Aye. Are you sure I can't bring anything? That's usually the way we do things around here."

"Thanks, but no. This is for Dave. We want to treat everyone to a Texas barbecue, especially you. My sister loves throwing get-togethers, and I'm good at following orders."

"Well, it's lovely of you to do this for my poor Dave. You've had a bit of a rough start here in our wee town, and it is kind of you to think of him, and me."

I smiled. "It has been interesting. And of course we're thinking of you. This has to be one of the hardest times of your life."

She sighed. "Aye, it is. I don't know what to do with myself. That's why I'm here at the shop. Keeping busy working on inventory and taking care of odds and ends."

"Well, I'll let you get back to it. Lizzie is expecting me."

She shooed me away. "Go on with you, then. See you Saturday."

There was more to Linda than met the eye. That was for certain, but she was kind-hearted and helpful. I think possibly her being a part of so many committees and having ideas was her way of fitting in. I sensed she needed to feel important, even though she felt like an outsider.

I could relate.

It didn't explain why Rob and Scott disliked her so much, but some people just weren't meant to get along. I learned that lesson the hard way years ago with a group of writer friends.

Still, Rob and Scott had shown up for her with food and company. They were good guys and there when it mattered.

"Thanks," Lizzie said as I joined her behind the counter. "Your little friend Liam is upstairs. His mom is in the cookbook section. I promise I won't be long. Caro is already back there making us tea. She seems like a sweetheart. I can't wait to hear about what it was like to work with our granddad."

I would have liked to have been in on that conversation. "Take your time," I said. Yes, I had a book to write, but I had a solid plan for it in my head.

A few minutes later, Liam came downstairs with an armload of books.

I smiled. "That's a serious pile," I said.

"You didn't tell me how much fun the books would be," he said seriously. "Mam says this is the last lot for a while. We went to the library, but the ones I wanted to read were checked out."

"Man, I don't like it when that happens."

"Have you seen my mam?"

I took the books from him and sat them on the counter.

"I think she's over here. Follow me."

He did. His mother had a pile of books about baking in her arms.

"Have you been watching reruns of the *Great British Bake Off*?" I asked. I recognized some author names of cast members on the show.

Her eyes went wide. "How did you know?"

"I've never missed a season. I don't bake or cook. But I love the show. I always end up buying books on the subject, but I have no talents in that regard. I'm the last person who should go near an oven."

She smiled. "It's my hobby and has been for years. But they take it to the next level."

"They do. I think the creativity is part of the big appeal for me."

"They are all so clever. My birthday is coming up, and Liam's da said to buy myself whatever I wanted."

I laughed. "Most women would go for clothes or purses. Maybe some shoes."

She giggled. "I live in Shamrock Cove, and I can walk everywhere, so I don't need a car. And I need sensible shoes, and as a mammy, I carry so many things with me all the time, I couldn't live without my *mála droma*." She pointed to the back-pack on her shoulder. "Books are my treasure."

Funny, my grandfather felt the same way, and so did I. Maybe that really was what he'd meant by his mysterious letter.

"Did you find some more books?" she asked Liam.

"Yes, Mam." The little dude was adorable. "A lot."

"And are you going to do your chores if I buy them for you?"

"Yes, Mam."

"There's a good boy," she said. She was so tender with him.

"Would you like me to set some of those on the counter? And Liam can wait with me while you shop."

"Oh, that's kind of you. I won't be much longer."

After setting Liam up on the stool behind the counter with one of his books, I checked in his purchases and decided to wrap them.

By the time my sister and Caro came out of the back, I had finished serving Liam and his mom, and they had left.

Lizzie made the introductions.

"Thank you for speaking to Linda," Caro said. "She's a lovely woman, but she doesn't need me much. I've been picking up the slack with some cleaning, but I much prefer working here."

She was a bit older than us, probably in her fifties with brown hair, and a gray streak that went down the front.

"We're happy to have you," Lizzie said. She smiled broadly. "Caro has promised to share her stories about our grandfather."

"You would have loved him. He was quiet and bookish, and

so smart. He had a gift for knowing the kind of books someone needed. Not wanted, mind you, but needed."

"I think my sister may have that same gift," Lizzie said. "That little boy who just walked out wasn't interested in books until Mercy got ahold of him."

They laughed.

"Don't count yourself short in that department," Caro said to my sister. "I watched you with the customers. You have it as well."

"I agree," I said.

Lizzie blushed.

"Well, I best get on," said Caro. "I need to let the folks I've been cleaning for know that I'm back here. I've missed the bookshop. I love this place," she said wistfully.

"We do, too."

After the door shut, my belly growled.

"Sounds like we need to break for lunch," Lizzie said as she put the money from the register in a bank bag. "Did you go to the station? What happened?"

"I'll tell you on the way home." I locked the front door and turned the sign around to *closed*. I was about to head to the back when I sensed someone watching me.

At the edge of the window was a shadow. I ran to the window, but I didn't see anyone.

Could have just been someone peeking into the store.

But the hairs on the back of my neck tingled.

"Where are you?" Lizzie asked.

"Coming."

When we arrived home, our front door was open.

"Did you leave it unlocked?" she asked.

"No. I locked it. I remember... Oh."

"Oh?"

"I went back for a jacket and maybe I left it unlocked, but I didn't leave it open."

She stayed there on the doorstep. "We should call the detective," she said. I glanced down to find her hand shaking.

"I'm sure it's fine," I said. "Let me check it out."

"No." She pulled out her phone. "I'd feel safer if we call the police."

I put a hand on her shoulder. "They are short-staffed as it is. I probably didn't shut it properly. You stand here. If I see anything, I'll scream loud, and you can run for help."

"I don't know..."

She'd argue with me all day if I didn't just do it.

I stepped inside, and then grabbed one of the pointy umbrellas in the stand.

I brandished it like a weapon. "Is anyone here?"

"What's going on?" Rob asked from beside my sister.

Lizzie and I screamed and then laughed.

"You scared us to death," she said. "We're worried someone broke into the house."

"She's worried. I think maybe I forgot to shut the door the right way or the wind blew it open."

He took the umbrella from me and pointed it at me. "I've got you.

"We've got you surrounded. Come out with your hands up." His voice was loud, dramatic, and completely believable.

Lizzie giggled nervously behind me.

Then the back door slammed.

We looked wide-eyed at one another, and then ran to the back of the house.

Rob was in front of me, and I couldn't see past him.

"Do you see anyone?" I followed him down the path to the back gate.

"No," he said. Then he bent over to catch his breath. "There's no one back here."

"But you heard it, right?" I wheezed. "I didn't imagine the door slamming. And I know I locked the back door when I left."

"Aye, I heard it. Someone was definitely in here." By the time we made it back through the house, Kieran was at the front door with my sister.

"Lizzie says you had an intruder," he said.

"They did." Rob put the umbrella back in the stand. The detective watched him carefully. "I'm calling a meeting of the council. This is unacceptable."

"It is," the detective said. "Could you take Lizzie to your house and maybe get her some tea?"

"I'm fine," Lizzie said shakily. There was white around her mouth. "We need to see if they took anything."

"I can help with that," I said. "Rob, I'm starving. It's rude, but could you maybe fix us something to eat?" My sister didn't need this.

"I'm happy to," he said. "I'm trying out a new recipe..." he said to Lizzie as he led her down to the front gate.

"Why would they break into our house?" I asked.

"They think you know something," he said. "I was worried about this when you were attacked last night."

"You don't think it was someone here to rob us? Like just a regular kind of criminal?"

"Regular criminal? I thought you were a writer?"

"Rude. You know what I mean."

"Given the circumstances, I understand why it's difficult for you to believe, but we don't have crime in the court. It's too well protected."

"So, you keep saying."

"Fair point, but it is the truth. The timing of all this, with your arrival, is unfortunate. But it is also unusual."

"I'll take your word for it." I'd gone through this in Manhattan. Someone had prowled through my things and moved them around just enough that I would notice. It was more than disconcerting and I'd lost a great deal of sleep and security because of my stalker.

I'd hoped to be away from all of that.

But had they followed me here? I'd asked myself that more than once.

After checking downstairs, I followed him upstairs. "Do you see anything out of place or missing?"

"Not that I've seen so far," I said. Then I remembered something. I headed back downstairs. When I opened my bathroom cabinets, I sucked in a breath. I'd put the slightly damp files I'd taken from the judge's house in there. The ones that had been about my family.

"What is it?" He was at the door to the bathroom.

"I... some papers I had are gone."

"From the loo?"

"Private files," I said. "I had them in the cabinet."

"Seems an odd place to keep something so important. What would the intruder have wanted with them?"

I had no idea. I didn't have a chance to look at them.

"I've no idea," I said.

"Is anything else missing?"

I went to my office, and double-checked my laptop was still there. As awful as it sounds, that was the only thing that mattered to me in this house—my sister of course—but my life's work was on that machine.

And yes, everything was backed up in the cloud, but still.

"I'll need to bring Lizzie in to check, but I don't think so."

"I need to know what the papers were," he said. Then he held up a hand. "Just a general idea so I can understand why someone might want to take them."

I took a deep breath. I didn't want to lie to him anymore, so I changed the subject.

"Could you maybe test for fingerprints here and around the house?"

"Aye. I've texted the team. They'll send someone soon."

My stomach growled. "I need to eat. When my blood sugar gets low, I can feel kind of woozy." I held my hand to my head. I was fine, but the blood sugar thing was true. Usually, when I'd forgotten to eat, which happened only when I was working and forgot to put snacks on my desk.

"Why don't you go next door? I'll let you know when we're done here."

I nodded.

I grabbed my laptop. I didn't like the idea of people traipsing in and out with it just sitting there. I stuck it in my backpack.

"Do you want a coffee? I'm grabbing one to take over to Rob's."

"Aye."

He followed me back to the kitchen. I filled my travel mug. Then filled a cup for him.

"Again, before you go. About those papers?"

I sighed. I'd hoped my diversion worked.

It didn't.

"They were files on my family... that I found at the judge's house last night. I brought them home to take a look. Except, they were slightly damp, and needed to dry out, so I put them in that cabinet because the floors are heated, and those cabinets stay warm.

"Now, if you're going to arrest me for stealing evidence, I ask that you give me the courtesy of lunch first. No one wants me hangry in jail."

Then I left him standing there with his eyes wide and mouth slightly open.

TWENTY

By the time Saturday afternoon rolled around, the break-in had mostly been forgotten. No fingerprints had been found or traces of clothing. The only thing they'd taken were the files—ones that included information about our family.

Since I had no idea what was in the files, I hadn't been much help with the investigation. That hadn't kept Kieran from grilling me, but I hadn't blamed him.

Lizzie had been shaken up, and she'd ended up sleeping in my bed the last few nights. She tended to jump when there were loud noises, but she was better.

Today, she was using Lolly's huge outdoor grill to cook a brisket and some other food. She'd left me in our kitchen slicing vegetables. It was about the only thing I was qualified to do when it came to preparing a meal. I'd also helped clean the house and set tables up in the backyard.

She truly wanted this to be a Texas kind of party and the weather had cooperated. It was warmer than usual in Shamrock Cove and the sun peeked through the clouds. The perfect day for a barbecue.

While I'd been distracted this past week, my book brain had

kicked in big time. I'd written more words the last few days than I had the last year. It felt good.

But I'd set all that aside to make a plan of attack for tonight. I had questions that needed answers. I'd sort of promised my sister that I'd stay out of things going forward. After the break-in, she told me enough with the Nancy Drew. I didn't blame her.

The back gate creaked shut and I looked out the window to find Rob and Scott carrying some benches down the garden path.

I opened the door. "Do you need help?" I asked.

"We've got it," Scott said. "We promised Lizzie she could borrow the benches for one of the tables."

On my list of suspects, I'd marked Rob off because he'd been with me when someone went out of our back door. Scott had been out of town that day. And I'd ruled out Lolly because she'd been at home when I'd been attacked on the back path the night I broke into the judge's house.

That left Linda, Matt, and his mother as suspects. Or I could be totally wrong, and it was one of the criminals from the judge's past. But my gut said it was someone here in town.

They placed the benches on one side of the long picnic table we'd put up in the middle of the lawn.

The men wore khaki shorts and checkered cowboy shirts with snaps.

"Where did you get those shirts?" I smiled.

"We're gay," Scott said as if that answered the question. Then we all laughed. "Let us grab the other bench and we'll come back to help with prep."

"Did Lizzie send you to check on me?"

The two men shrugged and looked at each other comically.

"Whatever. The onions were next on the list, you're welcome to them."

This was supposed to be a casual party to send Dave off in

style, but that didn't mean I couldn't use the opportunity to find a killer.

By the time the others started arriving, we'd set everything out. Lizzie and Lolly had brought steaming foil trays of meats and sides. We set everything up buffet-style on the tables nearest the house.

In true Texas party fashion, we had a big silver tub stuffed with ice, beer, sodas, and waters. Well, technically back home everything would have been in a cooler, but we didn't have one here. There was a selection of wines, as well.

My sister was circulating a tray of jalapeno poppers which were more cheese than pepper.

I watched everyone like a hawk going after their prey. My plan was to swoop in and strike, without them ever knowing what I was doing.

Linda showed up in jeans and a ruffled pink shirt. I'd never seen her in such a bright color. And though we had a theme for today, which was Texas, I hadn't expected her to show up in something so bright.

"I love your blouse."

"Thank you." She smiled but it didn't reach her eyes. "My Dave loved me in pink. I wore it for him." Her voice caught, and she blinked as if trying to stem a tide of tears.

"Then he would say you are beautiful today," I said. "And if it all gets to be too much for you, we will understand if you need to go home."

She sniffed and then cleared her throat. "Thank you."

"What would you like to drink?" I asked.

"Wine," she said.

"Which color?"

She gave me a tight smile. "I'll take the red," she said.

"How are you? This isn't too much too soon, is it?"

She blinked. "What do you mean?"

I poured her wine. "Just that you might not be in exactly a

party mood after everything that has happened. And we worried about having a Texas theme for a celebration of life might be a bit much."

"I think it is wonderful that you are doing this," she said softly. "Dave always did love a themed garden party. And he would have loved that it was Texas."

"Oh, good. You two always seemed so happy together. You mentioned that you read a lot of romance, is that the secret to a happy relationship?"

Linda choked on her wine. I patted her back. "Are you okay?"

She waved a hand. "I'm fine. I swallowed wrong. And to answer your question, I honestly don't know the secret to relationships. I've been lucky with Dave, but even with him..."

"Was everything okay?" I asked.

"Oh, it's just married people stuff," she said. "Most days are wonderful. And then, other days, you want to take them out with the rubbish. But in the end, we were grateful for one another. I miss him."

"Back home, everyone gets divorced for any kind of reason," I said.

She blanched. "I've thought about it on occasion. One time I was even serious about it."

"What happened?"

"I talked to the judge about it."

Wait. What?

"I'm confused. I thought you two didn't get along."

"Only about the revamp. He was... difficult. But he cared about the people on the court. He looked after us in his way. Anyway, he went behind my back and spoke to Dave.

"At first, I was furious. If I could have, I would have ruined his career, but he'd already retired. I mean, who does that? It was such a betrayal."

Now, that was a motive to kill the judge.

"But you two were still together until... You seemed happy."

"We were. After the judge talked to him, Dave was a different man. He was attentive and tried to find ways to make me happy. And I did the same for him. That's why I read so many romances. I was always looking for new ways to keep the relationship on course. The funny thing is the judge saved our marriage. In a way, he was a hero. Dave never told me what he said, though." She brushed her hair behind her ear.

"Well, you two set an example. I hope it isn't too painful talking about him."

She gave me a weak smile. "This is a celebration of him, right? Who else would we be talking about?"

"True. Well, I hope we do him justice today."

"Thanks." She grinned. "How are you and Lizzie? I was so sorry to hear about your trouble the other day. Did they take anything?"

I shook my head. "No," I lied. "I guess we interrupted whoever it was."

"Strange. In all the years I've lived here, we've never had so much trouble on the court."

While she hadn't stated it exactly, she meant since Lizzie and I had arrived.

"That's what people keep saying, but that hasn't been our experience."

Her eyebrow went up. "Are you thinking of moving out?"

"No, at least not yet. We want to give it some time. My sister has been through a lot, and I'm hoping things settle down so she can move on with her life."

"And what about you? Is this what you want? I mean, you came from the big city to this place."

I grinned. "I do miss home a bit. More that I can't get Chinese food twenty-four-seven. I live on the stuff when I'm writing. And I miss American donuts."

She laughed. "I've never had an American donut. But

Paisley has almost finished the revamp of her patisserie. You'll love her pastries. They are some of the best I've ever tasted. But the shop has been closed for several months. She needed a bigger space."

"Is there more than one bakery? Lizzie came home with some goodies the first week we were here."

"Yes. That was John's. He's mostly a bread baker, and he's very good at it. If you had any sort of pastries from his place, they were made by Paisley. Since her shop's been closed, he's been letting her sell things there. And even when they were both open, she sold his bread in her shop, and he sold some of her pastries."

"But aren't they competing?" I asked.

She shrugged. "They used to be married and discovered they were better friends and business partners. Together, they own the bakery and patisserie. Lovely people. They are your age. I'm surprised you haven't met them yet."

"Lizzie probably has. She's the more social twin. When I'm on a deadline, which is most of the time, I tend to be a hermit."

"Is it very exciting be a writer? I haven't read your books yet, but I did pick one up with my order the other day. I don't read much mystery."

"That was kind of you to buy the book," I said.

"Well, I like to support local artists." It was as if she'd practiced that saying so much she'd made herself believe it. "So, what's it like to be so famous?"

"I'm not," I said. "Famous, that is."

"Oh, but you are. I read about you. You sell millions of books every time one comes out. That's why I don't understand why you'd want to live in our tiny town. And in a cottage. You could buy a castle with all that money."

I never liked discussing money.

"I love the cottage," I said. "It's the perfect size for Lizzie and me. I stayed with her a lot over the last year, and I realized how much I missed her. She's grounding for me, and, in a weird way, I think I'm the same for her. We're pretty compatible roommates for family."

"Oh, that's sweet. I grew up with four brothers. They are all a mess in one way or another. I couldn't imagine living with them again."

I shrugged. "Maybe it's different for women or twins. It's a huge cliché but when she's not around, I feel like a part of me is missing. I mean, I had a great life in New York, but I didn't realize how lonely it was until I'd stayed in Texas for a bit."

Linda stared at me thoughtfully.

"As for living in Shamrock Cove, it's been eventful. But it's also quite beautiful. The air is clear, and the sea is right there."

"You're surrounded by water in New York." Why did she seem so determined to remind me what I'd been missing?

I laughed. "But it's not like I can just walk down to the beach. Lizzie and I needed a change. At least for now, I think Shamrock Cove is the perfect place."

"Lizzie says it's time to eat," Rob announced loudly.

"It is," my sister said.

Everyone sat down at the long tables we'd set up.

"My sister would like to say a few words," Lizzie said.

I would?

I'm sure I had a deer-in-the-headlights look.

I'm going to kill her.

I cleared my throat. "We're gathered here to celebrate the life of Dave. While Lizzie and I didn't have the pleasure of knowing him near long enough, we know through your stories what a great guy he was and such a good member of the community on the court. We hope that you will continue to share your stories about him with us." I held up my glass. "To Dave."

Linda dabbed her eyes with her napkin.

"We hope you enjoy our food tribute to Dave," Lizzie

added. "We were told he was quite the foodie. Today's fare is humble but a part of many celebrations back in Texas. As my sister said, we're looking forward to your stories."

I waited for everyone to get in line at the buffet. Lizzie and I would make sure everyone had their food and drinks before grabbing some for ourselves. It was the Texan way.

I whispered to her about what Linda had said.

"I thought you were going to stop investigating," she whispered back.

"Come on," I said. "If you'd seen those divorce papers, you would have tried to find a way to ask some questions just out of curiosity. Besides, it was your idea to get everyone together like an Agatha Christie novel."

She sighed. "True. Matt and his mom never showed. I hope they are okay. You didn't insult them, did you?"

"Why is it always me that's to blame?"

Her eyebrows rose.

I laughed. "No. But I will call the pub to make sure they're okay."

Just as I pulled my phone from my pocket, Matt and his mother came through the gate. She only looked a few years older than him, and I'd never noticed how pretty she was.

"So, sorry we're late," he said. "Our bartender was running behind coming in with supplies from Dublin—"

"Doesn't matter, Matty." His mom patted his shoulder. "Thank you for inviting us. Your garden is lovely."

"Thank you," Lizzie said. "Our grandfather had excellent taste. Come, let's get you some food." She guided Matt's mom to the banquet line.

"I really am sorry," Matt said. "I don't like being late. Between Josh arriving late and the detective questioning me for the millionth time, I didn't think we'd ever get away."

"Why would he question you?"

"Something he found in the judge's papers. He said I didn't

pay off the whole loan, and that's why the ownership hadn't transferred, but that wasn't true. I have papers to back up my side of the story, and I showed him.

"I have no idea what the judge was doing, but the loan he'd given my mother had been paid in full."

The paperwork I'd seen said the same thing. "I had to help the detective with the judge's computer," I said. "They are probably looking at a different set of papers."

"Why were you helping him?"

I shrugged. "Computer skills I picked up along the way."

"I have the paperwork he signed off on. But he had to be the one to file it. That last bit was the only thing we'd been waiting on. He was taking his time with it. I've no idea why."

"I'm glad you have that proof," I said.

"Thanks to Lolly, it's now been filed. We're finally in the clear. You know, after I talked to you the other night... I think the judge might have cared more about my mom than he let on. Like, maybe that's why he hadn't filed the paperwork once everything was paid off. It was his way of staying connected to her."

I led him toward the buffet. "When it comes to the judge, I wouldn't be surprised. The more I hear about him the more confused I become. There are those who see him as a hero, others as a nuisance. But I think he was like all of us, a bit of both."

He chuckled. "Just grumpier about life in general than anyone I'd ever met."

"You may be right about that. Did he ever treat you..." I wasn't sure how to pose the question. "From what I've heard, he wasn't always so accepting of Rob and Scott."

Matt's eyebrow rose. "Oh, you mean, because they're gay?"

I shrugged.

"Never discussed my private life with him," he said. "I'm

not sure he knew about my sexual preferences. I certainly wasn't one to discuss them with him."

"Sorry," I said. "You know I don't care about that sort of thing."

He laughed. "No harm, Mercy. Truly. You're just trying to understand the old man, but I promise it's impossible. I will say, when it came to law, he was fair. But when it came to judging people..."

"Understood. Come on, let's get some food."

As we headed toward the food line, the detective and Sheila came through the gate.

Oh, no. What now?

TWENTY-ONE

Trying to head them off at the pass, I moved quickly across the lawn. Kieran was dressed in jeans and a blue button-down shirt. Sheila wore jeans and a Thin Lizzy T-shirt. They weren't in uniform. Not that the detective wore one usually. Unless it was his mackintosh that said *Police* on it.

Had my sister invited them?

"We had to wait for James to get back from the Corselys' farm," Kieran said.

"So, we're a wee bit late," Sheila said.

"I... uh..."

"Welcome," Lizzie said from behind me. "I'm so glad you could make it. I didn't know you two were a couple."

I didn't either.

Sheila and Kieran glanced at each other and then busted out laughing.

"So, you're not a couple," Lizzie said.

"Goodness, no," Sheila said. "Best mates, maybe. Can you imagine?"

He shook his head.

"I need a man I can boss around," she said. "Any single men tonight?"

This time it was Lizzie and I who laughed.

"Unfortunately, with the exception of the detective, and maybe Matt, I don't think we've met any in Shamrock Cove," I said.

"Matty's here? I'm not his type, but I've never had a better drinking buddy." She took off toward the food.

"He's her wingman when they go out," Kieran said.

"You could have brought your girlfriend—or boyfriend," Lizzie said. "I don't want to presume anything."

"I'm not dating anyone at the moment. I don't like to date women in Shamrock Cove. If it doesn't go well…" He shrugged.

"That makes sense," she said. "Well, come on. Let's get you fed."

He hesitated. "I do appreciate the gesture of you two inviting me. I haven't made your stay very easy."

I smiled. "But you have made it interesting."

He chuckled.

After grabbing some food, we all joined the table. Since there were only seats at the end, I was forced to sit next to Kieran.

"I gather you didn't know we were coming," he said as he cut into my sister's tender brisket.

"Well, no. At first, I thought you were here to arrest me again. Any news from your investigation? I know you can't say specifics, but do you have a suspect yet?"

Someone had killed the judge and Dave and had broken into our house and stolen files. I had no way of proving they were the same person, but I had a gut feeling that was a fact.

"We are looking into a few things. How about you?"

Lizzie gave me evil eyes across the table.

I shook my head. "I'm leaving the investigating to you. But I do have a favor to ask later." I whispered the last bit. "Just not with Lizzie across the table."

Lizzie stood with her beer. "As Mercy said earlier, this is all for Dave. We're looking forward to hearing your stories about him. Sláinte."

People around the table clinked glasses.

Then she motioned toward Lolly.

"We're going to miss our Dave," Lolly said. "He was a good bloke, who always lent a helping hand when needed. Last summer I don't know what I would have done without his help for the garden show. He never complained once, and even stepped in as a judge. I'll be forever grateful for him, and that's just one of many stories about a young fellow who was taken from us much too soon. Sláinte." She held up her glass.

Each person at the table told a nice story about Dave. As the afternoon wore on, people relaxed, and it turned into a lovely celebration. Every now and then, Linda would dab her eyes and give whoever was speaking a watery smile.

I was glad we'd done this.

Now, if we could just figure out who killed the judge, and possibly Dave—I didn't believe it was just a heart attack—broke into our house, and shoved me into a tree, everything would be perfect.

I left that part out of my speech.

Later, my sister made us play The Hygge Game, where everyone is asked a big life question. The question that brought forth some of the most interesting answers was a simple one.

What has been the best day of your life? And the person answering wasn't allowed to say births or marriages.

For me, it was when my editor called and said she'd be acquiring my first book. "I still feel that rush of happiness and excitement when I think about that day a hundred years ago," I said.

Everyone laughed.

Lizzie's eyes watered a bit when she gave her answer. "The day I met my fiancé was the same day my lavender business got a big push on a morning show, thanks to my sister."

"What?"

She nodded. "You mentioned it on a national morning show, and they put my website down on the bottom crawl. Our sales took off that day and it's been great ever since."

"I had no idea," I said. She'd never mentioned it, and I didn't remember saying anything. Though, I'd always been proud of her business, and I was often asked if my twin was also a writer.

"And that night, I went out to celebrate with some friends and I met John... it was a good night." She sniffed. "How about you, Lolly?"

I handed Lizzie some extra tissues. She still couldn't say John's name without getting kind of weepy, and I wondered if that day would ever come. I didn't judge or blame her. I'd never seen two people more in love or perfect for one another. That he had a daughter was a bonus for my sister.

I'd loved John and Audrey, too. But Lizzie had lost her heart the night they died.

After Lolly, it was Kieran's turn.

"The day I graduated and became a part of the Garda," he said. "That probably doesn't surprise anyone here."

Lolly patted his cheek. "You've always been a good boy," she said.

"Ma and Pa might disagree." He laughed and shook his head.

"All boys have growing pains. You found your way. I couldn't be prouder."

It was hard to tell in the dark, with just the twinkle lights overhead, but I think Kieran blushed.

I was curious about his growing pains. I remembered what he'd said about the judge setting him straight years ago. There was a story there.

By the time people started saying their goodbyes, it was nearing nine thirty that night.

"That was one of the best meals I've ever had," Lolly said. "And I've been around the block a few times."

"You should bottle that sauce," Rob said. "You'd make millions."

"Thank you for everything," Linda said. "I was wrong."

"What do you mean?" Lizzie asked.

"I shouldn't have listened to Dave. He deserved a wake whether he wanted one or not. But today helped. It was good to hear so many stories about him. Thank you both."

"It was our pleasure," Lizzie said.

I nodded.

"I'll walk you home," Matt said to Linda.

She smiled up at him. "Thank you, Matty. You are a sweet young man."

Rob and Scott wouldn't go home until they helped us clean up.

"That's a new record," Rob said.

"What do you mean?" Lizzie asked.

"That's the latest one of the court parties has ever gone. Usually, someone ends up in a fight around seven and half the people go home," Rob said.

"Or there is a hard out at nine," Scott finished his sentence. "Part of that was half of the crowd used to be over seventy."

"You aren't wrong," Rob agreed. "It's weird to only have Lolly left from the old guard."

"Were our grandfather's parties like that?" I asked.

The two men looked at one another and smiled.

"We've been wondering when you'd ask," Scott said. "Yes, to the parties, but usually, he held them at the bookshop. The man knew his way around wine and cheese. He had the best pairings.

"Personally, I thought he was a magical old man. I mean that in the nicest way. He reminded me of some of your old-time American actors. Like a Cary Grant or a James Stewart."

"Yes," Rob added. "He had a quiet strength about him, but he had a dry sense of humor that would make you laugh hours after he said something. And he was smart. I mean, get him in a pub quiz, and he held his own with the judge.

"But for the most part, he just looked out for people. And I don't just mean here on the court."

"He sounds too perfect," Lizzie said. "You can tell us the truth. We really want to know who he was."

That surprised me. My sister was quite adept at looking only for the good in people.

"I just... except for the books he curated, there aren't many personal things here in the house," she said. "There are a few old photos, but we have no idea who the people are in them.

"I even snooped in a few boxes," she continued. "He was in the military. I found a few medals and certificates. But there's nothing with our grandmother or our father. We didn't know him either."

The two men looked at one another again.

"You'll want to ask Lolly about that," Rob said. "She may have some of the old photos. But it was my understanding, and I heard this from Linda, that when your grandmother died at a very early age, he sent your father off to boarding school. And he got rid of anything that reminded him of her."

"Mind you, that's hearsay," Scott said. "Your grandfather was a very private man and quite a bit in his years when we met him. But he never spoke of the past. Once when we were celebrating Remembrance Day—it isn't as big a holiday here as what you have in the States, but many Irishmen fought in the First and Second World Wars—Lolly asked your grandfather to speak, but he refused. Said there was no sense rehashing the past. He just didn't like talking about any of it. We even tried a few times, but he'd change the subject."

"I think he may have had some regrets later in life," Rob added. "Maybe, that's why he was so nice to everyone. He'd lost his wife and son, and perhaps he hadn't been as good to them as he might have been."

"But if you really want to know him, ask Lolly," Rob said. "She likes keeping the history and the people of the court alive."

"We'll do that," Lizzie said. "And thank you both so much for helping out tonight."

"It's our pleasure. You two are a lot like him in a way," Rob said.

"How so?"

"You're kind and you've fit right into our little group. Oh, and you throw a great party," he said.

It's weird but I never thought of myself as kind.

"My sister throws a great party," I said. "I'm just good at following orders."

They laughed.

After everything was done, I said goodnight to Lizzie. She was yawning like crazy, but at least she had the next day off at the bookstore.

I was still a bit wired, so I went to my office, and had a small panic attack when I found my laptop was missing.

Then I laughed. I'd taken it and put it under my pillow on my bed. The study door didn't lock, so I'd thought it was the safest option since my bedroom door did have a lock and key.

After making certain it was still there, I went to my grandfather's private library.

I had a feeling this room meant something special to him. While he'd curated books for his shop, these tomes were his private collection. I thought, perhaps, I could get to know him through some of his favorite books. The ones that were a bit more worn than others.

As I reached for a copy of *The Picture of Dorian Gray*, there was a blood-curdling scream.

Lizzie ran down the stairs as I ran out of the room.

"Did you hear that?" she asked as we stopped in the front entry.

I nodded. "I thought it was you."

"I thought it was you," she said.

"Let's check out front."

We raced out, me carrying the huge umbrella. Lizzie grabbed a spade by the bench in the garden.

As we moved to our gate, there was a figure on the ground near the entrance to the court.

"It could be a trick," I said.

"Is that Linda?" Rob said from beside us.

Lizzie and I jumped, and we may have screamed.

"When did you get ninja skills?" Lizzie asked.

"Scott is a light sleeper, so I've learned to walk softly. Is she dead?"

We ran toward her.

I knelt to take her pulse. "No. Her pulse is strong. I left my phone in the house, does someone have a flashlight, or torch?"

Rob turned the app on, but it wasn't nearly enough light out in the darkness so close to the wall.

She was face down in the grass just off one of the paths. She wore a flowery top and yoga pants, which were not what she'd worn to the party.

I followed the emergency procedures I'd learned from my classes, even going so far as to check for broken bones in her legs.

"How much did she drink and why is she out here?" Lizzie asked.

"I've called emergency services." Scott came up. He turned the light on his phone as well. "Did she pass out?"

"Oh dear," Lolly said as she walked up. She wore a robe and fluffy house slippers.

"I'm afraid to move her if she's fallen. I don't feel any broken bones, but she could have hurt her neck when she hit the ground." There were small cuts on her hand, as if she'd tried to stop herself as she fell.

Everyone gasped, including me, when Linda groaned.

"Take it easy," I said. "You've fallen and we can't be certain of what's been damaged."

"I didn't fall," Linda complained as she rubbed her head. She pushed herself up to a sitting position, and she appeared a bit dazed. "Some bloody idiot hit me from behind. I heard them, but before I could turn around..."

"I can't find the bloody gate, someone yelled on the other side of the wall. They need lights out here."

Scott ran over to open it.

Two medics ran in, and Sheila trailed after them. She too had changed into knit shorts, a The Cure T-shirt, and wellies.

"I need you to all back away please," Sheila said. "Let the medics do their jobs."

Lizzie helped me off the ground, and we did as Sheila asked.

"Where's Kieran?" Lolly asked.

"Handling something at the pub. I was already in bed when he called to see if I could come here. Can you tell me what happened?" She pointed to me. "You were over the victim."

Victim?

"She was checking to make sure she was alive," Lizzie said.

"She's right," Rob added. "We heard a scream. I saw Mercy and Lizzie headed into the garden, and I told Scott to call you. And then I joined them."

"That's right," Scott said.

"Thank you, everyone, for your answers, but I asked Mercy the question."

I bit the inside of my lip to keep from laughing. Though, I was grateful they all stepped up for me.

"It's as they said. I heard a scream. My sister and I ran out here with Rob. We found Linda face down."

Sheila gave our umbrella and spade a hard look.

"We weren't sure if it was another intruder," I said.

"Did you hit her with one of the items you're carrying?"

"No. Of course, we didn't," Lizzie said. "We were protecting ourselves."

"Ms. McCarthy, if you don't mind, I'd like to speak to your sister first."

Lizzie huffed.

"Well, she's right," I said. "Except to check her pulse and for broken bones, I didn't touch her."

One of the medics came over. "She's had a hit on the head, but she seems okay. We're going to take her home and call for the doctor," the medic said. "She doesn't want to go to the hospital."

"Is there anything we can do to help?" Lizzie asked.

"I'll be all right," Linda said. "But there is someone up to no good on the court." She gave us the evil eye as if we were the guilty party.

Linda had suffered enough and now someone had tried to kill her.

We needed answers fast.

TWENTY-TWO

The next morning, I woke up to the scent of coffee. I checked my phone, and it was almost eight. We'd stayed up late the night before trying to find out what happened to Linda and to make certain she was okay.

I'd fallen asleep wondering if our murderer had tried to kill her. And why would someone want to do that?

None of this makes sense.

I made it to the hallway before I heard the voices.

I turned around and went back to my room. I was not presentable for company. After brushing my teeth, and changing, I headed to the kitchen.

Everyone in the court was there.

Even Linda, with bruises on the side of her face where she'd hit the ground.

"Morning," Lizzie said as I came into the kitchen. "I asked everyone to come over to address our security concerns. You know the ones we discussed last night." She gave me a look.

We had discussed no such thing, but I picked up on what she'd been trying to do. This was a keep your enemies close sort of thing.

"Oh... good idea. Linda, how are you feeling?"

"Thanks to that coffee machine of yours, loads better. The cappuccino helps with the headache. I've never seen a machine that can do so many things. It's like having your own barista in your house."

I smiled. "It is. Hello, everyone. Sorry I'm late to the meeting I didn't know we were having it so early."

They laughed.

"I've just arrived," Lolly said. "I was busy checking with Kieran to see if they had any suspects in Linda's attack."

I glanced around the table dramatically. "And?"

"Nothing so far," Lolly said.

"Why were you out there?" I asked Linda. It sounded more accusatory than I meant.

"Please pardon my sister, she hasn't had her morning medicine." Lizzie set a cup of coffee in front me.

I smirked. "She's not wrong. It's just, we were really worried about you last night. Given what's been going on lately, it might be best if we don't go out alone after dark."

I was kind of proud of myself. I sounded perfectly plausible.

"I can't believe we've come to that," Lolly said. "I never thought changing times would affect the court. We've always been so impervious to crime."

"Maybe it's my mystery-writer brain, but everything that has happened feels personal."

But who was it? Rob had been coming up the path from his house the same time we were, and it took Lolly even longer.

"I'd been going to the shop," Linda said. "I couldn't sleep because I couldn't remember if I turned the light off in my office. I tend to obsess over silly things like that, especially before bed."

Lizzie put a platter of blueberry and cranberry muffins, along with some cinnamon scones on the table. I could barely get myself out of bed and dressed by eight in the morning.

Meanwhile, my sister, had called a meeting and made breakfast for the attendees. *She truly is a marvel.*

We had not discussed security concerns the night before, but we had stayed up late wondering how we could find out more information about Dave. I very much needed to know if his death really was a heart attack or if it was suspicious. My bet was it was the latter.

After what happened to Linda, she was off the list. Luckily, she'd survived her attack, unlike the others.

"I could have sworn someone was watching me," Linda said. "It was creepy. I'd almost thought about going back to the house, but once something gets in my head, I can't turn it off. I was just about to the gate when I heard the footsteps. I screamed, and then everything went black."

Lolly reached over and patted Linda's arm. "That's awful, dear. I'm sorry for your trouble. I'm hoping these criminals will cease their shenanigans once Kieran moves into the court."

"So, he's definitely moving in?" Scott asked.

Lolly nodded. "I'm working on him. For some reason, he's not certain he wants to live next door to his gran. He's probably worried I'll be spying on him if he brings women home. If only. That boy has never brought a woman home to meet his gran. It's time he settled down."

There was silence and I felt certain the detective would be properly mortified if he knew what she'd just said.

"Do you have a bump on your head?" I asked Linda. "Do we need to worry about a concussion?"

She pointed to the side and back of her head. "My husband used to say I have a hard head and he must have been right. Only left a small bump. I did hurt my shoulder when I fell, though. That's way worse than my head."

Once again, something niggled at my brain. But there was not enough caffeine in my system to figure out what it was that bothered me so much about the situation with Linda.

"Until the detective figures out what's going on, I feel like we need some kind of high-alert neighborhood watch sort of thing," Lizzie said. "Like we keep an eye out for one another. If one of us needs to go out for any reason after dark, we ask someone to go with us."

Lolly sniffed, and a tear rolled down her cheek.

I put a hand on her arm. "Are you okay?"

She shook her head. "I know it's difficult for you to believe, but we've never had to worry about crime here. Not behind the wall, that is. And even in town the worst is a brawl or a pickpocket. No one who lives here would do such a thing."

Lizzie leaned forward. "You're not saying it's our fault are you, Mrs. O'Malley?" Her tone was more surprise than anything.

Lolly waved her hand. "Oh, no, dear. Not at all. Your grandfather wanted you safe behind that wall. He was so worried about you living in the States. I mean, one hears stories of violence there. Not that we haven't had our fair share. This is Ireland, after all. But Shamrock Cove is one of the safest places in the world to live."

"Or it was," Scott said.

Lolly scowled at him.

He shrugged.

"The thing that confuses me is the *why* of the situation," I said.

"What do you mean?" Lolly asked.

"No one at this table is responsible for what's going on, right?"

"Right," they said at the same time.

"Then why is someone targeting the court? This all started the day we arrived, but why? That's what I can't wrap my head around."

I tapped my chin with my finger. "Is there someone who desperately wanted into the court but couldn't find a way?"

Linda and Lolly glanced at one another, and their eyes went wide.

"What?" Rob asked.

"Loads of people apply for the lottery in case one of the houses... leaves no heirs," Lolly said. "When Driscoll, your grandfather, found out he was dying, we opened the lottery. Goodness, it's been almost two years ago now. We didn't know then about you two.

"Though, I assure you he was so happy to have found you." She sniffed again. "I only wish you could have known him. You would have loved one another."

The rest of the table nodded.

"We called off the lottery... and then when the judge died, I had talked to the court council and the Shamrock Cove village council about reopening it. And then we found out he'd left it to me, which is one of our loopholes to keep it within the families. But we hadn't officially opened the lottery again."

"So, it's possible there's someone who really wants to live here," Lizzie said, "but was denied their chance by the heirs of the court."

"And they might kill to make their dreams come true." I followed her train of thinking.

It made more sense than someone at the table trying to kill us. The shrimp and overdose of the judge could even be explained if it was someone in Shamrock Cove. At least, it was a motive. And now, I was short on those and real suspects. I had a difficult time believing that anyone sitting here had anything to do with this. I'd ruled out Lolly, Rob, Scott, and now Linda.

Besides, they already lived on the court. They'd have no reason to kill to do so.

"Lolly, we need to get a list of those lottery applicants," I said. I held up a hand. "Before anyone says its Kieran's job, I agree with you. But I also know he has his hands full with suspects from the judge's past. I say we get the list and go through it together.

"You all know the town and its people better than anyone. Maybe there are a few names we can give the detective to check out."

"It's almost like you know how to solve a mystery," Rob said. We all laughed.

"I'm pretty sure she saw that on *Midsomer Murders*, or was that one in an Ainsley McGregor book?" Lizzie asked.

"No telling," I said. "I watch and read a lot of mysteries."

"Did you really think it was one of us?" Linda asked.

I opened my mouth and closed it. And then I shrugged. "I didn't know what to think, to be honest."

Rob's hand went to his heart. "We are really suspects?"

"My sister's overactive imagination has to run through all the probabilities. It's what makes her such a great writer." Lizzie waved a hand.

That was a good save, and she didn't have to lie. It was the truth.

"So, is anyone busy tonight?" I changed the subject.

"Why?" Lolly asked.

"I thought we could order pizza and go through the list of lottery applicants," I said. "With all of us, it shouldn't take long."

"There's just one problem with that," Linda said. She frowned.

"What?" I asked.

"We don't have a pizza restaurant in town."

"Don't fret," Rob said. "I've got your pizza craving covered. Just tell me what toppings you want."

Later that afternoon, I was five chapters into the book's second half when there was a knock on the door.

I opened it to find Rob holding several large trays, one stacked on the other and wrapped in foil.

I glanced down at my watch. "Oh, wow, thank you. I didn't realize what time it was. Come in."

"Scott's grabbing drinks and will be here in a minute. We could do this at mine if you need to keep working."

I frowned. "What?"

"I saw you hunched over your computer, looking demonically possessed."

I laughed. "I'm three-quarters of the way through and heading toward the end. I probably look exactly like a demon."

After waving him through, I followed him to the kitchen.

The scents from the food made me want to eat the air. "How many pizzas did you make?"

"About eight," he said. "It's been so long since I made one, and I was having fun." I helped him spread the trays out on a long counter that Lizzie said would make a great buffet.

"Wow, these look amazing," I said as my stomach growled. "I wonder where she is?"

"Who?"

"My sister," I said. "She's never late, especially when she has company coming. Can you hold down the fort, while I go see what's happening?"

When I opened the front door, she was there looking a bit flustered.

"What's wrong?"

She screwed up her face. "I'm mad at myself, I couldn't find my keys to lock up the shop. Like, I have no idea where I left them. I had them when I let myself in to work on the window display while the shop was closed. I looked all over for them, but they're just gone."

I was usually the forgetful one in the family.

"I'll get the set I have and go lock up for you. Why don't you help Rob with the pizzas? Scott should be here any second with the drinks."

"Are Lolly and Linda here?"

I shook my head.

She frowned. "I guess we're all running a bit late. Don't be long."

"I won't." After grabbing the keys, I headed outside to find Lolly and Kieran walking down the path in front of the houses.

"Where are you going?" Lolly asked.

I explained the situation.

"Kieran, go with her. The sun is going down. I don't want the girls going anywhere after dark."

I shook my head. "I'll be fine. I'm just going to lock the doors and I'll be right back."

But the detective followed me through the gate.

"This isn't necessary," I said.

"If I don't do what Gran asked, I'll hear about it for at least the next month, maybe longer."

I laughed.

When we arrived at the backdoor to the shop, it was open.

The detective stopped and stared at it, and then at me.

I shrugged. "It's an old door, maybe she didn't pull it tight enough. She was flustered when she couldn't find the keys."

He cocked his head, as if he were listening to something. "Stay here," he whispered.

Were we being robbed? I wished I'd grabbed my pointed-tipped umbrella. I waited more than a minute, but he didn't return.

"Detective? Kieran?" A sense of dread filled me when he didn't answer. I dialed 999, and a phone rang within the store. Great, he was the one taking the calls. I hung up and then brandished my phone like a weapon.

It was pitch black inside, but I left the door open for the last bit of remaining light.

"Detective?" I whispered.

I stepped into the office. Someone shoved me from behind. I tripped over something and landed hard against the chair, knocking the side of my head against the back of it. I hit the same place I had the tree the other day.

What is happening?

Feeling woozy, I tried to stand up, but then someone hit me in the back of the head and I fell to my knees. I glanced down to see what caused my fall.

Kieran lay sprawled on the floor.

I glanced up to find a figure looming in the darkness.

"Where is it?" Linda snarled. "Tell me, or I'll kill you both."

"Linda," I said again, confused. "What's wrong? Why would you want to kill us?"

"You've done nothing but get in the way. You were helping him with the investigation. Where are the files? I must erase the past so no one else finds out what happened."

I cleared my throat. *Linda* was the killer. But no, she'd lost her own husband. I struggled to keep up with what was happening. My head screamed in pain, but I had to focus. I had to keep Kieran and me alive. But she'd had no motive to kill the judge, or her husband. Apparently looks were deceiving, and we'd all been duped.

"I don't understand," I said, trying to figure out my next move. "What are you talking about? Do you mean about the divorce papers?"

"I don't have time to answer your stupid questions," she shouted. "I have to get to your house, so I have an alibi. Hasn't anyone ever told you that you're a writer? You have no business running around like some detective out of your books. But you're not a very good one. You had the evidence in front of your face, and you missed it."

"I don't understand," I said. I was genuinely confused.

"Just tell me where the file is, and I won't kill the detective. He didn't see me."

Crud. Her meaning was clear.

But I had.

That's when I saw the letter opener in her hand. It was pointed straight at the detective's jugular.

"Okay," I said. "Don't hurt him."

She stood brandishing the letter opener. I was still on my knees, but I had no wish to find out how she planned to kill me with that thing.

If I told her what she wanted to know, she'd have no reason to keep me alive. It helped that I had no idea what she was talking about.

"Where are the files?" She stepped over the detective.

"They're locked in the safe." I played along. I cleared my throat. "But you'll need my fingerprint to get into it."

"Fine. I'll chop off your hand after I kill you. Where is the safe?" She pointed the letter opener toward the detective again. When she turned slightly, I popped up.

I headbutted her right in the stomach. She tripped over Kieran, only she went backward. It was like slow motion, as her arms windmilled around and around. The letter opener went flying toward me as I twisted away just in time.

And then she smashed into a wooden file cabinet. I was grateful Lizzie hadn't moved things around in here.

But the crash didn't take Linda down. She stumbled a bit and then snarled as she came for me.

My former Krav Maga training kicked in and I threw a punch at her throat with my right hand, and then smashed the heavy stapler I'd grabbed off the desk into the side of her head. I'd been taught by experts to use the tools at my disposal. She fell back again, but this time she couldn't right herself. She fell into the back hallway and into the cupboard that hid the secret doorway.

The heavy silver owl figurine toppled off the top and hit her head with a thud.

She blinked and then fell to the side.

"What the bloody hell is going on?" The detective sat up from the floor, holding his head.

Everything in my body hurt. My hand, head, back, all of it. It was all I could do to stay standing.

"I found your killer."

TWENTY-THREE

I'm not proud of it, but I blackmailed the detective. I had my reasons. I mean, I did find his killer for him. Okay, technically, she found me. But I kept her from murdering him. The least he could do was let me listen to her confession.

But it wasn't like the movies. The day after Linda had tried to kill us both, I watched his interrogation play out on the computer in his office, as it was the closest he would let me get. He'd said something about playing it by the book and proper procedures, which was why I wasn't allowed in the room with her.

Not that I wanted to be that close. She was a cold-blooded killer, and more devious than any of us could have suspected.

I just had to know why she'd tried to kill me and had murdered the judge, and possibly her husband. While they stared each other down, I opened the judge's laptop. There was something on here about her that she didn't want people to know.

"What are you doing? You shouldn't be touching the evidence," Lizzie said from beside me. She sat next to me in

Kieran's office. "You heard what he said. And I can't believe you blackmailed the man. I mean, really."

I waved her away. "I'm still helping him," I said. "Besides, you're every bit as curious as I am."

She smirked.

The medics had cleaned me up the night before. I had a few bruises and another conk on the head, but I'd survived worse. The detective and I were declared fit not long after the ordeal, but Linda had to go to the hospital for the night. They'd released her into police custody early this morning. Lolly had been the one to share that information.

No one on the court had slept much. While I'd held ice on my head and hands, we'd gone over every conversation with Linda. None of us could come up with a reason she'd done all of this.

It didn't make sense.

I'd missed something important in the judge's things. And while she'd be going away for assault at the very least, we needed to find out her motive for murder.

I'd come down to the station earlier in the morning and blackmailed Kieran. Well, all I said was, "If you don't want everyone to know I saved your life, you'll let me listen in when you interview the suspect."

I mean, he hadn't even said thank you for taking lunatic Linda down. And I know we're not supposed to use derogatory names for the mentally ill, but that witch tried to kill me.

"Why is he just staring at her?" Lizzie asked. "And why is she just staring right back? She should at least try to clear her name."

"It's not like in the movies," I said. "He knows what he's doing. Cops weaponize silence. It makes people feel uneasy."

Another officer from Dublin was there, and Sheila was in the corner of the room as well.

"Why did you need the judge's computer, Linda?" Kieran asked.

She glanced at her lawyer, and then crossed her arms. "No comment."

There was another long pause.

No one in the room spoke. They all just stared at her.

I opened the files that pertained to Linda and her divorce. That was the only thing the judge had on her, except for the Main Street revamp.

"He's going to kill you if he finds you snooping. Wait, who's that?" Lizzie moved her face closer to the screen.

"What do you mean?" I stared at the document.

She pointed to the name in the middle of the third paragraph. The name wasn't Dave or David. This was a divorce decree between Linda and another man: *Darnell Jones*. In my hurry and in the dark, I'd missed it when I snooped in the judge's house.

"Do you think Linda was married before?" my sister whispered the question. "Or maybe that is Dave's real name?"

And then all the pieces fell together in my head. Why had I not noticed this before? I felt like an idiot.

"No. It's a different man," I said. "These divorce papers were never signed or filed, but this means Linda was married to another man. That's it. That's the secret she didn't want anyone discovering. But the judge must have figured it out."

"And possibly her husband figured it out," I said.

"Do you think she killed poor Dave too?" Lizzie shivered.

"It wouldn't surprise me. The toxicology reports still haven't come back. But if she killed the judge, it would follow that she did the same to her husband. He must have found out the truth. Or maybe the judge told him before he was killed."

"What do you mean?" Kieran asked from the doorway. "And why are you still snooping?" He didn't bother sounding surprised, but he was obviously annoyed with me.

"What happened?" I asked as I glanced back at the screen where Linda sat with her lawyer.

"The solicitor asked for a ten-minute break. I don't suppose I could trouble you for one of your cortados. I've got a massive headache."

"I'll get it, and one for you," Lizzie said. "How about a cortado for you, Detective Inspector?" she asked the other man who had been in the room with the detective and stood behind Kieran.

"I don't know what a cortado is but if it has coffee and perhaps some espresso, I'm in," the other man said. "Can I help you with the cups?"

"Oh, that would be lovely," my sister said.

They went off. Like I said, Lizzie can charm most anyone without really trying.

"There's something I need to show you." I showed him the divorce decree on the laptop.

"You told me about this before," he said.

"Yes, but my sister noticed something we didn't. Look at the names."

His eyes went wide. Then he scrolled up to the dates.

"This doesn't make sense. She and Dave have only been married for—"

"Ten years," I said. The date on the document was for more than fifteen years ago. "Do you think Dave's real name is Darnell?"

"No," he said. "Why would his last name be different?" He sat back in his office chair. "Blimey."

"This means she's still married to someone else," I said.

He nodded.

"What if her husband didn't know she was still married to someone else? I don't think she took the papers to the judge to look them over. I think the judge found these documents and realized what was happening.

"He may have threatened to tell her husband. You said he was a fair man and hated injustice. I mean, how far would she go to keep that truth from coming out? It would ruin her reputation and her marriage.

"Plus, bigamy is against the law in Ireland, right?"

"Aye, it is."

"This helps you connect her to the judge. You don't have a lot of evidence for his murder. And technically, right now, we, I mean you, can only charge her with assault and attempted murder."

I pointed to the computer. "But that document gives her motive. And we know she had the opportunity. And if Dave found out..."

Kieran turned to me then and smiled. "You really are quite brilliant and beautiful."

Did he call me beautiful? My cheeks heated.

He was such a handsome man. I sometimes forgot that when I spent most of the time so utterly frustrated with him.

"We have her," he said. "And it's all thanks to you and your sister."

An hour later, Linda sang for her supper. Well, in her case, it was the possibility of a slightly reduced sentence. When the detective presented only a few of the facts, she crumbled. In between sobs, she spilled everything.

How she'd killed the judge by crushing his heart pills into his drink and making sure he tried something with the shrimp in it in case that didn't work. Then, how she'd broken into our house on the hunt for the judge's computer.

She even admitted to changing out Dave's heart pills, so he wasn't taking the right prescription. The judge had told Dave the truth, but her husband hadn't thought it was a big deal. He'd been ready to tell everyone in the court she was a bigamist. And she couldn't let that happen.

Through her blubbering cries, we discovered that she married right out of high school, and it had only lasted a few months. Her ex had run off, and she'd tried to file for divorce but she hadn't been able to find him to sign the papers. Eventually, she'd given up and assumed he was dead.

The judge had been digging around when she came to him saying she was considering divorcing Dave and found out the truth. He had given her two weeks to tell Dave, before he told her husband. But the judge had gone behind her back.

Once Dave knew the truth, he hadn't been angry. He believed everyone would understand. He even offered to help find her ex. But she didn't want anyone finding out how messed up her life had been or that she'd broken the law.

Everything had come to a head before the judge's wake. When Dave had suggested they talk to a lawyer to sort things out, she was furious. The last thing she wanted was for anyone else to find out what she'd done.

To save face, she killed Dave that night the same way she had the judge—by poisoning him with his own meds.

The satisfaction of catching her and knowing she'd go away for a very long time, felt good. And at the same time, I'd been exhausted. She was a troubled woman and while the judge certainly hadn't deserved murder, he had pushed her over the edge.

"I can't believe you solved the case," Lizzie said on the way home.

"*We* did it, sis." I paused. And then I pulled her into my arms. "I'm sorry this place hasn't turned out the way we hoped."

She squeezed me as tight as I did her. "I know, it's much less boring than I'd thought it would be."

I pulled back. "All of this hasn't frightened you into going back home?"

She shrugged. "I grew lavender for a living. Except for worrying about pests, prices, and launching new products... I was bored. I don't think I admitted it to myself until a few days ago."

I nodded slowly, a little surprised.

"Don't get me wrong. It was different when I had John and Audrey to focus on, and building our new life together. I had my little family, which made everything there more fun. But without them... it's just a place with good and bad memories and not much left for me. Why? Do you want to go back to Manhattan? I wouldn't blame you."

"Are you saying you want to stay?" I asked. I was surprised. "Your business was very successful. I mean, it still is, even though you aren't there."

She sighed. "Exactly, it's a well-oiled machine. I have the right people to take it to the next level. But here, I have a struggling bookstore and a town that needs it desperately. As silly as it may sound, I have purpose again.

"We have new ride-or-die friends with Rob, Scott, and Brenna, and they live right next door. I've had more excitement in this first month than I've ever had."

I'd had a text from Brenna, who had been shocked by the news. Now that things were safe, she'd be heading home soon.

I shook my head. "You can still surprise me, sis. I thought for certain you'd have our bags packed and would be ready to roll out on the next flight."

"I really love it here," she said. "Even with all the trouble, I feel like this is our place."

If someone had told me two years ago that I'd be living in a small Irish town today and loving it, I would have sent them to a psychiatrist.

But I would have been wrong.

"You're right. It's home."

My phone dinged in my pocket. I pulled it out to find a text from Carrie.

Lizzie says you solved a real-life murder. Now, get to work solving the one in your book.

I laughed. "I guess it's time to get back to work."

"First, lunch," she said.

"I heard there's fish and chips at the pub today," I said.

She laughed and turned us around on the sidewalk.

When we walked into the pub, everyone cheered and waved at us.

Lizzie and I laughed.

"Yep, all we had to do was solve a murder, and now they love us," she said.

"Today's lunch is on the house," Matt said. "And that includes unlimited coffee for you, Mercy."

"Thank you, but you may regret that."

They all laughed.

Just after our fish and chips arrived, Kieran came in and headed toward our table.

"Oh. No. What now?" Lizzie said.

He smiled. "I guess we had the same idea." He waved a hand toward our food. "I'm here to do a takeaway for everyone at the station. Thanks to you, we're celebrating this afternoon."

"It's the best fish and chips I've ever had," I said.

"Aye, Matt's mum is a great cook."

He stood there awkwardly.

"Is there something wrong?" Lizzie asked.

He stared down at me. "No. I just... if you wanted to get that drink sometime, Mercy? I'd be happy to help with any research you might need for your book."

My sister looked from the detective to me and grinned. "*Research*, right," she said under her breath.

I tried to kick her, but I missed.

"That would be great." Why did I sound so breathless? I cleared my throat. "Uh. Thanks."

"I still have one question," Lizzie said.

"What's that?" Kieran and I said at the same time.

"Why did the judge point up at you and blame you for killing him?" Why would she ask that? Was she trying to stir up trouble?

"I do believe he pointed to the heavens, not your sister," Kieran said. "The chemical reaction happening in his body most likely interfered with his sight, which wasn't great to begin with. But we don't believe it was anyone in particular he pointed at."

"Order is up, Kieran," Matt shouted.

He nodded. "Right. I best be going." Then he strode away quickly.

"He likes you," Lizzie said.

"He's just being nice since we helped with the case."

She snorted. "Right. He's very good-looking."

I sighed. She wasn't wrong.

Later, when we were leaving the pub, we ran into Liam and his mother. He was crying as he held a box.

"What's wrong?" I asked.

His mother sighed. "We found this wee pup, and Liam wanted to keep him. But Liam started sneezing and the doc says he's allergic. Now we need to find him a new home, and the boy isn't happy about it."

"It isn't fair." Liam sniffled. "I've always wanted a dog."

"Can I see him?" Lizzie asked softly.

He lifted the box to us. Inside was a small bundle of black

fur with the kindest eyes. He cocked his head and then lifted a paw as if to say hello.

"Would you look at that," I whispered. "He's smart."

"He is," Liam said. "He's the smartest dog ever."

I picked him up from the box, and he snuggled into my neck.

"He's so sweet," I said.

"Let me hold him," Lizzie said.

I reluctantly handed him over. He snuggled with her as well, but not before he licked her chin.

He was an adorable fluff ball, and I was already smitten.

Lizzie and I looked at one another, and she nodded.

"We could take him," I said. "I've always wanted a dog, but I've lived in apartments most of my adult life. I promise you, Liam, we'll give him a good home."

"And you can come visit him at number three any time you want. Sometimes when you have an allergy, it's easier in small doses," Lizzie added. "As long as your mom says it is okay; we don't want you to get sick. And I'll keep him at the bookstore so you can also visit him there as well."

The pup yapped softly as if he agreed.

She smiled.

I hadn't seen her smile like that in a year.

"Are you sure?" Liam's mom asked. "You've both been so kind, we don't want to be a bother."

"The pup will be no bother," I said. "And I promise we'll love him."

Liam handed me the box. "Super promise?" he asked.

"Yes. I super promise."

"Okay." He didn't seem happy, but he nodded. "What will you name him?" he asked.

He had what looked like a mustache and, for some reason, reminded me of Edgar Allan Poe.

"I like the idea of calling him after one of my favorite writers, Edgar Allan Poe. What do you think, Liam?"

"His name could be Mr. Poe," Liam said.

"Oh, I love that. And he'll be our dog," Lizzie said. "We'll just look after him until you can come play."

"Provided you take allergy medicine beforehand," his mum said. "The doctor said only short visits."

Liam nodded. "Thank you."

"We have some food and a wee bed we can drop by later if that's okay," his mother said.

"That's fine," I said. "Or I can come by and pick them up."

"You know what this means," Lizzie said to Liam.

"What?" he asked.

"You've given us a new family member, and that means I'm going to owe you a lot of books."

He perked up, but then eyed her suspiciously. "The kind I like to read?"

"Yes, your favorites, for sure."

He nodded.

A few minutes later, we put Mr. Poe in the backyard and watched as he sniffed the grass and plants. We followed him as he checked out the fairy garden. He paused in front of the little door at the base of the tree and cocked his head as if he could hear something.

"Do you think he hears the fairies?" Lizzie said and then laughed.

He cocked his head the other way and gave a soft yap. Then he headed toward the backdoor.

"We have a dog," she said. "And he's adorable."

I smiled. "He is. Maybe he'll be the one who finally finds our grandfather's secret door and his journals. He already fits right in so I guess we really have found a home." I crooked my arm in hers.

"Yes, Shamrock Cove is everything we didn't know we needed." She was relaxed and happy.

"Agreed." Our fresh start may have come with a few bumps in the road, but we'd found our place in the world. Tension I didn't know I'd been holding left my shoulders, and I took a deep breath.

The air here was so fresh and full of flowers. So different than what I'd left in New York.

"You okay?" She glanced over at me.

"I am. Let's build a fire in the living room. I can sit and write."

"And I can play with our friend Mr. Poe," she said.

"Sounds like the perfect afternoon," I said. Coming to Ireland truly had been the best decision we'd ever made.

A LETTER FROM LUCY CONNELLY

Lovely reader,

I want to say a huge thank you for choosing to read *An Irish Bookshop Murder*. If you did enjoy it, and want to keep up to date with all my latest releases, just sign up at the following link. Your email address will never be shared, and you can unsubscribe at any time.

www.bookouture.com/lucy-connelly

One of the things I loved about writing *An Irish Bookshop Murder* was being transported to Ireland and Shamrock Cove, a village I made up but very much want to live in. How about you? And what do you think of the twins Mercy and Lizzie? I've never had a sister, but I adore their relationship. How did they make you feel? What do you think about Mercy and the good detective working together?

I'd love to hear what you think, and it makes such a difference helping new readers to discover one of my books for the first time if you write a review. You can get in touch through my social media or my website.

Love to you all,

Lucy Connelly

KEEP IN TOUCH WITH LUCY

www.lucyconnelly.com

facebook.com/LucyConnellyBooks
x.com/candacehavens

ACKNOWLEDGMENTS

I'd very much like to thank my editor, Maisie Lawrence, and the team at Bookouture for believing in *An Irish Bookshop Murder*. I'm grateful for your guidance and for helping me to make the best story possible.

Without my agent, Jill Marsal, who has the patience of a saint, I wouldn't be the writer I am. Thank you for always knowing when a story is ready for the rest of the world to see it.

Dear husband and the rest of my family and friends, thank you for being my literary and life cheerleaders. You have no idea how grateful I am for you.

And don't tell the rest of them, but you are my favorite, dear readers. Sharing my stories with you is one of the great joys and privileges of my life. Love to you all.

PUBLISHING TEAM

Turning a manuscript into a book requires the efforts of many people. The publishing team at Bookouture would like to acknowledge everyone who contributed to this publication.

Audio
Alba Proko
Sinead O'Connor
Melissa Tran

Commercial
Lauren Morrissette
Hannah Richmond
Imogen Allport

Cover design
Lisa Horton

Data and analysis
Mark Alder
Mohamed Bussuri

Editorial
Maisie Lawrence
Ria Clare

Printed in Great Britain
by Amazon

51071176R00158